"Yes, Mum... I Made It!"

Henry Harvey

"You came into existence for a purpose."
\- Sheila Clary

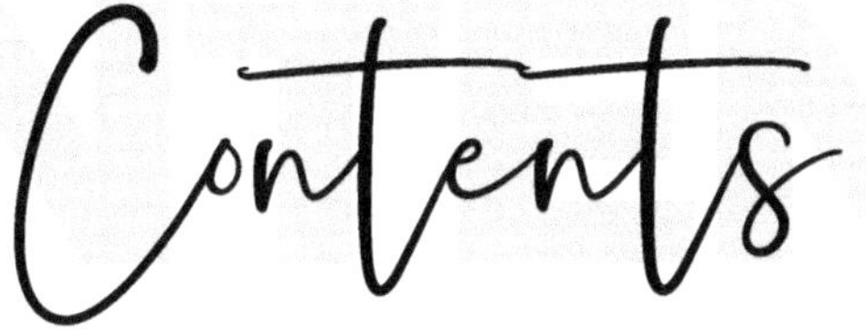

Contents

INTRODUCTION

The Letter

"You came into existence for a purpose."

As the little boy sat on the old worn-out cardboard, he looked hopelessly at his mother who laid motionless next to him. His tugging at her clothes did not cause her to wake up that morning. His cries and eventual screams alerted the other addicts living in the abandoned house to walk over and investigate. One of the women bent over the woman on the cardboard and shouted: "Sheila real sick! Somebody call the damn ambulance quickly!" One of the occupants dialed the Emergency number from an old mobile phone.

Within fifteen minutes, the ambulance arrived, and medics wasted no time in placing Sheila and her meager belongings on the stretcher and into the ambulance. Her little boy was also placed in the back before it took off for the nearby Providence Hospital. With sirens blasting, the ambulance wended its way through the light traffic while the medics worked tirelessly to pump Sheila's chest. Another medic turned to the scared little boy who, by now, was staring at his mother through tear-streaked eyes, looking confused at the scene unfolding in front of him. The friendly medic patted him on his head and asked him his name. "Mikey," he whispered as he continued to stare at his mother, who, by now, was hooked up to IV lines and monitors. "Do not worry Mikey," said Andrea, the female medic, "My name is Ms. Andrea, and we will take good care of you and your mum." Her smile and kind-hearted attitude served to calm his spirit.

In about twenty minutes, the ambulance arrived at the hospital and the medics rushed Sheila into the emergency room. Andrea held the little boy's hand and walked in briskly with him. On reaching the emergency room, she told him to sit on a chair while she updated the nurses who were in attendance. In five minutes, Andrea came over to where Mikey was sitting and informed him that the nurse was going to do a little check on him. As he held her hand, his grip tightened, and he refused to leave her side. Andrea soon realized that he was overwhelmed with the situation and offered to take him to the room herself. Nurse Gray then gave him a small stuffed toy that she had on a shelf telling him it was his to take. She then began her initial examination of the child while Andrea held his hand.

Fifteen minutes had passed, and the initial triage was completed, and he left the room with Andrea and his new stuffed toy. Andrea then said to him, "Good, Mikey. Now we will go check on your mum." As they walked to the next room, Andrea realized that Sheila was still being attended to and offered instead to go to the food court with Mikey. "Are you hungry?" she asked. He nodded in response. "What would you like to have? I see that they have burgers, fries, and chicken bites. What would you like Mikey?" He pointed to the fries and chicken bites and then grabbed her hand once more. In ten minutes, Andrea was walking back to the waiting room with Mikey and his food in hand. She told him to sit on the chair and eat while she checked on his mother. The child nodded and began quietly eating his food while Andrea went to the ER.

On reaching the door, she noticed that Sheila was still being worked on. She searched for Nurse Gray who informed her that it was not looking positive for Sheila and that they had to brace for the worst. They then both looked at Mikey who sat devouring his meal. "Did she have any documents with her when you brought her in?" asked Nurse Gray. "I do recall that she had a worn-out brown bag which probably held her dearest possessions," responded Andrea. Nurse Gray went into the emergency room and eventually located the bag which was placed there by one of the other medics. On rummaging through the bag, they noticed a bundle of papers inside a dirty brown envelope. On opening it Nurse Gray observed that there was a birth certificate among the documents. Both Nurse Gray and Andrea took turns reading the contents of the document which had the name "Mike Clary" typewritten as well as the Date of Birth and the mother's name. However, in the section for father's name, it was blank. They both realized that Mike Clary was five years of age. As they looked through the other documents in the envelope, an identification card was found with the name Sheila Clary. On the card, it was noted that Sheila was only twenty-nine years of age and looked quite attractive in her photo which highlighted her brown braided hair and light brown eyes. In the picture she smiled shyly at the camera and her full lips curved into a most beautiful smile. It was certainly hugely different from the drug-induced woman who now lay fighting for her life in the emergency room. Both women stayed silent for a minute or two doing their best to absorb and even comprehend what could have led such a beautiful woman to turn to drugs. There was one more document in the bag and it was a letter handwritten with the name Mikey on the cover.

Since the letter was already in an open envelope, both Andrea and Nurse Gray read the letter quietly to determine if there was any information that could assist them at that time with their records. What surprised them was that even though Sheila was on drugs, she cared enough to write a letter for her son if anything should happen to her. Andrea began reading the letter quietly.

"Dear Mikey, I must apologize for bringing you into this world and being unable to provide for you as I would have wanted. You are my heartbeat, my life, my only reason for trying to struggle from one day to the next. If anything should happen to me, I want you to always remember that you are special, that when I first saw you, I knew you came into my life for a purpose which is yet to be fulfilled. I destroyed my own life by following friends who led me to drugs. I was weak to do so and soon those friends left me on my own without anything to call my own. You are my only possession, and I would never leave you no matter what happens to me. You must never feel that you were responsible for how my life turned out. You are the only good that came out of my life. My love for you went beyond anything and for that, I did not want to leave you with anyone. I did what I had to do to ensure that you had food each day. If I had to do it all again, you would still be my only focus. Each day your face gave me joy and I want you to never forget that. If something should happen to me, I want you to live with a good family who will love you like I do. If anyone should find this letter, all I ask is that my Mikey be given a chance in life and that he be provided for in the best way possible. Thanks for helping me and please let my little boy know that he will always be my heartbeat and that I loved him with my whole being."

- Sheila Clary

Both women wiped their eyes as their eyes traveled to the little boy who, by now, was finished with his meal and was now drinking his juice. Nurse Gray hurried back into the Emergency room to check on Sheila. Approximately twenty minutes later she returned with her face now saddened and her eyes redder than before. Andrea looked at her and could not utter a word for Nurse Gray's gentle touch on her arm as she swayed her head from side to side, confirming that Sheila had passed away. Andrea could not help but wipe her own eyes as her gaze rested on Mikey.

They both knew that based on protocol, the Child Services Division had to be notified about the situation. Given that Mikey did not have any other kin, he would now become a ward of the state. As much as it hurt them to think that Mikey would be taken to an orphanage, they also remembered that they could not become emotionally involved in the lives of the patients. Andrea took a moment to check her watch and realized that her shift had ended about half an hour prior, and she was still at the hospital. While she could have walked off, her heart tugged in her chest and somehow, she could not leave Mikey alone there. She walked over to him as he ran towards her. "Is my mummy, ok?" he asked. Andrea sat down with him and decided to adopt the direct approach.

"Mikey," she started off in a trembling voice, "Let us sit a bit. The doctors did their best to help your mummy, but she was too ill, and she went on to be with the angels." She looked at the child looking so hopeless and sad that she had to control her emotions and not hold on to him and cry. "Do you understand what that means?" she asked. Mikey looked at her and asked, "Is my mummy dead?" Andrea could only respond with a nod of her head. She noticed that Mikey's eyes became red, but surprisingly he did not immediately burst into tears. He seemed to look up into the sky for a moment contemplating his situation. Andrea then placed her arms around his small shoulder and drew him towards her chest. It was then that he released his pent-up emotions, crying uncontrollably in her arms while she, too, released the tears that she tried so valiantly to control. Both did not even notice when Nurse Gray came and sat beside them stroking Mikey's mop of black curls on his head.

After what seemed like an eternity, Nurse Gray asked Andrea if she would consider taking him home that night and in the morning, they would contact Child Services since she would be back on duty at that time as well. It was already late, and it would be too much to have the child moved to an environment where he knew no one. Andrea contemplated, but not for long. She lived alone and had no children and was extremely happy to help this child, who somehow seemed to cling to her. "No problem," replied Andrea. Nurse Gray gave her a slight hug when she gave her response.

"We can sort out all the matters tomorrow. I guess an announcement would have to be made to locate some family or next of kin for Sheila." Nurse Gray replied, "Yes. We would have to put out an advertisement in the newspaper asking for any family members to contact us. That will be for one week. In the meantime, Sheila's body will remain at the hospital morgue and if no one comes forward, she will be buried as Jane Doe. Mikey, here, will have to be taken to the Orphanage until a family member can come forward and accept him as well." All this time while they spoke softly between themselves, the child rested his head on Andrea's lap. His crying had now subsided, and he was sleepy. Andrea collected Sheila's bag, making sure to replace the letter in the envelope and proceeded to her car. She lifted Mikey and proceeded to her vehicle which was parked at the southern end of the compound.

She placed Mikey on the back seat and strapped him in. She was worried that she had no car seat for him but the distance to her complex was about fifteen minutes away and she was anxious to get off the road. On the way to her home, she took short glimpses of the child, who, by now, was fast asleep. She managed to get to her home safely and was able to get to her apartment with much more ease than she had anticipated while carrying the sleeping child.

He looked so innocent while sleeping but she had to wake him up to get a shower and get into some clean clothes. While she had an extra toothbrush, she laughed to herself when she realized that the smallest of her jerseys would be too big for Mikey. She made a conscious decision to stop at the neighborhood, Tracey's Department Store and pick up a few items for him. As she bathed the child, she noted that he had no marks of violence on his body as one may have expected. His mother had done an excellent job of protecting him against the rough environment which she had traversed. That was a feat, and she did a surprisingly decent job given her circumstances. She was able to brush his teeth and put on her smallest jersey on him. She then showed him his spot on the guest bed and within five minutes, he fell asleep. She gently placed the comforter over him and smiled at how the jersey had swallowed him. She then proceeded to get herself a shower and wind down for the day. As she took off the light in her room, she muttered to herself, "What a day it has been! Who would have thought this was how my day would end?

As the sunbathed the small town with its first light, Andrea stirred in her bed. She would usually arise at that hour to pray and get her thoughts together for the new day. It was then that she recalled that she had a guest in her next room, and she included him in her prayer. "Lord, while today is not going to be easy, make it bearable for Mikey," she prayed. She remained with her eyes closed for a further two minutes as though to ensure that her prayer was heard. Andrea got off her bed at 6:30 that morning and proceeded to get her day organized. In doing so, she made a quick call to one of her colleagues, Shawn Chadshaw, who had three small boys of his own. "Hi Shawn," she began, "Sorry to bother you right now. However, I have a bit of an emergency, and I am looking for some clothes to fit a five-year old boy. Would you happen to have any from your boys that you would no longer need?" "Absolutely!" replied Shawn. "As our boys are growing so quickly, Jan and I usually have clothes that we can donate to another child. Look no further. I can drop it off for you in about half an hour if you would be home by then." "You are a savior. Thanks much Shawn," said Andrea.

With that out of the way, Andrea stopped by the guest room to peep in on Mikey. He did not stir at all, and she decided to let him get his rest; he needed it. She then proceeded to the kitchen where she began to prepare a breakfast of scrambled eggs and toast, hot chocolate, and oranges. Once she was finished, she sat quietly sipping a cup of hot chocolate and looked at the morning news on television. At around 7:15 am that morning, she heard her doorbell buzz and through the peephole, she saw that Shawn had arrived.

She hurriedly opened the door, and he stretched out his hand to give her a navy-blue canvas bag that was well packed.

"Thanks so much Shawn. Bless you and Jan for such a generous gesture," she said as she reached out and gave the short, balding man a big hug. He smiled gleefully and soon made his way back to his parked car. Andrea then went to her room and began perusing through the contents of the bag. She was completely surprised with the amount of clothes that were neatly packed there. In addition to that, there were two pairs of shoes and a pair of tan sandals that would seem to fit Mikey. She smiled and prepared the clothes that he would wear that day.

In fifteen minutes, she heard Mikey calling out for his mummy. She rushed to the room where the child was, sat next to him and held him. "Hello Mikey," she said tenderly, "I heard you crying for your mummy. Do you remember what happened and where she went yesterday?" "Yes, with the angels," he said shyly, rubbing his little red eyes. "Why not let us say a prayer together for her so that she can know that you are thinking of her? Whenever you miss her, close your eyes, and know that she is right near you even though you cannot see her." Those words somehow soothed the child and together with Andrea, they said a prayer. Once that was over, she took him to the bathroom and after ten minutes, he was showered and ready to put on his clothes.

He looked so smart in the blue jersey, khaki pants, and tan sandals. She brushed his hair, and she told him how handsome he looked. She then guided him to the table to have breakfast and he ate his meal heartily. Andrea ate her breakfast with him, chatting with him about things that he liked to eat, what was his favorite color among other topics. Eventually they were finished with breakfast, and she put on the television at a cartoon station. As the little boy sat glued to the television, Andrea washed up the wares and then sat together with him. She had decided to sit him down and explain as best as she could, what would take place that day.

When the cartoon was finished, she sat facing him and said, "Mikey today we will be going back to the hospital to meet Nurse Gray, the lovely nurse who attended to you yesterday. You will then have to go to another home where you would have many other children to play with. Does that sound like fun?" Mikey looked at her and shockingly asked her, "Will you come with me?" For a moment she found herself speechless, unable to find the right words to say. However, she knew that she had to ease the shock for the child seated across from her given the expectations that he had. "I am too big to be at that home, but I promise that I will come to look for you each week," she replied. "Ok," he responded. "Will you bring my favorite snack when you come to look for me?"

"Of course. You just say let me know and I will get it for you," said Andrea feeling relieved that the child did not take it as hard as she had expected. She then left him to watch cartoons while she got herself dressed and organized. They left her house at 9:30 am and got to the hospital in around thirty minutes due to the traffic. Andrea parked the car in her usual spot and with Mikey's bag on her shoulder, she carried him in her arms towards the entrance. On arriving at the nurse's station, she saw Nurse Gray, who walked up to them with a smile. Andrea placed Mikey on the floor and took him to a seat. Nurse Gray then asked Mikey how he was doing and went to her desk, taking something out of the drawer. She hid it behind her back and said, "Do you know what I have here?" Mikey shook his head to indicate that he did not know. "Tah Dah!" shouted Nurse Gray and the child's eyes lit up. "Look what you forgot in the waiting room," she said playfully to Mikey. He then took hold of the stuffed toy that she had given to him the day before. She then left it with him and quickly informed Andrea that they needed to contact Child Services so that the necessary steps could be taken as easily as possible. No one had come forward to claim Sheila's body thus far, but they still had a week for this to happen.

Nurse Gray then proceeded to contact Child Services while Andrea sat with Mikey. As the child played with the stuffed toy and swung his legs, Andrea could not help but wonder how he would make out at the Orphanage. Her thoughts also centered around Sheila and who would come forward to claim her body. As she contemplated, she saw when the official from the

Child Services Division had arrived. The young woman standing at the desk was of medium height, with curly black hair. Andrea overheard her ask for Nurse Gray, who appeared from a room at the side of the receptionist's desk.

Both women walked over to where Andrea sat with Mikey. Nurse Gray smiled at Mikey and said gently, "Hello Mikey. Meet Ms. Pam. She is here to meet you and take you to your new home." Andrea quickly added, "Mikey do you remember what we spoke about when I told you about the place with lots of children to play?" The child nodded in the affirmative and this was the cue for Ms. Pam to introduce herself. "Hello Mikey," Pam Strudel said, "I heard that you are a smart boy, and I look forward to having you at the Precious Children's Orphanage." She then asked if she could sit next to him, and he inched around on the bench to give her space. Mikey looked at Pam for a moment and then asked, "Can Ms. Andrea come too?" Pam smiled and realized that the child had taken a liking to the medic who sat next to him. "Well, the beds there are too small for Ms. Andrea to fit, but I tell you what, she can come to visit you at any time that you wish. Would that be ok for you?" He then looked at Andrea and said, "Will you cry if I am gone? You can look for me any time and bring any snacks so that we can eat together." This made the three women laugh and Andrea gave him a hug. "That surely sounds like something good to me, Mikey. I promise not to cry if you do not," said Andrea. Pam then got up and held out her hand towards Mikey, who got up and took it with his right hand, while he held the stuffed toy in the left. Nurse Gray had briefed Pam about the documents which were retrieved from Sheila and which she had placed in the blue canvas bag. As both Mikey and Pam began walking down the corridor toward the door, he suddenly released her hand and ran back to Andrea. Mikey wrapped his little arms around her waist and rested his head on her stomach. After what seemed like an eternity, he ran back to Pam who stood waiting quietly. Andrea wiped the tears from her eyes and returned to the bench while Nurse Gray herself dabbed at her eyes with a tissue and joined Andrea on the bench. Both women then sat there staring blankly into space, their individual thoughts reeling around in their minds until they were jolted back to reality by a code red announcement on one of the wards.

CHAPTER 1

Orphaned Dreams

"I sing myself happy!"

(Four Years Later)

"Mike and Prince stop the fighting!" shouted Mr. Gosine, the Director of the Orphanage. "What is the matter with both of you? Why do you continue to have these scuffles?" Mike was crying and had a bruise on his cheek while Prince glared at him. It was Mike who said, "Each time I pass by, he would put out his foot to trip me. This time I hit my ankle, and I decided to hit him back." "Is this true Prince?" shouted Mr. Gosine. Prince did not answer but continued to stare at Mr. Gosine and Mike. "I asked you a question boy!" demanded the Dean, who, by now, was showing little patience towards Prince. The child never answered, and Mr. Gosine held him by his shirt collar and marched him off to his office.

In the meantime, he instructed Mike to go to the first aid station and get his bruise cleaned. After his bruise was taken care of by nurse Harding, Mike then limped to the Julie Mango tree and sat on the bench. He had now been at the orphanage for three years and he was not happy. He had to put up with the other children who, by now, would have stolen some of his clothes that he had when he got there. The most important thing for him was the envelope which was placed in the bag by Nurse Gray. That envelope contained the most precious piece of connection to his deceased mother, Sheila.

He had been able to attend her funeral about one month after she had died. No one had turned up to claim her body and Ms. Andrea had something to do with the funeral arrangements. She came to the children's home with a driver to take him to the funeral home. There, he saw his mother dressed up all in white looking just like an angel. Ms. Andrea, Nurse Gray, Ms. Pam and even Mr. Gosine were in the small gathering which also had some of the addicts from the abandoned house. It was during the service that Andrea read out the contents of the letter for all to hear. She had arranged with Pam to have the brown envelope brought to the funeral. When Mikey heard what his mother had written, it was then that he was engulfed in a sea of tears. He was given the brown envelope after the reading, and he held on to it knowing that was the connection to his now deceased mother. When he returned to the orphanage, he placed the envelope at the bottom of his canvas bag and placed his clothes on top of it. Since he was now learning to read, he would take it out from time to time and try reading it to himself, then hug the envelope and replace it in his bag. On her usual visits to him at the orphanage, he would sometimes read the letter to Andrea as they sat on the bench. "You are becoming a fantastic reader Mikey," she said encouragingly. This would make him beam from ear to ear and he began asking her to bring books in addition to his favorite snacks whenever she visited.

Mikey looked forward to Andrea's visit for this was the break that he needed to take his mind off the environment in which he now lived. As much as he had lived in an abandoned house with his mother, there was a warmth that he knew among the addicts for they would often look out for each other and share some of their stuff. At the Orphanage, however, this warmth was not felt. While he did his best to stay away from fights with the children, at times he had no choice but to defend himself. On most occasions, he would emerge with a scrape or two but there were times when he came out the worst for it and would sit and long to be taken to a home where he could be loved as his mother had once loved him. In as much as they had lived in a homeless situation, his mother was his protector. No one dared to come near to her Mikey. The long, cedar stick which she kept at the house was often used to ward off anyone who felt they could threaten her child. Now there was no one to protect him and Mikey soon learned to use his fists and legs to protect himself.

Despite the altercations from time to time, Mikey made friends with some of the students and became close with another boy by the name of Chad, who, like Mike, had lost his mother and had no family to take him in. He had come to the Orphanage about six months after Mikey and kept to himself. It was Mikey who developed a friendship with the little boy after he noticed him one day, sitting in a corner sobbing quietly. Mikey gravitated towards him and hugged the little boy until his chest stopped heaving. From that day, they became inseparable always finding time to chat and interact with each other.

In his quiet moments, Mikey would often go under the huge starch mango tree located on the southern side of the large compound, where he would often day- dream about having the warmth of a family, having meals, and doing things together, being hugged and told that he was loved. Sometimes he felt that he heard his mother's voice reminding him that he was not alone and that she was always close to him. This, together with Andrea's visits and encouragement, he managed to get through the days at Precious Children's Orphanage.

Mikey was soon able to join the Basic Business program for the children at home. This supervised program was geared towards giving the children a sense of responsibility by attending for three hours in a community service and earning a stipend to help with their personal expenses. The program was also meant to teach the children about keeping records with respect to how their money was utilized.

Mikey had looked forward to being a part of the program and could not wait to join. Mr. Gosine had approached him and had a conversation with respect to the program. "Mikey would you like to join the Basic Business program and earn money for yourself?" asked Mr. Gosine. "Yes, sir," he replied unhesitatingly.

"You have been doing quite well in your classes and this program would help you to put into practice some of what you have been taught in your social studies and math classes. The program is for one day a week only and requires that you help with some community service for three hours and be paid a stipend. In addition to that, you must keep a record of the money you receive and how you spend it," said Mr. Gosine. "Yes, sir. I know what takes place in the program," said Mikey his eyes gleaming with the thought of earning his own dollar. "Very well. I will get back to you," Mr. Gosine replied.

Mikey later had a chat with Chad about the upcoming program. Chad was not yet of age to join and would have to wait at least two more years. "I cannot wait to earn my own money. I will save all because I want to be rich when I grow up. I want to have a family, and a house filled with lots of love," said Mikey dreamily as he poured out his thoughts to Chad. Chad only smiled for he was too young to even think of what he wanted to do. He asked Mikey, "What kind of car do you like? I like cars and would want to have one when I get older." Mikey then said to him, "Hmm…I do not know. All I know is that I want one that does not shut down for sure." They both gave each other a bounce of their fists and laughed heartily as they ran onto the field to play a game of football with some of the other children.

As they played, the children observed that a grey station wagon was parked outside of the head office and a man and woman got out. The pair proceeded to the office door and were met by Mr. Gosine, who shook hands with them. After a half an hour, Mr. Gosine came to the playground and summoned Chad, who was still playing football. He placed his arms around the little boy and had a chat with him before he walked with him to the office. After another half an hour had lapsed, Chad ran back to the playground with a look of glee on his round face. Mikey ran to him to find out what was the matter, and he pulled him away from the other children. "Those people whom you saw, they want to adopt me. Seems like they never had children, and my photo was sent to them. They came to meet me and find out more about me. They asked if I would want to spend a week with them to make up my mind and I said yes," Chad blurted out as if it was in one breath. Mikey hugged him but at the same time, could not help but feel sad with the thought that his only friend would soon be gone, and he would be left alone. What bothered him more was that Chad was going to a home where he would be loved; something that he yearned for deep within. "Boy, I will miss you, but I am happy that you would be out of here. At least you would have a family now. I hope that when you move to your new home, you are not going to forget me," replied Mikey trying to sound happy. Both boys once again hugged each other and promised to never forget each other.

Three weeks after their conversation, Chad left to stay a week with the Richards family so that he could familiarize himself with the family. Chad's departure that morning coincided with the start of the Basic Business program. The excitement of starting the program cushioned the pain Mikey felt from separation. Fortunately for him, he would have been leaving before Chad left the Orphanage that morning. When Mr. Gosine came to meet him, he took a minute to say goodbye to Chad who was having breakfast. "Hey Chad," he said, "Just hoping you have an enjoyable time in your new home. Remember not to snore and wake up everyone." Chad replied, "You are so funny Mikey. I will miss you." He then got up and gave Mikey a quick hug before he settled back to the table to finish his breakfast.

Mikey soon joined Mr. Gosine and two other boys who were also starting the Basic Business program that day. The drive to the city was about twenty minutes and during that time, Mikey took in the sights on the way. He had told Andrea about the program when she last visited, and she reminded him about the importance of being pleasant to others and being honest in what he did. Soon enough Mr. Gosine stopped at a diner which was located next to a men's store. There were several tables stacked up on the sidewalk where the customers would usually sit and have their meals. It was now empty, and Mr. Gosine escorted the boys to meet the owner, Mr. Mack.

"Welcome to Mackey's Diner boys!" shouted Mr. Mack as he walked across to meet three young men. Mr. Mack was a short man with a mop of grey hair and friendly brown eyes. The boys also noticed that he walked with a limp, but this did not keep back the speed at which he moved towards them. He shook the hands of each boy as they introduced themselves. He outlined to them what they would be doing for the time that they would be there. Mr. Gosine then left them in Mr. Mack's care and told them that he would return at noon.

Soon enough, Mr. Mack took them to the back to place their bags in the locker and then introduced them to the rest of his five-member team. The diner would soon be open, and they would have to assist with getting the chairs and tables cleaned and the general area ready for the customers. Mikey ran ahead of the other boys and began taking down the red chairs that were stacked in a corner. The other two boys, Mervyn and Emmanuel soon joined him, and they laid out about twenty round blue tables on the sidewalk in front of the diner. After doing so, Mr. Mack showed them where to get the cleaning cloths and utensils.

Mikey sang a little song that he remembered his mother used to sing for him: "If you happy, move your feet, if you happy, move your feet, happy am I, so I move my happy feet." As he sang, he wiped the chairs and placed them in fours around each table. Mervyn and Emmanuel focused on wiping the tables and putting tablecloths on them. When this was done, they all got brooms and cleaned up the area where the customers would soon come in.

At 9:00 am sharp, Mr. Mack put on the sign to show that the diner was open for business. The boys were told where to position themselves when the customers came in and what to do when customers moved from the tables. Mikey noticed how effortlessly the servers moved from one table to the next taking orders and how busy they were bringing food to the table and ensuring that the customers paid the bills. He noticed too that even when a customer was rude, the servers put on their best smiles and functioned as though they did not see that rude behavior. "Wow!" he said to himself quietly, "I wonder if I could be so patient." He was soon jolted out of his thoughts when the first customer left, and he and his colleagues had to spring into action to clean the table and chairs. Once this was done, another customer was led to the table, and they once again assumed their positions out of sight. At about 10:00 am, Mr. Mack told them they could have a ten-minute break and a snack and a drink on the house. This, he said, was part of the benefits of working in his business. Mervyn had his break first, then Emmanuel and finally Mikey.

During his break, he observed that the servers got extra money from the customers. He had to find out more about that from Mr. Gosine. When his break was finished, he went back to helping with the cleaning of the tables and chairs. At one time he had to get the broom to clean up around a table. Mikey did all of this with speed and with a dance in his step. He enjoyed getting the area prepared for the customers and seeing the smiles on their faces when they were ushered to a clean table.

He and the other boys were so caught up in what they were doing, that they did not notice when Mr. Gosine walked through the door. He waved to Mervyn who alerted the others that he was there. This signaled the end of their first tour of the Basic Work program. Mr. Mack came across and sat at a table with Mr. Gosine and the boys. "Well," he started, "If these boys keep up as they have started, I see some very good workers here." The boys all smiled and were told to go for their bags. Upon their return to the table, Mr. Mack gave each of them a small brown envelope. Each boy opened his envelope gingerly, and smiles appeared on their faces when they realized that they had just been paid for their services. Mr. Mack commended them for their attitude towards the tasks that they had to do, and they said their goodbyes. "See you all next weekend boys," said Mr. Mack as he hustled off to take care of his customers.

On the way home, Mr. Gosine asked, "Well what did you think about today?" "I had fun," replied Emmanuel. "It was all right. I am so tired though," said Mervyn. "Tired?" said Mr. Gosine. "Imagine if you had to work for eight hours." "What about you Mikey?" asked Mr. Gosine. "I wanted to know about the money that I see the customers giving to the servers," he replied. "Why did they do that?" "Good observation Mikey. That is called a tip. Customers show their appreciation for the service given by the servers and give them something extra for their hard work," explained Mr. Gosine. "Oh, ok," said Mikey as he rested his head thinking of how many tips he may be able to get while working. A little smile crossed his lips as he began dozing off as they made their way through the traffic back to the orphanage.

Andrea came to visit Mikey that evening and he was excited to tell her about his first day on the work program. Mikey could not wait for her to take a seat and begin rattling off about his day at the Diner. After he rambled on for about twenty minutes with her nodding and smiling, he somehow sensed that something was wrong. He stopped mid-sentence and looked at her. She did not seem like her usual bubbly self and Mikey could not help but ask, "Is something wrong Ms. Andrea?" She smiled once again and told him to sit next to her on the bench in the courtyard. "Mikey, I have something to tell you," she said quietly as she placed her arm around his shoulder.

Mikey looked her in the eyes trying to understand what Andrea could have to say to him. She let her gaze fall on him for a few seconds before she said, "I got a job offer in another country and I will soon be leaving to start working there." She paused for a moment so that Mikey could process what she had just mentioned to him. He sat on the bench staring at nothing and said nothing for a while. After an uncomfortable silence between them both, he finally said, "I will miss you Ms. Andrea. You are like my mummy even though we do not live together. I will miss my snacks and your visits. Do you really have to go? Beside you, my only other friend was Chad. If he goes with his new family, I will have no one left. What will I do? I wish I could get a family to adopt me and give me love just like Chad." Having said this, he burst into tears and hugged Andrea tighter than ever. Her heart was breaking, and she said to him, "My moving is not because I do not love you Mikey. I wish that I could have taken you in myself, but I could not sustain you financially. This new job will offer me the opportunity to improve my situation, which I cannot tell you too much about. I am sure though, that very soon you will get a family to love you. You are smart, you are lovable, and you learn quickly. You can become anything that you want to be in your life Mikey. Never ever let anyone make you feel less than you are because of where you started in life. Always remember the qualities that would make you shine, and money cannot buy that. I heard you talk about your first day on the Basic Work Program and if you continue with that attitude, you will soon become a supervisor there. Just always do your best and treat people with respect. I know that you will do well Mikey. I feel it in my bones. I will continue to stay in touch by writing to you and calling if you want that. Who knows? One day you will visit me in Grenada." "Where is that?" he asked with a small frown on his forehead. "It is a small island in the Caribbean. You can google it and learn more," Andrea replied. "When do you plan to leave then?" he asked.

"In one month's, time, so we still have time to hang out," said Andrea with her lips curving into a smile. Mikey's brown eyes darted across at her as he leaned back with his head resting on her shoulder. "I will start reading up about Grenada so that I can know everything about where you are going and where I will one day be visiting," he said dreamily.

With this, they remained seated on the bench just quietly absorbing each other's company. For the first time Mikey did not want to eat the snacks which Andrea brought for him. When it was time for her to leave, he took the bag with the snacks and told her that he would eat them the next day because he was not hungry. They both hugged again, and she patted him on his head as she made her way to her car. It would be a long night for Mikey, for he just could not go to sleep with the thought that he was now going to be all alone in this orphanage and in the world. It was then the thought hit him. "If I focus on the work and get tips, I will save that money to one day achieve my dream. I must be rich one day and see Andrea and check on my friend, Chad," he said to himself. It was enough for him to pull the blanket over his head and doze into a sweet sleep.

The next morning, Mikey flew up out of his bed when he felt something wet. On opening his eyes, he saw Prince standing over his bed with a mug of water having a good laugh. "Wake up stupid! It is late and you have chores to do!" taunted Prince. Mikey was so angry that he simply rushed headlong into Prince knocking him over and into the rail of one of the beds. The other boys began shouting and urging them to fight. There was no need to, for both boys were now tumbling all over the dormitory and may have continued for much longer had Mr. Gosine not rushed in to part the fight. Mikey was sitting on top of Prince pounding away at his face until he felt hands grab him off Prince. Prince's mouth was now bloodied, and his right eye was swollen as he tried rising from the floor. One of the other boys assisted him in getting up and took him to the nurse to get attended to. In the meantime, Mr. Gosine held on to Mikey who, by now, was not only drenched with water, but with blood dripping from a cut he had sustained on his right hand. Mr. Gosine looked at the cut and felt that it was not life-threatening. He told Mikey to get his shower and report to his office after.

Mikey was never so angry, and he stormed off down to the dorm to organize himself for his shower. "I need to leave this place! I wish someone could take me away from here!" he said to no one in particular. The anger, mixed with the feelings he had pent up in his bosom, somehow found expression in the tears that flowed like a dam down his face. He stood in the shower and allowed the chilly water to wash over him, and he soon stopped crying. The hurt and the pain he felt were now replaced by a determination to overcome. As he stood under the water, he could not help but smile as he recalled how he had beaten Prince. "Now he would respect me," he smiled to himself.

After a half an hour had passed, Mikey was dressed but had to go to see Mr. Gosine before he had his breakfast. Mr. Gosine was seated at his desk brooding over a document when Mikey walked into his office. He looked up and pointed to the old red chair that was in front of his desk. Mikey sat down slowly and allowed his eyes to meet Mr. Gosine's intense gaze. Mikey felt uncomfortable but decided that he would not show it. He folded his arms and looked directly at Mr. Gosine, who, by now, had rocked back in his chair. He stared at Mikey for a few more seconds before he shook his head and burst out laughing. "The damage that you did to Prince showed the kind of talent that you have within you," he said with a smirk. "Have you ever thought about wrestling? For a boy who is always so quiet, you taught

Prince a good lesson. I am not saying that fighting was good, but you proved that you could handle yourself well if you were pushed." Mikey did not know what to say and sat there in shock for he thought he was going to get the scolding of his life. Mr. Gosine continued, "In the world out there, you will have to learn to stand up for yourself. Life is not easy and there are moments when you must stand up for yourself. You have shown that you can do that today. However, be careful, for there are times when you must make the decision whether it is the right time to engage the person who is taunting you. At times, there is no need to respond to everything."

"Thanks Mr. Gosine," Mikey responded. As he was about to get up from his seat, Mr. Gosine said, "On another note, I understood that you worked quite well on your first rotation. I want to urge you to keep it up. Who knows? You may own a business one day, and this is a start. Many wealthy people have started off with small businesses. Keep your chin up and always do your best while being courteous and respectful." Mr. Gosine dismissed him from his office.

Mikey walked out the office feeling lighter than when he had gone in and proceeded to the hall where he had a hearty breakfast. The fight with Prince and the fear of the unknown with Mr. Gosine had taken up room in his brain and food was the last thing on his mind. At the breakfast table, he realized that he was famished.

Mikey spent the rest of the day in his classes and avoided any interaction with Prince who was now wearing bandages on various parts of his body; evidence of his recent beat-down. Mikey was never bothered by Prince after that incident. Chad had also returned for a few days to collect the remainder of his personal belongings and had informed Mikey that he liked his new home, so he was going to stay there with his newly adopted family. With Chad gone, Mikey spent more time on his schoolwork and particularly liked Mathematics. Aside from the Business Program, which he looked forward to with a heightened eagerness, he did not care to have too many friends and preferred spending time on the internet researching many topics which interested him.

Andrea continued to visit him and increased her time with him to two visits per week to ensure that they spent as much time together. He had told her about his fight with Prince and what Mr. Gosine had said to him. She reminded him of the talks they had in the past and even told him that Mr. Gosine had provided him with sound advice. On her last visit with him, she gave him a green leather journal. She urged him to use it daily to write about his feelings, his thoughts, his dreams and about anything he wanted. She even told him to think of the journal as though he was chatting with her. She departed that evening with the promise that she would remain in touch, and he retreated to his bed hugging his journal close to his chest as the tears fell quietly. With the thought that he was now alone, he slept fitfully that night.

As the months passed by, Mikey began to get more involved in the business program and asked Mr. Mack to be given more work in the areas where he could directly interact with the customers. He was happiest when that day finally arrived. One day, when Mr. Gosine had dropped him off at the diner, Mr. Mack called him and informed him that he was now moving him up from busser to assist the waiters. In this new role, Mikey would be taking orders from the customers and bringing their meals to them. He would be under the guidance of one of the seasoned waiters. He was bubbling with excitement and hurriedly ran to the changing room to put on his gear.

On getting back to the main lobby, he was paired with Sonya Hastings, a young lady who worked at the diner for the past five years. She greeted Mikey with a smile and told him that he would go with her to the table when she was taking orders. In that way, he would get a first-hand view as to how to operate. He had no objections to this and stayed close to Sonya when she made her rounds to the customers' tables. He soon learned how to provide the menu to customers, how to explain and advise on the offerings and how to help Sonya with the bills. He soon realized that his calculation skills would be in use at the diner. He also noted that Sonya got generous tips when she worked, and he hoped that he would soon be the recipient of tips as well.

Among his observations, he noticed that any rotation that he worked, a tall gentleman sporting a thick well-groomed gray beard, always arrived at nine in the morning and sat at table eight located in the right-hand corner of the diner. "Who is that customer who sits in that corner and at that table each time?" he asked Sonya one day, pointing in the direction of the gentleman. She turned around and replied, "Oh, that is Bob Kramer. He owns Kramer Real Estate Company. He has been one of our faithful customers for much longer than I have worked here. When he enters, you know that it is 9:00 am. He is pleasant so you will get to meet him one day in your rounds."

That day did not take long in coming for it was about two weeks after his chat with Sonya that Mikey was asked to attend to Mr. Kramer. Mikey was doing quite well with the customers and now Sonya wanted to evaluate him to see how he would conduct himself without her being there.

Mikey went directly to Table Eight and said, "Good morning, sir. My name is Mike, but everyone calls me Mikey. I will be assisting with your order today. Would you be having your usual toast, scrambled eggs, sausage, and coffee today?" The gentleman smiled as he looked up from the table. "Hello Mikey. I am happy to make your acquaintance, and I must say that you have a keen sense of observation. How do you know what my usual young man is?" "Well sir, I usually pay attention to what customers order as part of my training and I noticed that you would order the same thing each time that you are here. I do need to ask though, in case you changed your mind," replied Mikey. Bob looked at Mikey with a smile and gave a nod of his head. "Sure. I will have the usual," said Bob with an approving nod of his head. "No problem, sir. Your order will be coming right up," said Mikey as he moved quickly to take the order to the kitchen.

In about ten minutes, Mikey was moving like quicksilver among the tables, bringing Bob his order. "Bon Appetit!" he remarked, just as he would usually hear the seasoned waiters telling their customers. Bob once again smiled and became engrossed in the meal before him. In the meantime, Mikey served other tables and moved to take an order from an old lady who had seated herself at one of the tables close to the door. The lady walked with the aid of a cane and Mikey introduced himself while ensuring that she was comfortable. He then did the routine provision of the Menu, chatting with her about what she wanted and finally took her order to the kitchen. When she was finished with her meal, he held her bag and her hand as she was trying to lift herself from the chair. Quite unexpectedly, she said to him, "Young man, thank you for the care and attention which you gave to me. You have helped me to feel relaxed while at this diner. Not many young people have the patience to deal with old folks like me. Please hold this as a token of my appreciation." Mikey was stunned when he saw her place forty dollars in his right hands. He gulped hard before he stuttered, "Thank you miss." "Call me Ms. Viola," she replied with a smile. "Thank you, Ms. Viola," he said as he beamed from ear to ear placing the money securely into his deep pocket. Once the lady was gone, he went back to check on Bob, who, by now, was just finishing his meal. "How was your meal sir?" asked Mikey. "Delicious as always," replied Bob. "Is there anything else that you would like now?" asked Mikey. "No, I am filled. Just bring me the bill," replied Bob with a smile. When Mikey returned to Bob's table, he was surprised when Bob said to him, "What area are you from Mikey?" The young boy bent his head and whispered, "Precious Children's Orphanage."

"The orphanage at Fair Meadows Avenue?" Bob asked. Mikey nodded. "That is interesting," Bob continued. "I have been watching how you dealt with the customers all morning and especially that elderly lady. You have shown great qualities young man. Keep it up!" Mikey smiled and nodded his head. "Thank you, sir," he said, still beaming from his encounter with Ms. Viola. With that, he took up the wares from the table and placed them in the sink. After that, he took Bob's bill to him and provided him with his change. As Bob was leaving the diner, he gave Mikey a twenty-dollar tip. Mikey smiled even more now that his mental calculator had indicated that he had received sixty dollars in tips for the morning. He was so happy that he did not even notice when Mr. Gosine arrived to pick him up along with the other two boys. "How was your morning?" Mr. Gosine asked in his usual fatherly voice. While the other boys sounded tired when they responded to Mr. Gosine, Mikey had a fresh burst of energy and said to Mr. Gosine, "The morning was great sir!"

On the drive back to the Orphanage, Mikey said little and preferred to stare out the window quietly gloating in the happiness of receiving his little haul that morning.

It was exactly two months after her departure that Mikey got a call from Andrea. She had been trying to settle into her new home and was unable to communicate with him before that. She sounded exhausted but happy to chat with him. He, too, was brimming with excitement and could not hold back all the fun that he was having doing his weekly rotation at the diner. He told her everything as well about how he had gotten tips and where he hid his money from the other boys. In any case, Andrea told him it would be nice to have a bank account one day where he could continue to save his money and get interest. "What is interest?" he asked. She then spent time explaining that to him. After twenty minutes of conversation, Andrea told him that she had to go. She gave him her mobile number if he wanted to contact her and encouraged him to one day purchase his own phone so it could be easier to stay in touch. "Talk to you soon," Andrea said to Mikey.

"Remember that you are special, and I love you." Mikey smiled when he heard those words, he never thought he would hear someone saying to him "I love you." "I love you too, Ms. Andrea," he replied. As the phone clicked off, he returned to his room and sat pondering on whether he would see Andrea any time soon. He missed her and he missed their talks. In the time being, however, he knew that he had to do what he must do to make her proud of him.

Three weeks later, Mikey had just finished a class when Mr. Gosine met him in the corridor. "How are things Mikey? "He asked." "Not bad sir. I am doing the topic of interest in Mathematics and only some weeks ago Ms. Andrea told me about Interest. I see that what we do in math is what takes place in all that we do. I enjoy that subject." "Indeed, math takes place all around us," Mr. Gosine reiterated. "I needed to ask; did you meet a gentleman by the name of Bob Kramer recently at the diner?" "Oh, Mr. Kramer! Yeah! He comes in at the same time, sits at the same table and orders the same menu each time I am there," Mikey answered with a slight smile. "Why do you ask sir?" Mr. Gosine simply shrugged his shoulders and with a smile he said, "Well, he called today to compliment us on how well we are doing in helping the children to develop based on how well you and your two friends were doing at the diner. In fact, he asked to visit the orphanage to see how he can further assist us in any way. What do you think about that? "Well sir, I think that any help that we get for the Orphanage would be good for all of us. The old Music Room needs to be fixed so that we could begin to learn different instruments. Barry would also get a place to sing his off-key tunes and not disturb us when he is bathing." As he said this, he let out a loud boisterous laugh that even caused Mr. Gosine to laugh until his slightly round belly trembled. "Ok Mikey, I will chat further with Mr. Kramer, and we will see what can take place. With that, he walked briskly to his office.

On his way to his room, Mikey pondered on the conversation and was surprised that Mr. Kramer had in fact called the orphanage after asking him where he resided. He felt good that his encounter with him would, in fact, work out in such a way that the other children at the orphanage would get improved facilities. With those thoughts, he smiled and did not notice that a window was opened near to the dorm's entrance, and he bumped into it hitting his forehead. The sudden pain caused him to drop the book which he had in his hand, and he massaged the spot. After the pain subsided, he picked up the book and continued to his room angry with himself for not being more careful. He made a mental note to inform Mr. Gosine that the direction in which the window opened needed to be reversed. This could be added to the list of things that needed to be fixed at the orphanage.

The next morning, his forehead was swollen the size of a small ball, and he needed to get to the nurse to get a pain killer. That day, he realized that he needed to stay in bed because his head throbbed badly. This was the first time that he could not attend class, but he knew that he would be no good to himself if he did attend and had to rest his head on the desk.

In the sick room, he was examined by the nurse and given painkillers. He was given a sick slip to take to his teacher, Mr. Boswell, after which he proceeded to the dorm. Within ten minutes of taking the painkillers, Mikey fell asleep with his blanket pulled tightly around him and there he remained for the day.

It was around 5:00 pm when he woke up confused wondering what time of day it was. It was when one of his roommates told him the time that he remembered. "Wow!" he said to himself, "Those pills really knocked me out." As he said this, he touched his forehead and gave a little wince. He observed that the pain was not as bad as before. He remained on his bed for a while and around 6:00 pm, he went to shower and organize himself for dinner.

CHAPTER 2

Making Cents of Work

"Teamwork is the essence of business success."

"A visitor?" he asked Sharon, the clerical officer, who had come to the classroom to get him the next morning around eleven. He excused himself from his class and followed her to Mr. Gosine's office, wondering who this visitor could be. As he entered, he was totally surprised to see Bob Kramer sitting there, smiling, and chatting with Mr. Gosine.

Mikey entered the office with a surprised expression on his face. "Have a seat," said Mr. Gosine, pointing to the chair on the left of the gentleman. Mikey sat on the edge of the chair and focused his eyes on Mr. Gosine who proceeded to explain the reason for the visit. "Mikey, do you remember Mr. Kramer who is a regular customer at the diner?" Mikey nodded without uttering a word. "Well," continued Mr. Gosine, "He has been observing how you worked and interacted with the customers at the diner and when he found out where you lived, he felt that he should do something for the orphanage. Because it was your qualities that led to this, I thought it only fair that you be the first to know the impact that your behavior had for the orphanage." At this point, Bob chimed in, "Yes, Mikey. Sorry I did not tell you anything before but after I had asked you where you lived, I went home and thought about what I could do to assist the children at the home since they were doing a wonderful job in instilling the right values in not just you, but your colleagues as well. You and the other children can let Mr. Gosine know what you would like for the home, and I will do my best to help. Are you fine with that or am I being too nosey?" Mikey smiled when he heard this and said, "Not at all Mr. Kramer. Thank you very much. We will give Mr. Gosine our list." He was told that he could leave and as he rose, Bob got up and shook his hand.

Mikey left the office deep in thought wondering how best this Mr. Kramer could help make things better at the orphanage. He decided to chat about it with his two other friends, Mervyn, and Emmanuel, who worked on the Program at the diner on Saturdays. They were both surprised to hear about it, and he asked them to keep it quiet but think about what they, too, would want to see improved. Both guys thought it was wonderful that their presence at the diner could result in something positive for the home. They promised Mikey that they would think about it and get back to him.

Three days after their conversation, the boys met under the tree and exchanged ideas which they had. "The bathrooms are in need of repair as well as the broken dryer in the Laundry Room needs to be repaired," said Emmanuel. "Yeah, I noticed that too," said Mervyn. "Do you think Mr. Kramer could put in a library for us?" said Mervyn in a timid voice. "We do not know, Merv, but nothing is wrong with adding it to the list," said Mikey. The boys continued their conversation until they exhausted their thoughts. All that time, Mikey was jotting down the ideas. They were all smiling when they left the bench that evening. Mikey went straight to Mr. Gosine to hand over the list of ideas and told him that Mervyn and Emmanuel also contributed. Mr. Gosine smiled when he realized that Mikey had involved the other boys who worked with him. "Good teamwork from you boys," he replied as he patted Mikey on the head.

After that, Mikey did not see Mr. Kramer return to the orphanage but saw him at the diner. He would be his usual self but her never mentioned his visit at the home and Mikey did not speak about it either. He went about his usual business dealing with the customers and enjoying the tips that came his way.

It was not until one month after that the children at the home noticed a construction crew turn up at the orphanage. Mr. Gosine seemed to have been caught by surprise and called the children into the lunchroom where he briefed them about the work that was about to take place. The students all cheered, for they too were happy to have improved living conditions. They were all instructed to keep away from some areas where the work would begin and told that they may hear some noise and there may be dust. As such, they must keep away from those areas that would be worked on. The children were excited and could not wait to see the finished project. Emmanuel, Mervyn, and Mikey gave each other high-fives after the meeting; their ideas were about to become a reality.

Mr. Kramer had in fact, asked one of his colleagues, Joe Miller, to render assistance to the Orphanage and Joe's company, Tips Construction, had willingly obliged to do the work at no cost. Mr. Gosine knew but did not provide those details to the boys. He could not stop thanking Mr. Kramer whenever he came by to look at the progress with respect to the project.

One day, however, while in conversation with Mr. Kramer, he was casually asked about Mikey and his background. Given Mikey's impact on the man, he was not surprised by the question, and he started off by telling him that Mikey's mum had passed away and so he was brought to the orphanage. He mentioned that he had no family but had been loved by those who had taken care of him from the time that he entered the hospital with his dying mum. He mentioned Andrea and how she had taken a special interest in the boy, but she had migrated and continued to stay in touch with him. He spoke about Mikey's dream to one day have a family but for now, the only family he had was at the orphanage. He also spoke of Mikey's love for Mathematics and his determination to be a success. When he was finished, Mr. Kramer could not help but notice that Mr. Gosine wiped away tears of pride which welled up in his eyes. He recognized that Mikey was dear to this man who managed the orphanage. At the end of their conversation that day, Mr. Kramer shook Mr. Gosine's hand and commended him on the excellent job that he was doing with the children under his care.

"Wow!" was the collective response from the children when the new wing was unveiled about two months after. "Our building looks great!" shouted Evan, one of the young boys looking on as the ribbon was cut to open the renovated building. The children ran towards the door to explore what was inside. The chatter from them created a great vibe and Mikey felt proud of what was accomplished. He gave Mervyn and Emmanuel a high five since they, too, had an input in the project.

He walked over to where Bob Kramer, Mr. Miller, the contractor, and Mr. Gosine were chatting. "Excuse me Mr. Kramer," he said with all the pride he could muster, "Thank you for what you have done for us. All of us are happy and I for one will not be bouncing my head anymore." With that comment the men laughed, and Bob patted Mikey on his head. "It was a pleasure Mikey," he replied. "But the praise should really go to Mr. Miller here for his hard work."

Mikey turned to Mr. Miller and thanked him for the work that was done by his team. He then ran off to join his friends. Not long after, Mr. Miller took his leave, having to visit another job at another location. As Bob and Mr. Gosine stood chatting, he suddenly stopped and asked Mr. Gosine, "What are the procedures to adopt a child from the orphanage?" As Mr. Gosine advised him, Bob listened carefully, asking for clarification when he did not understand. "Why do you ask?" Mr. Gosine questioned.

"I have a friend who mentioned to me a while back that he and his wife had two daughters but were unable to have any more children of their own. They always wanted a son and were thinking about adopting a boy. That was a year ago, so I do not know if that is still the case with them. I do not usually see them and may have lost their number. However, I can make a check," said Bob as he looked at his watch. He made a sign to Mr. Gosine that he had to go, and, in a few minutes, he was driving out of the compound leaving behind a group of children who were running around ecstatically. Mr. Gosine himself went to join his charges and tour the newly renovated building.

Five weeks after the opening of the renovated building, Mr. Gosine received a call from Bob. He informed him that he was able to get in touch with his friend Evan Andrews and that he and his wife were still contemplating adoption. He then asked if Mikey could be the boy that they could consider since he believed that Mr. Andrews and his wife would take loving care of him and provide him with a comfortable, loving home. Mr. Gosine was happy that Mikey was being considered since he felt that Mikey was so deserving of a nurturing environment and a family where he could be loved. Mikey was special to him, and he would not allow the child to go with just anyone. He advised Bob that Mr. Andrews and his wife must come in to meet with him and a date was arranged. In the time being, he wondered if he should tell Mikey anything or simply surprise him. He opted for the latter.

On the date that was agreed, Bob and his friends, Mr. and Mrs. Andrews were all seated in Mr. Gosine's office discussing the process of adoption. When the couple was satisfied with the process, they were anxious to meet with Mikey. Mr. Gosine, as well as Bob, had spoken highly of the little boy. Before Mikey was brought to meet the Andrews family, however, Bob decided to take his leave. He did not want Mikey to know that he had a hand in his adoption. "I would prefer that he did not think that there was any connection to me. All the best," said Bob as he slipped out of the door and headed towards his car.

Mr. Gosine then sent for Mikey to come to his office. Mikey sat at the edge of the chair as though he would fall off. He took a few seconds before he uttered, "I do not know what to say. This is a surprise for me. I am happy to know that I am being considered." As he said these words, he smiled and bent his head. There was an awkward silence as he sat there with tears brimming in his eyelids, uttering not a word, and simply staring at the two people who were thinking of adopting him. For a fleeting moment he wished it were Ms.

Andrea sitting there. However, she was not in the country, and he had to move on. She would always be there for him; he knew that. Many thoughts raced around his head at this time. How was he supposed to react? He had waited for this for such a long time and now that the day had indeed arrived, he did not know what to say. It was Mr. Gosine who broke the silence when he said in a fatherly voice, "Mikey." He paused as the young boy turned to look in his direction and then he continued, "These folks already have two daughters, but they always wanted a son and when they connected with us at the home, they heard about the wonderful person that you are and could not wait to see you. Please meet Evan and Diana Andrews." Mikey looked over at the two people who now rose to greet him. He observed that Evan was tall and handsome with an endearing smile and Diana was a beautiful woman of medium height with curly black hair and well-dressed in matching heels and handbag. He rose from his seat and shook hands with them. "Pleased to meet you,'" he said to each of them. Mr. Andrews not only shook his hand but patted him on the head as he would do to a son. This gesture warmed Mikey and he smiled.

Mikey realized that these people were the answer to his prayer. He had been hoping to move in with a family where he would be loved. He sat back in his chair feeling a bit more comfortable. His surprise and timidity were now replaced by curiosity. What would it be like to live with these two people? What were their daughters like? Would he then have sisters as time went by? The thought of sisters made him smile.

Mr. Gosine then guided the discussion when he said, "The procedure here is that the child to be adopted would usually stay with the family for a week to determine if he himself would want to live with the family considering him. It goes both ways. If Mikey has no objections, we can arrange a time when this can be done. Would you be interested Mikey?" The boy looked at all the adults seated in the room. He then gave a slight nod in response. "Is that yes?" asked Mr. Gosine. "Yes, it is," he replied shyly. It was a happy moment for everyone in the room including Mr. Gosine, who was fighting hard to hold back the tears. After signing up the necessary documents, a time was agreed upon a time when Mikey would go to Andrews' residence.

Mr. Andrews, upon getting ready to leave, stretched out his hand and shook Mikey's again. With a smile he said to Mikey, "We have been told so many good things about you that we would be happy to have you as part of our family. We look forward to welcoming you to our home." Diana Andrews, however, had not said much and simply smiled and walked out with her husband.

As he left Mr. Gosine's office, Mikey could not help but smile as he returned to his class with an extra bounce in his step.

That night, with so many questions floating around in his head, Mikey tossed and turned in his bed sweating beads of perspiration. The fan in his room seemed unable to cool him down. What would it be like? Would they like me? Would I like them? He finally got up to get a drink of water and returned to his bed.

The next morning Mikey got up later than usual but hastened to get dressed to go to his work rotation. He was still sleepy, but he was excited about the day ahead of him. When he got to the diner, he went about his routine with the same level of efficiency. When Bob Kramer came in that morning, Mikey took his order and chatted with him as usual. There was nothing to indicate that he knew what was taking place with Mikey. However, that morning, upon leaving, he gave him a bigger tip than usual, and the boy smiled thinking of his increased savings over the past few weeks.

Upon returning to the orphanage after his routine at the diner that morning, Mikey hastened to pack his bag. Since he had arrived at that home, he did not really have an opportunity to pack his bag to go anywhere to spend time. It was a strange, yet joyous feeling that engulfed him. One thing he made sure to pack was the brown envelope which his mother left for him. It was always his comfort when he was not in a good mood, and he was surely not going to leave it behind. He made sure, as well, to pack his money saved from his tips. He had asked Mr. Gosine to get him a lock for his locker and he had made sure to hide away his savings.

At around 2:00 pm, Mr. Gosine came to inform him that Mr. Andrews was there to pick him up. "Are you ready?" Mr. Gosine said with a smile. "I guess I am sir," he replied quietly. "Well off you go to see what it would be like outside of these walls. Do remember to be you Mikey. I have watched you develop since you came here, and I must say that you are one of the best boys that we have had here at the Orphanage. Make me proud of you." With that, Mikey gave him a long hug before he walked down the corridor with him.

Upon reaching the vehicle, which was parked at the front of the office, Mr. Andrews walked over to Mikey and greeted him with a handshake and offered to take his bag. Mikey declined since he did not trust anyone with his bag which contained his only precious belongings in the world. Instead, he said to Mr. Andrews, "Thanks sir, but my bag is light. I can carry it." Mr. Andrews then went to the other side of the car to open the door for him and after saying his goodbye to Mr. Gosine and Pam Strudel. She was one of the counselors who had joined them at the front of the office. Mikey walked towards the car without looking back. As the car was slowly driven out of the compound, Pam said, "There is something about that boy. I look forward to hearing wonderful things about him." With that, both she and Mr. Gosine returned to the office.

Along the way, Mikey took in the sights of the city with the many tall brown stone buildings, the huge park where many children were at play and the well-kept lawns and homes which formed part of the landscape through which they drove on their way to the Andrews' residence. As they drove, his mind was upon Andrea. He had not heard from her for a couple of weeks, and he was beginning to wonder if all was well with her. He promised himself that he would somehow try to contact her when he settled in. He missed her tremendously and he wondered if Mrs. Andrews would be like Andrea. If she were going to be his new mother, what would she be like?

After forty minutes or so, Mr. Andrews pulled into a driveway that was edged on both sides by a neat green hedge. The light green, two-storey house that stood before them was surrounded by a garden filled with palm trees and rose trees. Mikey smiled as he saw the garden. He always wanted to have a home with a garden, and this was like a dream coming through here.

When they had parked, Mr. Andrews unlocked the front door and ushered Mikey into his home. "Honey, we are here!" Mr. Andrews said with some degree of excitement. Soon enough, the woman he had met at the orphanage sauntered into the living room. Mikey expected that she would hug him. However, she stood there smiling and looking at him from head to toe and said to him, "Welcome to our home Mikey." "Thank you miss. Mike Clary is my full name," he explained, "but everyone calls me Mikey." "Good to hear that explanation. Do make yourself comfortable. You can call me Mrs. D instead of miss. Be relaxed here. Evan will take you to your room and you can get some rest. Dinner will be at six this evening." She turned and walked back to the kitchen.

Mr. Andrews then proceeded to walk up the stairs with Mikey in tow. The room which Mikey got was simple and neat with a small bed and television in it. There was a window which opened out onto a tree outside. He told Mikey that the two girls, Cindy and Hetty, were out to dance class and would be home by five. He gave Mikey a short tour of the house and explained where things were. Mikey noted that the bathroom near to the bedrooms was a shared space with the girls. He wondered what it would be like living with them and sharing the space. He had been sharing space with several boys since he was at the orphanage. He smiled to himself and let out a quiet sigh. After being shown around for about fifteen minutes, Mikey was left to get some rest. He laid down on the small bed and drifted off into a sound sleep. About an hour after, Mikey was awakened by the sound of laughter and chatter coming from the room down the corridor. The girls had arrived. This prompted Mikey to straighten up his bed just in case they came calling; and that they did. Within five minutes, he heard a knocking on his door, and he said, "Come in." Soon enough, standing in front of him were two girls who introduced themselves. Cindy, the taller of the two girls, shook his hands and said, "Hello Mikey, I am Cindy. Nice to meet you." Then it was Hetty's turn, and she too shook his hands and said, "Welcome to our home Mikey. I am Hetty and I am pleased to meet you." Mikey smiled politely with both girls and felt a bit awkward being in the room with two girls. He had lived in a boys' dormitory for the past few years. He noticed that while Hetty was shorter, she resembled her father more and had shoulder-length black hair. Cindy, on the other hand, had short brown hair and a dimpled smile. Mikey felt that it would be fun to get to know these girls. It was Hetty who said, "Come on Mikey, let us have dinner before mum gets annoyed. She never likes her dinner to go cold." With that, she grabbed Mikey's hand and the three rushed out of the room, closing the door behind them.

At the dinner table, Mr. Andrews blessed the meal and then proceeded to dish out the food. Before them was a simple dinner of baked chicken with mashed potato and garden salad. The aroma of the food made Mikey's mouth water, and he could not wait to eat. Mr. Andrews blessed the meal before the plates were passed around to be filled. While they were eating, Mikey noticed that each time he raised his head, Mrs. Andrews would be staring at him. Each time he would smile. At one time she asked, "Are you enjoying the food?" "Very much so Mrs. D. It is delicious," he replied. With that answer, she smiled approvingly. After the meal was finished, they had sponge cake for dessert. The girls then assisted with clearing up the table and washing the wares. Mikey too, chipped in by taking some of the dishes to the kitchen sink.

After that, they proceeded to the television room where they watched a movie for about an hour. During that time, Mikey noticed that Mrs. Andrews had fallen asleep on her husband's lap, and he woke her gently to guide her upstairs to her bed. When he and the girls were left alone, Cindy and Hetty bombarded him with questions about the orphanage and what they did there. Mikey was able to chat about what they did there, about Mr. Gosine and even told them about his Basic Work program. "Wow! That sounds cool," said Cindy. "I wish I too could one day meet customers like you do." Mikey beamed with pride as he spoke about the orphanage.

"What sport do you play?" asked Hetty. "None really, but sometimes I play football in the field with some of the other boys," said Mikey. "I mostly read books in my spare time." "Well, we also like girls' football at school and we do dance," said Hetty. "Perhaps you can come and see what we do at another time."

They then switched off the television and the three went to get their shower and prepare for bed.

When Mikey was tucked up in his bed, he heard a slight knock and saw Mr. Andrews enter the room. "Sleep well Mikey. You had a long day and I know the girls almost talked off your ear," he chuckled. Mikey smiled and as he was about to leave the room, he patted Mikey on his head and turned off the light.

The next day Mikey woke from his sleep around 6am and looked around his room. His first night at the Andrews' home was welcoming. He sat up on his bed and contemplated what the day ahead would be like at home. His mind ran across Andrea, and he promised himself that he would try to contact her that day. It was a while since he had heard from her, and he wanted to give her updates on what was taking place with him. Mikey snuggled under his blanket and fell asleep with a deep sense of contentment.

He then decided to get up and do his morning routine before the girls got up. He tiptoed around to make sure that he did not wake anyone. In about twenty minutes he was showered, dressed, and went downstairs to do some exploration by himself. He went through the living room and opened the door. He went out into the garden and smiled when he saw the birds flitting from one tree to another. He enjoyed the chirping sounds and the smell of fresh air. He continued his exploration and went to the back of the house where he noticed that there was a small room adjoining the house. He opened the door and saw a bed smaller than the one he had slept on. In that room there was a table and chair but no television. Next to the room was a small bathroom. He pondered why this room would be there and promised to ask when he got back in. One thing, though, he noticed that the room was just under the tree that was outside of his room and so the birds gathered a lot in that area. Mikey continued his walk around the house and after about fifteen minutes decided to return to the house. As he opened the door, the smell of bacon and eggs greeted him at the door. He smiled and went to the kitchen. "Good morning, Ms. D," he said chirpily. "Oh, good morning, Mikey," she replied. "How was your night?" "I slept well thank you and I already did some walking around outside." Mrs. Andrews responded by saying, "I see that you did not waste time in getting to know your surroundings. That is good. Would you like to help me set the table?" "Of course," replied Mikey. She showed him where the cutlery, plates and other items were stored. He soon had the table set for he learned how to do this at the Orphanage. He was looking over the set table when Mr. Andrews sauntered into the dining room. "Wow! Excellent job Mikey. "You did quite well there," he said encouragingly. Mikey beamed from ear to ear. "Thanks Mr. Andrews. I have already taken a walk around the house. Why do you have a room outside of the house?" "Oh, when we bought this house, that room was there as well as the small bathroom. At one time we had a guy who looked after the garden, and he used that room and the bathroom whenever he came by. It was convenient at the time. Since he got ill, no one else was hired, and I try to trim the trees and mow the lawn from time to time," said Mr. Andrews. "Oh, ok. The garden looks nice. The birds like it too." said Mikey.

They then went to the kitchen to help take the food to the table. In about ten minutes everything was ready, and Mr. Andrews called out to the girls to let them know that breakfast was ready.

Cindy and Hetty soon clambered down the stairs and hugged their parents before they both said in unison, "Good morning, Mikey." Cindy said, "I heard when you got up. You are an early bird." With that they laughed and took their seats at the table. Mr. Andrews said grace, and they all ate a hearty breakfast.

Once the dining table was cleared, Mr. Andrews washed the wares while his wife and the girls got dressed for church. Mikey was invited to attend church, but he indicated that he did not come prepared to attend. After half an hour, Mrs. Andrews and the girls were ready. They said their goodbyes and Mrs. Andrews drove off leaving Mr. Andrews and Mikey behind. "How are you doing so far?" Mr. Andrews asked Mikey. "I am doing well thanks sir," Mikey replied. "What do you like to do in your spare time Mikey?" Mr. Andrews asked. "Oh. I read a lot, and I enjoy a good game of football with my friends at the orphanage at times. I also enjoy speaking with my friend, Ms. Andrea," he responded. He then went on to tell Mr. Andrews about Andrea and how he wanted to contact her but did not have the means to do so. "Do you have a number for her?" Mr. Andrews asked. "Yes, she gave it to me the last time we spoke," said Mikey. "Ok, well bring it and let us see if we can get in touch with her," Mr. Andrews said with a smile.

Mikey rushed to his room to get the slip of paper with Andrea's number. In three minutes, he was back with Mr. Andrews and gave him the slip of paper. The elder man dialed the number from the house phone and after one minute of ringing the phone went to voicemail. Mikey looked disappointed. Mr. Andrews said, "Let us try again." He dialed the number again and waited for the phone to be answered. After four rings, he was about to hang up when a voice answered at the other end. "Hello," said the sleepy sounding voice. Mr. Andrews quickly passed the phone to Mikey, and he gushed out, "Ms. Andrea! This is Mikey!" "Oh, Mikey darling, how are you doing?" replied Andrea on the other end. "It is such a wonderful surprise to hear from you. I have been meaning to call you for some time now, but I am so busy with work that I am exhausted when I am in. I pray for you often though. How are you doing?" Mikey embraced the opportunity to tell her about his stay with the Andrews family and his Work Program. He told her how much he missed their talks and that he was happy to hear her voice. "I am happy to hear you too Mikey. I am so excited that you will finally have a home where you will be loved. Someday you will visit me where I am. For now, you just keep on getting good grades in school and making me proud of you. You are forever in my heart. Let me have a word with Mr. Andrews please," said Andrea.

For about a minute Mr. Andrews listened as Andrea introduced herself and told him what she felt he needed to know about taking care of Mikey. He smiled as he returned the phone to Mikey to say his goodbye. Mr. Andrews looked on as the little boy seemed so happy speaking to this woman.

Her short conversation with him made him realize the bond that the boy shared with her. He smiled as Mikey hung up the phone and thanked him for making the call. "Ms. Andrea is a lovely person, Mr. Andrews. She took really loving care of me when my mama was sick. One day I do hope that I can visit her," he said with a smile. He sat and closed his eyes for a while and Mr. Andrews chose not to disturb him in that space. Mr. Andrews then turned on the television and they both watched a game of football. During that time, the newspapers were delivered, and they sat reading for about half an hour. Mr. Andrews then invited Mikey to go out into the garden where they did some weeding and cleaning up around the yard. As soon as they came to the end of the yard work, the girls and Mrs. Andrews returned from church. Before the car was even parked, Cindy was waving frantically and shouting, "Hey Mikey, we are home! What have you been up to?" Hetty chimed in, "Seems like dad got a gardening partner now." They both laughed as their mother brought the car to a stop. The girls got out and scrambled inside the house to change their clothes while Mrs. Andrews walked around the car and stopped to survey the work that was done. "Hello Mikey, I see you are getting acquainted with the garden routine. Nice to see that you like plants," she said. Without waiting for a reply, she walked into the house.

Mikey and Mr. Andrews soon joined the girls and Mr. Andrews in the house. It was time to start cooking lunch and that started amidst chatter from the girls. Lunch was finished in about an hour's time and it was then time to set the table. Mikey and Mr. Andrews helped with the setting of the table and soon enough they were all seated ready to eat the lovely meal that was spread before them. Mikey was asked to say grace that day and he did so without hesitation. After lunch and cleaning the kitchen, the family took a nap. Mikey chose to watch television and so he stayed in the living room.

Later that evening, the family went for a drive and to purchase ice cream. Mikey enjoyed himself and chatted non-stop with the girls. He did notice, though, that while the girls and Mr. Andrews did a lot of talking, Mrs. Andrews did not talk much. Somehow, though, her husband sensed what she wanted without her saying much. At the ice-cream shop, he bought her Coconut ice- cream and said, "Here dear, your favorite flavor." She had taken the cone without even saying thanks but somehow, he ignored this and smiled through it all. Mikey had observed all of this while enjoying his Passion Fruit ice- cream. The family then went to the Botanic Gardens where they spent another hour or so before setting out on the trip back to the house. During the drive back home, Mikey took in the sights as the car rolled by. He liked the view of the buildings and the well-designed landscape that formed the backdrop. "I think I would like to live here," he said to himself.

On arrival at the house, they all hustled out of the car and went directly to the bathrooms to get ready for bed. Luckily, there was no school for the rest of that week and this pleased the children even more because it meant sleeping later than usual.

After the week had passed, it was time for Mikey to return to the orphanage. Having packed his bag, Mikey walked down the stairs slowly, contemplating what the next move may be. Did they like me enough for me to live with them? Would I have to remain at the Orphanage? While these thoughts occupied his mind, he did not see the girls hiding at the bottom of the stairs. As he got there, they pounced on him, throwing him to the floor and showering him with hugs. Mikey was completely taken by surprise. "We will miss you Mikey. You were fun to have around." said Cindy. "Yeah, hope we see you soon to play more pranks on you," Hetty joined in. Mikey could not help but smile when he heard these words. "Take care, you pranksters," he replied with a laugh.

He proceeded to the kitchen where he approached Mrs. Andrews and gave her a hug. This surprised her, and she barely responded. "Thanks for everything Ms. Diana," he said. She patted him on his shoulder and without a word, she went back to her chores.

Mr. Andrews came into the kitchen and said, "Are you ready Mikey?" "Yes sir," he replied. After saying goodbye to the girls and waving to them, Mikey settled in the car as they made the return trip to the Orphanage.

"How was your week with us Mikey?" Mr. Andrews inquired. "I had fun with the girls, and I also enjoyed helping you in the garden. Ms. Diana is also a good cook. I like your family," Mikey said. "That is good news. We like you as well Mikey," said Mr. Andrews. With that being said, the rest of the journey was quiet, and Mikey took the time to snooze until they arrived at the Orphanage.

When he got there, he ran to Mr. Gosine and hugged him. "Well, welcome back Mikey. We will chat later about your stay with the Andrews family. You can join the other children as they prepare the hall for dinner." With that, Mikey ran off to his familiar territory and Mr. Andrews chatted a bit with Mr. Gosine for about twenty minutes before he left for his return trip home.

After dinner that evening, Mr. Gosine, and Mikey had a heart-to-heart conversation. It started off with Mikey chatting about his fun time with the family and his gardening chores with Mr. Andrews. His only observation was that Mrs. Andrews was a bit strange since she did not say much while the rest of the family had fun. "Everyone is not the same and we just have to find the ways to interact with them," Mr. Gosine reminded him. "Other than that, she is a good cook.

Her "Well, tomorrow we shall get the necessary paperwork done and it seems to me that you will have delicious pies," Mikey said with a smile. "So, the big question is, would you like to live with them?" asked Mr. Gosine. Mikey pondered for a moment and then with a smile, he replied, "I believe that I would like to live with the Andrews family. Yeah."a new home within the next few weeks once all goes well Mikey. Mr. Andrews also mentioned that they like you and the girls were clamoring to have you stay with them. He also mentioned that he made a call to Miss Andrea, and you chatted with her. Seems you are a boy who is loved by so many Mikey. Your mum must be proud of her boy as she looks down on you," said Mr. Gosine with a bit of emotion.

Within five weeks, all was in place for Mikey to move in with the Andrews family as a full member. That evening when Mr. Andrews came to meet him, he did not realize how hard it would have been to finally leave the place that he knew as home since his mum had passed away. He stood looking at the building and the good and tough times floated past his mind. Mr. Gosine was like a father to him, and he hugged the man so tightly that the older gentleman was having a tough time breathing. "I am just a call away Mikey, never forget that. You will be missed, but I look forward to remarkable things from you in this new chapter of your life," Mr. Gosine said as he released his hands from around Mikey.

As the car pulled away from the Orphanage, Mikey looked back at the building, which was growing smaller in the distance. He could not stop waving to Mr. Gosine who never left until the car was out of sight. His face was wet as the tears could not be controlled any longer. "As much as I wanted a family, this was home. However, I look forward to my new adventure," he said to himself. He eventually got his thoughts together and settled in the car, eagerly looking towards his new life.

CHAPTER 3

Clearing the Path

"Kick aside the rocks and pebbles in your path."

In the first year of his stay with the Andrews family, Mikey was happy. He had bonded well with the girls and even attended the same school, Bridges Government Primary School. Mikey did well in school and excelled in Mathematics. He even joined the school's football club and wore the green uniform proudly when he had matches. Cindy and Hetty wasted no time introducing him to their friends whenever they got the chance. "Meet my brother, Mikey," said Hetty one day to her friend Susan. As usual, she would pull Mikey's hair or run away giggling. When there was Open Day at the school, his teachers spoke highly of him, and he would beam from ear to ear knowing that his adopted parents were getting good reports about him.

At home, Mikey enjoyed doing outdoor chores with Mr. Andrews and learned a lot about taking care of plants. He was especially proud of the kitchen garden with the many herbs that were now used when cooking was done. In addition to this, Mr. Andrews taught him some plumbing skills and he was able to help with any plumbing issues which arose from time to time. Mikey enjoyed this for he felt that he could assist more around the place he now called home. His participation in the Work Rotation program had ended when he had moved from the orphanage and his new skills were embraced even though he was not receiving tips. He had even asked Mr. Andrews about selling some of the herbs from their garden. "That is a brilliant idea Mikey. We can look at it and see how we can make that possible. It would be a source of income for us," said Mr. Andrews in response to Mikey's idea.

While he did not have a problem with the girls nor their father, it was their mother who worried him. She was not very warm towards him and showed little emotion. With the girls, she would smile a little, but overall, she never said much. Mikey felt uncomfortable with this at times, but believed in his heart that she would get warmer over time. He often remembered Mr. Gosine's words and did not allow it to bother him too much.

The days rolled into months and soon enough he was into his third year with the Andrews family. Mr. Andrews had indeed worked with him in setting up the boxes for the increased herb garden and soon enough they were selling herbs to the neighbors. With Mikey's background with the diner, he was able to interact well with the customers. He felt proud of what he was doing and more so given that his new dad was a part of it. Mr. Andrews seemed to lap up every moment with Mikey and seemed to spend more time with him than with the girls who never really liked outdoor work. While Mikey and Mr. Andrews were out in the yard, the girls would spend time watching video games or assisting their mother in the kitchen. On evenings, they would all meet in the television room to relax. This is what he loved, and this is what made it feel like family.

It was in the third year of his stay with his adopted family when Mr. Andrews fell ill. He was diagnosed with a kidney ailment and within weeks had to begin dialysis. His ill health resulted in a drastic change at the home. At least three times per week he had to visit the clinic for treatment and many times he would return home tired. He spent most of his time in his bedroom for he often felt weak. The vibrant man who had loved the outdoors had now become a shadow of himself. He was unable to spend time tending to the garden and doing the outdoor chores. Mikey, however, seemed to have slipped effortlessly into that role taking care of the outdoor matters. With his movements having slowed tremendously, Mikey and the girls would go to his bedroom and spend time reading with him and even playing board games. His diet, too, had now changed and he got smaller in size. His attitude to life, however, was still strong and he would often be heard laughing with the children when they were in his room.

Yet, despite his gallant efforts to be light-hearted, there were many tedious days for him with the illness and the trips to and from the clinic for treatment.

Mrs. Andrews, on the other hand, was now forced to take charge of things in the home. She gradually began making changes around the home which contributed to a shift in the way things were. One of the things that she wanted was for the girls to go to their father's room before to check on him and to find out what he needed before they came down for breakfast. At first, they would do so without being told but it was now an instruction which they carried out with some level of annoyance. If they did not do so, their mother would shout at them to go back up the stairs and find out what their father needed. What was once a pleasure was now seen as a task and it began to show even in the way they began to interact with their father. Cindy would simply stay by the door and ask if he needed anything and whether he answered or not, she simply turned around and went downstairs. Hetty, on the other hand, would still go to him and make sure that he was comfortable. She was the one who would help her mother bring his meals and make sure that his needs were provided for.

While the girls were now forced to take care of their father, Mikey was now relegated to doing the yard work and to doing other outdoor chores such as washing the family vehicle, carrying out the garbage and cleaning the drains. While he did outdoor work, it now seemed as though it was a demand. Mrs. Andrews would seem to give instructions even though Mikey did his chores without being told. She wanted to assert that she was now in charge. When his chores were completed, she would instruct him to go to the kitchen and help to clean up. Sometimes she would even demand that he must help Mr. Andrews to get dressed. For Mikey, this was not a problem since he felt a special sense of care for Mr. Andrews.

As time progressed, the laughter that once filled the house was heard intermittently at the odd times that the three children came together to sit with their father. The games that they would usually play together were now rare. It was now obvious that Mr. Andrews was getting weaker and spent more time sleeping in between his dialysis appointments. During the day, Mrs. Andrews, herself, would visit with him in the bedroom now and then but left the children to bring him his meals and whatever else he needed. Somehow Mr. Andrews' illness created a sadness that the children themselves were trying to cope with. One day Mikey met Cindy crying and asked her what was wrong. "I wish things went back to how they were before dad got ill," she said quietly. "Do not worry Cindy. Dad does not want to be ill either. I know how you feel for I was worried and scared when my mum got sick, as well. Let us just try to make him comfortable," Mikey replied. With that, he patted her on the shoulder and went to tend to his chores.

Despite the increase in his responsibilities at home, Mikey continued to do well at school. No one at school would even know what was taking place. Even the girls kept up their grades. The only indication that something was different was that their mother had to take them to school now.

As the months went by, Mr. Andrews' condition took a turn for the worse and the dialysis days were increased. Yet, even as he suffered with his kidneys, he always had a smile on his face when Mikey visited him. On Mikey's last visit with him, in a weak voice he said to him, "Mikey, you have proven to be the son that I always wanted. We made a wonderful choice at the orphanage, and I could see why Mr. Gosine and Ms. Andrea felt you were special. I may not be here much longer, but I want you to help take care of your sisters. My wife may not talk much but do not let that bother you. Just do what she says and help around the house. Remember your goals in life and work to achieve them. Make me proud of you son." He fell asleep, and Mikey stood quietly for a while looking at the man on the bed. This man, who had treated him like a son and in fact, had just called him son. He quietly turned and left the room smiling to himself.

Three days after that conversation, Mr. Andrews passed away quietly in his sleep. It was Mrs. Andrews who noticed that he was gone when she got up that morning. She got so flustered that she rushed out of the bedroom and woke up Mikey asking him to come with her to break the news to the girls. Mikey felt as though this was deja vu having experienced the trauma when his mum had passed away. He was surprised that Mrs. Andrews came to him first and he quickly moved to assist her.

Before going to the girls, she went to the bathroom and Mikey took the opportunity to stop for a fleeting moment to look at Mr. Andrews who looked as though he was taking a nap. However, his chest did not move signifying the obvious. To him, there was a smile on his face. Mikey's emotions were now raw, and the tears rolled down his cheeks. This was the second parent that he had lost, and he still did not know how to deal with this type of pain. For the few years that he lived with the Andrews family, this man was his father in every way. He taught him some of his skills and he made him feel welcome into his family. He could not say a negative thing about the man who was now dead on the bed. He braced himself for the flood of emotions that would come from the girls when they were told.

In five minutes, Mrs. Andrews came from the bathroom and together with Mikey, they went to the girls' room. He stood by the door as Mrs. Andrews went and sat on Cindy's bed. "Girls! Wake up! Wake up!" she said in a hurried voice. Both girls awakened as if in a stupor. "What is it, mum?" asked Hetty as she dragged herself to a sitting position. "Is it dad?" asked Cindy, who was now sitting next to her mother. The only thing that Mrs. Andrews could do was shake her head and say, "Yes. Dad passed away in his sleep." Hetty began crying and Cindy grabbed her mother. Mikey went into the room and held Hetty, whose body was now racked with tears. The pain of losing their father was not easy and it was about fifteen minutes before anyone moved into the room. As the suddenness of the situation wore away and as the sobs subsided, Mrs. Andrews said in a hushed tone, "The police will have to be called since Evan has died at home. Girls you may go to the room and look at your dad, but we need to hurry since time is important with things like these."

All of them left the girls' room and walked slowly towards the bedroom where Mr. Andrews's body was lying. Upon seeing their father, the girls began wailing even more and had to be consoled once again. Soon enough they went to the bathroom to get themselves ready for the officials who would come. In the meantime, Mrs. Andrews made the call to the police.

It took them about half an hour to arrive at the house. They went to the bedroom and took notes. They also inquired if he was under medical care and Mrs. Andrews provided the responses to the numerous questions that followed. They then organized for the District Medical Officer to come to the house as well as the mortuary attendants who would remove the body. The District Medical Officer arrived at the house within an hour after the police and proceeded to pronounce Mr. Andrews as dead as well as provide an estimated time of death. The police then instructed the mortuary attendants to remove the body to the hospital morgue. Mrs. Andrews was advised of the next steps that she should take and with that the police left the house.

Mrs. Andrews, Mikey, and the girls sat at the dining room table in silence still trying to come to terms with the death of Mr. Andrews.

With funeral preparations being made, Mikey and the girls assisted Mrs. Andrews around the house. For the next two days before the funeral, they had to field several calls from neighbors expressing their condolences and from relatives, some who they would have met before and many whom they never knew about. Mr. Andrews did not come from a large family and like Mikey, his parents were dead, and he was an only child. Among the persons to call was Bob Kramer. While he did not speak directly with Mikey, he spoke to Mrs. Andrews and took the opportunity to ask about the boy. He was happy to hear that things were going well, and he expressed his condolences before he ended the call.

Mikey had called the orphanage and informed Mr. Gosine about his adopted father's death. Mr. Gosine expressed his condolences and inquired about information concerning the funeral. As Mikey hung up the phone, he stood for a moment taking in the silence in the home. With Mr. Andrews gone, he now pondered how things would be. "I guess time will tell," he murmured to himself.

The funeral was held three days after Mr. Andrews' death. The small group of mourners paid their respects to the man who looked resplendent even in death. Many echoed the sentiments that Mr. Andrews was quiet and pleasant, a hard worker and a caring family man. One neighbor said that for the years she had known him, she could not recall a time when she heard him raise his voice or got annoyed. In giving the eulogy, Hetty praised her father for his resilience in life, his deep sense of care and the commitment that he made to their family through the tough and good times. She considered her father a hero and made it clear that a part of her died when he died. "Daddy, you will always live in my heart. Our fun times will continue to live in my head. Even as you laid on your sick bed, you remained strong so that we would not be worried. You were an angel daddy and God needed you. Fly high. We love you dearly," she said mournfully and as she was finished, she broke down and had to be consoled by Mikey.

Mikey too spoke at the funeral and informed the small gathering that Mr. Andrews taught him about family. He mentioned the skills that he had learned and the small business that he supported him with. "This man right here treated me like a son, and not one day did I was an outsider when he welcomed me into his home and his heart. Thank you, Mr. Andrews; it was an honor to call you dad. Your pain is over. I will miss you dearly. Rest in peace," he said as he ended his short speech and took his seat wiping the tears which freely rolled down his cheeks. Someone patted him on his shoulder from behind and as he turned, he recognized that it was Mr. Gosine.

After the funeral service, Mr. Andrews was buried in the town's cemetery. Mr. Gosine spoke with him after the burial was done and reminded him that he was just a call away if he needed any sort of support. He took his leave and did not bother to go to Andrews' residence where a repast was to take place. At the home, about ten people came by to visit with the family. Sandwiches, coffee, and juice were served. Mikey did not know most of the people but saw the girls interacting with most of the visitors. Mrs. Andrews remained near the door greeting persons as they came and as they left. Mikey noticed that she did not have much interaction with the guests and merely moved around with a smile on her face, stopping now and then to say a word to someone.

Around six that evening, the family was left alone when the last guest departed. They all sat in the TV Room exhausted and still in their funeral clothing. Cindy was the one who made the first move to get a shower and a change of clothes. The others followed suit and by seven they were all having a light snack before heading to bed. No one was in the mood to watch television, and they went to their bedrooms. Only Mrs. Andrews remained in the tv room simply staring into space. Mikey had asked if she needed anything, and she informed him that she just needed some time alone. Mikey got up, gave her a pat on her shoulder and headed off to his room where he laid in silence staring at the ceiling. He could hear sobbing coming from the girls' room and he knew that the road ahead would not be an easy one in the home without Mr. Andrews. He even remembered that he did not inform Ms. Andrea about Mr. Andrews' death, and he made a promise to himself to contact her soon. With those thoughts floating around his head, it took him almost half an hour before he drifted off into a fitful sleep.

As a new day dawned, the rising sun spilled its brilliance over the hills and the birds chirped sweetly heralding the awakening. Mikey remained on his bed absorbing the melody that was being played by the birds and eventually opened his window to inhale the fresh air. As he stood by the window, he realized that his life was about to change in the home. What he did not know was how drastically this would be.

After getting dressed to do his chores that morning, he went downstairs to the kitchen and met Mrs. Andrews preparing breakfast. He greeted her as usual and then opened the refrigerator to take out the milk. Somehow the box of milk slipped from his hand and fell to the floor. "Gosh!" he exclaimed. However, before she could move to pick up the box, he felt a stinging in his ear and realized that Mrs. Andrews had just slapped him. "Clumsy fool!" she shouted, "Could you not hold the box better than that?" Mikey stood in shock looking at her for a moment before she proceeded to pick up the box and clean the floor. "Sorry Ms. D," he said humbly. "It seemed as though someone held the box before with a greasy hand and so it slipped form me." "Shut up with the excuses and try not to be so clumsy again!" she continued shouting despite his explanation. "Put away the box and go outside and clean the yard! When you are finished you can come back in for your breakfast!" Mrs. Andrews instructed. Shock registered across Mikey's face, and he made a dash for the door.

As he reached the garden, he sat on a small bench and began to sob. "Was this a sign of things to come?" he asked himself. "Was Mrs. Andrews now showing her real side and how she feels about me? Now with Mr. Andrews gone, is this how things will be here?" he continued murmuring to himself. He massaged his ear which was hurting him. He was angry because he could not recall Mr. Gosine or any of his Orphanage guardians hitting him. The fights he got into over the years were with his mates there. To be slapped by a parent was something new for him. The whole idea of running him off to do the outdoor work was another new twist and without breakfast at that. Mikey drank some water from the garden hose and went about his duties just as he would when Mr. Andrews was around.

He lingered in the garden for about an hour working and thinking whether he wanted to be around Mrs. Andrews for the rest of the day. When he was finished with his chores, he went into the kitchen and noticed that both she and the girls were already having breakfast. "Good morning Hetty and Cindy," he said as he proceeded to join them at the table. His breakfast was now cold, but he ate in silence. "Why are you so quiet today?" Cindy asked. He simply raised his head and looked at her and at Mrs. Andrews who, by now, was not looking in his direction. As he ate, the food did not seem to have taste given how he was feeling. He ate quickly and asked for an excuse leaving the girls and their mother at the table.

He spent the rest of the day selling his chives, tomatoes, and peppers from his garden project. Mr. Andrews would usually tell him to save the money which he received in his Savings account which was opened for him. He smiled as he thought of how his account would grow with each deposit. His little comfort was dashed when he closed off for the day and Mrs. Andrews informed him that he was to give her a fixed sum of money from what he collected from his sales. She informed him that was to maintain the area and pay for any repairs to be done. The explanation given did not make sense to Mikey since he was the one who was always fixing anything around the house. Mikey pondered whether to continue the garden project but decided to hold on to it a little while longer since this was what Mr. Andrews would have wanted. The thought of Mr. Andrews made him smile and somehow, he got the feeling that he was there with him in the garden. "I miss you dad," he said as he sobbed quietly. "I do not know what is taking place with Mrs. Andrews, but it seems as though she was waiting for something like this to happen to show how she really feels about me," he said softly.

He then wiped his eyes and decided that he was simply going to stay out of Mrs. Andrews' way as much as he could. The girls themselves seemed to be changing like their mother for he noticed that they were beginning to order him around as though he was there to pick up after them. While Hetty may have been a little kinder, Cindy behaved as though he was there to do her bidding. If he chose not to do so, she would complain to Mrs. Andrews, who, in turn, would approach him aggressively and order him to do what Cindy wanted. At times Hetty would tell him not to worry when she saw the look of disgust on his face. They no longer had fun in the television room and much of the laughter that used to take place was now almost non-existent. It was as though all the joy in the house died when Mr. Andrews passed away. The girls were either in their room or at practice. Many days Mikey watched television alone.

Mikey felt that he simply had to find the best way to deal with his situation and not go running to anyone. He could have easily called Mr. Gosine but he felt that he had to be able to stand on his own. The funny thing, though, was that while he disliked the treatment he was now being given, he still felt a sense of care for Mrs. Andrews, and he continued to treat her with respect.

As the months rolled by, things grew progressively worse in the home. One morning as he was about to go out into the garden to do his chores, Mrs. Andrews met him outside of his bedroom and told him that he was to move his clothes to the room outside in the garden. This was the same room that the gardener used in previous times. Mikey stood in shock when this was stated to him. Instead of asking her for a reason or instead of pouting when she accosted him, he simply shook his head and went to the bedroom to retrieve his belongings. He smiled when he was told this and Mrs. Andrews herself looked puzzled by his response. In his mind he believed that he would prefer to be outside of a house that was now so cold on the inside. He saw this as a blessing in disguise as opposed to something that would make him feel worse. At least he would be closer to his gardening that he loved so much and in a space that he had shared with Mr. Andrews.

Mikey grabbed his few belongings and his bags and went out to the room outside. The small room had a cupboard which had sheets stored in it. There was enough room for his clothes, and he decided that he would make a makeshift hanging closet to place his hangers. He did not have a television in the room and decided that if he wanted to watch a show, he would simply go to the television room. He then took a sheet from the cupboard and made up the bed. He began to place his small pieces of clothing in the cupboard. He then went to the laundry area and got a broom and mop. He then swept, mopped, and opened the windows to allow fresh air into the room. He saw an old mat and placed that in the room next to the bed. There was an old table in the room, and he recalled that there was an old, rickety chair in the garden shed outside. After completing the cleaning in the room, he went to the shed and began working on the old chair. After a half an hour or so, the chair was repaired, and he tested it out. He was all smiles when he noticed that the chair could take his weight. He took it back to the room and was pleased with the fit at the table. He promised himself to paint the chair at another time.

Mikey then did his chores around the garden and then went into the house to get this breakfast. He went to the breakfast table and noticed that there was no place set for him as usual. Instead, Mrs. Andrews told him his breakfast was on top of the stove and he could eat in his room. This time, Hetty asked, "Why is it that Mikey must eat in his room mother? What is wrong with him eating with us at the dining table?" Her mother gave her a long hard look before she said, "Around my table is for intelligent people, not foolish people who will become nothing in this life." "How could you say something like that mother? Mikey is a smart person, and I do not like that he cannot have breakfast with us at the table. Where is this coming from?" Hetty replied. "You are not the head of this home, and I would advise you to shut up before I give you a reminder," said Mrs. Andrews in a very cold tone of voice. Hetty quickly collected her wares from the table and went to the kitchen leaving Cindy and her mother behind. Mikey went to the kitchen and there he told Hetty, "Please do not worry Hetty. This will not last forever. Thanks for standing up for me. I am ok." With that, he took his breakfast as exited the house.

In his room, Mikey placed the plate with the eggs, sausage and bread on the table and then rested his cup of green tea next to the plate. Before he ate, he blessed his meal and then the tears simply rolled. Mikey sat awash in tears not knowing what to do. He felt helpless, trying to come to terms with the changes taking place at the house. It seemed that every week there was some new change that pushed him further away from home. In his prayer, he uttered, "I longed for a family for years and I genuinely enjoyed being here when Mr. Andrews was around. How things have changed since his death. I am now back to the days when I did not have a family. Yet, I am going to remember his words to me, and I will make him proud. I will also make Mr. Gosine and Miss Andrea proud of me. I am not going to allow Mrs. Andrews to make me feel bad." He went to the small bathroom and washed his face. He was determined that she must not see him crying nor must she feel that what she is doing is going to affect him. Mikey returned to the table and ate his breakfast, which, by now, had gotten cold; not that he even noticed.

After eating his breakfast, he returned to the kitchen to wash his wares and noticed that all the wares were still in the sink. He was the person to wash wares now. He said nothing and cleaned the kitchen without a murmur. He then went outside to his room and did his homework. He promised to stay focused but for all his efforts, he was still affected by what was taking place and it began to show in his grades. His scores in Mathematics, his favorite subject, had taken a nose-dive and his teacher, Mr. Trim had been observing this and asked him to see him in his office after school one day.

"Mikey," he began in his deep fatherly voice, "I am noticing that your grades have been slipping lately. This is not the norm for my star Mathematics student. Is there something wrong?" Mikey bent his head and shook it. "No sir." he said and tried to put on a brave smile. Mr. Trim looked at him for a few seconds and Mikey felt as though he was seeing right through him. He felt uncomfortable and felt as though he could go through the floor. Mr. Trim then rose from his chair and leaned on his desk close to where Mikey sat. He then said to him in a most caring voice, "Mikey, I too lost my father around your age. I know the pain and the longing that was there even to this day. If you need to talk to anyone, please feel free to call me. It does not matter if it is night or day. You can call me or even come to this office to chat with me if you feel the need to talk to someone. It is important that you know that. I see the potential in you, and I would not want you to slip back. Death of a parent is not easy and there is no cure for the pain. It is important to take it one day at a time. My door is open to you at any time." With that, Mikey rose from his seat and for a moment he kept his head bent before he finally looked up and said, "Thanks for your kind words, sir. I will remember that." He briskly walked out of Mr. Trim's office and walked to meet his sisters for the journey home. When Mrs. Andrews came to meet them, they all bundled into the car, said their greetings and all three children closed their eyes and dozed for the entire trip.

On getting home that evening, the girls went inside their room and Mikey went to his on the outside. Mrs. Andrews did not hesitate to remind him that he needed to clean the kitchen and take out the trash. Fifteen minutes had not even passed when he heard her shouting out his name from the doorway of the kitchen. "Where are you Mikey? Get in here and clean up this place!" she shouted gruffly. "I told you what you needed to get done and you have not yet gotten in here!" Mikey was startled by her shouting which increased each time she opened her mouth.

"I was trying to get my football clothes together to place in the washing machine," he replied from inside of his room. "I will be there shortly!" She continued with her ranting, "Get in here now! Forget bringing any clothes to put in this washing machine! From now on you wash your clothes outside. There is a bucket in the shed which you can use, and you can start to use your money to buy your own laundry detergent!" With that she stormed back into the house.

Once again Mikey stood in shock. The tears now rolled freely down his cheeks, and he realized that things were not getting any better. How did it reach to this? What did I do to upset Mrs. Andrews? He dropped the clothes on the floor and decided that he would wash them after he cleaned the kitchen.

He walked across the yard and entered the kitchen. He suddenly felt a slap behind his head and as he spun around, he stood face to face with Mrs. Andrews who looked like a raging bull about to pounce on him. That she did, with all her might, slapping him in his face, spitting out venom by telling him he would not amount to any good and that he would be a failure. Mikey shielded his face with his hands as she continued to pound away at him. It seemed like an eternity until Hetty entered the room and held her mother's hands preventing her from striking Mikey any further.

"Stop Mother! Stop hitting Mikey like that! He came to clean the kitchen. Let him do so!" Hetty shouted to her mother. Mrs. Andrews then turned to her daughter and walked out of the kitchen. "Sorry Mikey," Hetty said. "Are you hurt?" Mikey just turned without answering and proceeded to wash the wares. When he was done with his chores, he took his dinner and went to his room. He did not have laundry detergent to wash his clothes and decided that he would go to the neighborhood grocery mart and purchase some when he was finished.

Mikey pondered what was taking place with him at home. He remembered his conversation with Mr. Trim that evening and felt that he needed to reach out to someone. Mr. Trim seemed fatherly, and he believed in his heart that he had his best interest at heart. He did not want to call Mr. Gosine for it seemed like doing so would be like taking a step back to his past. He was here now, and Mr. Trim had extended a hand. "Maybe, just maybe I will talk to him," he said to himself.

When he completed his meal, he walked down to the Grocery mart and purchased some laundry detergent as well as some snacks. He did not notice that he had a black eye until Mr. Stone, the grocer, asked him where he had gotten that black eye. "Oh, I got that while playing football," he responded. Mr. Stone smiled and said, "That was a rough tackle you got there. Put this on it." He then gave him a small bottle of salve lotion, on the house and advised him to be careful. Mikey thanked him and left the grocery mart. He hustled back to his room and quickly got the bucket to wash his clothes. When he was finished, he realized that he did not have clothespins to hang out the clothes. He then used some material in the shed to make a makeshift clothesline outside. After washing, he hung the clothes hoping that they would dry in time for the next day and that they would not fall off.

He then went inside and began his homework. However, he was so tired that he fell asleep on his books and before he knew it night had crept in. He struggled to finish his work before he took a shower and climbed into his bed. Not all his work was completed though, and he promised himself that he would get up early the next day and finish before he got to school.

The next morning, he jumped up from his sleep when he heard knocking on his door. "Mikey! Where are you? Get up or you will be late for school!" It was Cindy's voice. He looked at the small clock on the table and realized that he had overslept. He got up and showered hastily, putting on his clothes. He did not even have time to check his football clothes on the line since he had to rush to meet the girls, who by now, were getting into the car. He had no time to go inside for breakfast and none was offered to him. Mrs. Andrews did not look at him that morning and did not answer when he greeted her.

On the trip to school, he took out his book and read his work while the girls chattered away. He paused when Hetty asked if he were playing in the match that afternoon and he indicated that he would not. He did not give a reason and continued his reading until they got to the school gate. He got out of the car quickly, said goodbye and proceeded to the gate without looking back. He went straight to the canteen and bought himself a patty and a drink which he quickly devoured before the bill rang.

He proceeded hurriedly to his first class which was English Grammar. He was able to follow along and managed to get through that class. The second class was math and as Mr. Trim entered the class, he looked directly at Mikey. For a moment he paused, looking at him, but said nothing. When he asked Mikey to respond to a question that was given for homework, he seemed offended when the boy informed him that he did not complete the homework. Again, he said nothing and simply asked the next student to respond. Mikey managed to get through the rest of the class without any issues. When the bell rang to signal the end of the class, Mr. Trim asked him to meet him at his office.

Mikey arrived at Mr. Trim's office about five minutes after the class ended. He was invited to sit, and Mr. Trim sat at the edge of his desk. He took a moment before he began speaking. "Mikey, this is not like you to not do homework. I am genuinely concerned about you currently. Is everything ok at home? Wait a minute! What has happened to your eye?" With that, he got up and held Mikey's face in his hands and looked caringly at him. As he looked at Mikey, the child's eyes welled up with tears which, by then, he was unable to control. Mr. Trim stooped in front of Mikey and held him as his chest heaved up and down, tears flowing like a river. He allowed the child to cry and when he was more composed, he gave him a napkin to wipe his face and a bottle of water. He then pulled his chair and said to the distressed child, "Mikey, please tell me all that has been happening with you to cause this much pain. I am going to be there for you, but I must find out what the issue is. I can promise you that what is said in this office will remain here. Talk to me son. Take your time and tell me what is taking place."

It took Mikey a while before he began talking and Mr. Trim remained seated waiting for him to begin. After about ten minutes of silence, Mikey began his story, at the end of which, Mr. Trim was aware of the issues that his student was undergoing.

After speaking with Mr. Trim, Mikey felt as though a weight was lifted from his chest. Somehow that conversation enabled him to unburden his mind, and the tears seemed to have washed away the pain. The next day, Mikey woke up with a resolve to get back on track with his schoolwork and not let Mrs. Andrews affect him. He remembered Mr. Trim's words from the day before, "Mikey you owe it to yourself to hold on to what is good about yourself. You must remember that the path in life is not smooth but with each day always make up your mind to kick aside the rocks and pebbles that may be in your path. Think of Mrs. Andrews as a rock or pebble in your path. Do what you can to move away from the rocks or pebbles and keep on going. She is suffering deep down inside and does not know how to deal with it. At times, adults too suffer from the death of loved ones but never want to admit it. Some deal with loss horribly, like Mrs. Andrews. Once day she may communicate why she is treating you like that. For now, your business is to be the best that you can be every day. God created you for purpose Mikey. You must have heard that many times before. Think always of the people who would be proud of you, your mum, Mr. Gosine, Ms. Andrea and even Mr. Andrews, whom you were proud to call dad. They believed in you. You must believe in yourself. If you need anything, call me. If you need help with your work, call me. There is no shame in that."

Mikey got up that morning and before he did anything else, he uttered a word of prayer thanking God for a new day and as he said to himself, for new beginnings.

With that, he decided on a routine that he could implement so that he could see little of Mrs. Andrews and the girls and be more on his own. He noticed that they woke up later than he would and, as such, he did his routine earlier than they did. He knew how to use the stove and instead of waiting for Mrs. Andrews to make breakfast, he did his own and left enough for her and the girls. He was not going to allow her to turn him into a selfish person.

Once he had finished having his breakfast, he cleaned the kitchen and went back to his room. There he got ready to do his yard chores and tend to his small garden.

The morning was still young, so he took a shower, got ready for school, and went inside the house to wait for the girls. He sat on the sofa reading a book. By the time the girls got ready for school and came downstairs, he was waiting for them. It was Cindy who asked, "Did you make this breakfast Mikey?" "I did," he replied. "Not bad at all," she responded. It was Mrs. Andrews who stated, "These eggs need salt. You did not find the salt container? You cannot do anything right. You are a waste of time." Instead of allowing her to irritate him, he smiled and said, "Would you like me to bring the salt Mrs. D? That is not a problem." With that, he got up and got the salt bottle from the counter and placed it on the table where she could access it. He smiled as he placed the salt on the table, and she observed that. Instead of flying off the hook as she did lately, she simply mumbled to herself and snatched the bottle from the table. Mikey returned to reading his book and continued to do so before they were able to leave for school.

That morning as he got to school, he met Mr. Trim near the assembly hall, and he inquired about him and how he was doing. Mr. Trim had noticed a change in Mikey's countenance, and he was anxious to find out what had happened since they last spoke. Mikey was able to tell him that he remembered his words and that he had made up his mind to deal with any insults like pebbles or rocks that were thrown his way. Mr. Trim smiled and patted him on his shoulder encouragingly. He even reminded Mikey that his National Examinations were to be held in the six months and that he needed to remain focused. "I do hope you know that if you do very well you can be considered for a National Scholarship. I never asked what sort of career you wanted Mikey," said Mr. Trim. "Honestly sir, I want to be able to do a job that involves figures and money. I was thinking of Accounting but still not too sure," replied Mikey. "Well, that is not a problem. Most students are not certain until they get a little further in their schooling. At least you know the area you wish to get involved in and that is good. Keep on plugging at the mathematics. I must go now since I have a class. I will see you later when I have your group," said Mr. Trim as he walked off briskly.

Mikey too walked off hurriedly for he had a Grammar class with Mrs. Knott. He had completed his assignments and was enthusiastic to get to her class. After Mathematics, he enjoyed Grammar. Mrs. Knott had even told him that his writing and phrasing were improving. He enjoyed the debates that she would have in class from time to time and one day she joked that he should think of being a politician or a lawyer. He laughed and said, "Me Miss? Nah., I do not like crowds and people staring at me. Just imagine me standing there scared when the judge is waiting for me to begin and all I could say is, sssoooooorrry your hhhonnnnoourrr." Mrs. Knott was in stitches looking at him and his antics. She then said, "You should think of becoming a comedian or even an actor. You are so funny Mikey. I like it when you are like this." For the rest of that day, Mikey enjoyed his classes. Not for a moment did he think about his home. He had a football match that evening and while his team did not win, he had a good game. He was totally drained at the end of the day and when Mrs. Andrews came to meet him and the girls, he tumbled into the back seat drained but happy. He had greeted Mrs. Andrews and as usual she mumbled. He acted as though he did not hear her while the girls chattered non- stop about their day. They told their mother that they all needed money for a contribution to something at the school and they needed the money for the next day. Mrs. Andrews then said, "Well I have enough to give you two but none for Mikey. He would have to get his own." He had overheard the conversation, and he said nothing. He had already made up his mind not to ask her for anything as far as possible. He had his money which he used wisely. The contribution was only ten dollars and that was not a problem for him to make. He leaned back on the car seat and dozed until they got home.

Nine months had passed since Mr. Andrews had died and Mikey was now literally taking care of himself. He had found ways to deal with the situation at home and he was using his time studying for the National Examinations. So too was Cindy. She was not in his class, but she had to sit the examination as well. In comparing their grades, Mikey's were better than hers, but he never said anything to her or to Mrs. Andrews. If she needed help with a question, he did so willingly. At times she was rude to him and behaved as though he was her courier. However, he had made up his mind to not be distracted by her as well. He made sure that he stuck to his routine so that he had enough time to study. He was happy that the football season had ended, so he used that free time to put in more work. He was determined that he had to pass all eight of his subjects with excellent grades. This was his personal challenge, and he had six months to do so.

It was during that six-month period, however, that things took another turn at Andrews' home. Mrs. Andrews fell ill with her heart. He remembered being up one morning studying when he heard Hetty pounding away on his door. When he opened the door, he found her breathless saying that her mother had collapsed in her bedroom. Mikey did not think twice about rushing to her aid. He met Cindy holding her and he immediately told Hetty to call for an ambulance. His First Aid training from the orphanage kicked in and he was able to tell Cindy what to do until the medics came. Cindy went in the ambulance with her mother while Mikey and Hetty waited for one of their aunts to get there for none of them could drive the family car. Aunt Rose did not waste time getting there even though she lived about forty minutes away in the other town.

As soon as she got there, the children got into the car, and they all rushed to the hospital. Aunt Rose was fortunate to get a park not too far from the emergency entrance. The three of them scurried in through the entrance and went to the receptionist's desk to ask for directions. They were advised what to do and soon enough they were in the lobby on the second floor. As soon as they got off the elevator, they saw Cindy, who rushed towards them and hugged Aunt Rose, who by now, was beginning to ask a lot of questions. Cindy asked her to sit and proceeded to update all of them on the current situation. "There is something wrong with mum's heart and whatever it is, led to a heart attack. The doctors need to do a few more tests to decide what was the cause and what they will do. They said that the Heart Specialist would see her this morning. The doctors and nurses attended to her, and she is asleep now," she said as her voice trailed off and the tears flowed. Mikey moved forward and hugged her. With that she placed her head on his shoulder and let the tears flow freely. Mikey, too, wiped away his tears, for despite how he was treated, this was the family that he knew and so wanted to come together. He eventually guided her to a seat, and he sat there holding her for a while.

In the time being, Hetty moved to a corner and stood looking heartbroken at the outside view. Her mind was racing as she tried to process what was taking place. Her father had passed away only a few months ago and now she was wondering if her mother would also be dying. "What is this?" she asked herself. "What was happening to their family? How long was mum ill? What will they do if she dies?" The very thought of this made her sob unashamedly until she felt a hand on her shoulder turning her around. On turning, she realized that it was Mikey. Without saying a word, she hugged him while releasing a torrent of tears. "We will get through this together," he said to her, trying to comfort the young girl. He then guided her to a seat until she eventually composed herself. The four of them sat in silence waiting for what seemed like an eternity.

In about another fifteen minutes a doctor came to the lobby asking for the parties for Mrs. Andrews. All four of them rose from their seats and walked towards him. He smiled and introduced himself. Dr. Burns was about six feet tall, so they all had to look up at him. He proceeded to update them about Mrs. Andrews's condition. "Diana has a blockage in her heart; a condition for which she may need surgery. I am awaiting one more test to be done before we are certain that this is the course that we deem best. She will have to remain on the ward since she cannot be moved around right now. In the interim, you are not to worry. Our medical team will take excellent care of your mum. You are free to visit but keep the talking to a minimum please. Do not tell her anything that would excite her. She must remain calm as much as possible. I will update you once we are completed with all tests. You can liaise with our Front Desk nurses for any further information. Have a good evening and do not worry," said Dr. Burns reassuringly as he returned from the direction in which he came. The four of them stood there not knowing what to do until Aunt Rose mentioned that they needed to get something to eat and that they needed to get clothing to take back to the hospital. It was going to be a long day.

CHAPTER 4

Strength in the Struggle

"Never let the personal pain of others get you down."

After refreshing themselves and getting a change of clothing for Mrs. Andrews, the four of them returned to the hospital. Thankfully, this was not a school day, so they did not have to worry about missing classes. As soon as they got on to the floor where their mother was checked in, they proceeded to the nurses station to inform them that they were there with her clothing. They were given the all- clear to visit her, but they must not have her talking for any length of time.

The four of them walked gingerly down the corridor until they got to Room 20. Upon pushing the door, they noticed Diana lying there with many tubes attached to her and to a monitor. She was fast asleep, so they tiptoed around the bed, whispering to each other. The clothes cupboard was empty, so they hung her clothes on the hangers that were already in there. As they were doing so, they heard a soft voice saying, "Were you here all this time?" They all turned to see Mrs. Andrews trying to smile though she was in some discomfort. Hetty dropped the hanger and ran to hug her mother while Cindy followed. Mikey stood at the foot of the bed and said, "Hello Ms. D." She ignored Mikey and looked at her sister Rose. "Hi Diana. How are you feeling at this time?" asked Rose. "As though I was hit by a bus," replied Diana. "Well, it could have been worse," said Rose. It was then Cindy asked, "Did the doctor come back during the morning?" "I cannot say. I was out like a light for most of the day. I guess you will have to talk to the nurses. I feel tired now," said Diana. With that, she pulled up her cover and drifted off to sleep.

That was a signal for them to leave her to get her rest. They exited the ward and Mikey stood for a while looking at her on the bed. Memories of his birth mother flooded his mind, and he could not help but think about how Ms. Andrea was there for him. He felt that he needed to be there for his sisters as well. Kindness is what he had learned from Ms. Andrea, and he was not going to forget that. He then hurried to catch up with the rest of them as they walked along the corridor heading towards the exit. Mikey also felt a strong urge to call Ms. Andrea that day and he decided that he would ask Aunt Rose to do him that favour. She did not appear to be like Mrs. Andrews because she treated him well.

On the drive home, they were all quiet; not even the radio was put on. The engine's hum was the only sound that shattered the silence. Each occupant of the vehicle was lost in thought. Upon reaching the home, they lazily piled out of the vehicle. Aunt Rose indicated that now that she knew what the situation was, she would have to make arrangements at her home since it seemed that she would have to stay with them for a while. She began walking towards the house with the girls to make sure that they were all right. She asked Mikey why he was not coming into the house. He looked at her, bowed his head and told her that it was nothing. Before she could press for an explanation, he walked off to his room on the outside. Aunt Rose stood looking on with a worried expression on her face but decided to leave it alone for now.

While she was in the house with the girls, Mikey threw himself on his small bed and could not help but think how unfair Life could be. "I always wanted a family and just to be loved. I had that when Mr. Andrews was around, but when he died that dream was shattered. The way Ms. D has treated me after his death, was not love. Yet, I could not hate her. I was happy to have someone to think of as a parent. I was happy that I had someone to wait for me after school. I was thankful for the trivial things that I would not have gotten if I were on the street or even at the Orphanage. I have my own room even though my feet hang off the bed and even though it is a tiny shed. I would not want anything bad to happen to Ms. D even though she tells me hurtful things. Mr. Trim told me those were pebbles, and I have not allowed her words to bother me for I kick them aside in my mind," he said to himself. He stayed on his bed for another ten minutes and then decided to go tend to his garden. This, for him, was a way to relax and forget all that was happening around him.

He was soon absorbed in pulling out weeds from among his plants and did not notice when Aunt Rose came up to him. "Did you plant all of these?" she asked with some degree of awe. "I did," replied Mikey. "These are certainly lush," she continued. "I see now that you all do not have to buy some things at the market or the supermarket. That is great Mikey. You do have a lot. What do you do with the extras?" she asked. "Oh, I started selling my herbs since Mr. Andrews was alive," he reminisced. "That is excellent!" said Aunt Rose encouragingly. "Well, I must be going now if I must get back here before it is too late. I will make dinner and bring it with me when I come back. You all do not have to worry about what to eat. Just stay with the girls. I left them in the living room. I know that they are hurting so be the strong brother for them. Make sure you all lock up the house and do not let in any strangers. I will see you all when I get back," she said as she started heading towards her vehicle.

Mikey walked with her towards her blue Camry car and closed the door behind her. As she pulled out of the driveway, they both waved at each other. As he promised, he went into the house to check on the girls. There they were sitting in front of the television but not really noticing what was taking place on the show. Cindy was lying on the couch while Hetty was curled up on the other chair. Mikey went and sat on the floor between them both and just said nothing for a while. "Do you want anything Cindy?" he asked. She just shook her head to say no. "Anything for you Hetty?" he asked. "No thanks Mikey. I am just trying to hope for the best with mum. I do not know what we will do without her," she said as she wiped away the tears. Mikey put his head on his knees and began to hum that song that his mother used to sing for him, "If you happy and you know it, move your feet, if you happy and you know it sing Amen, if you happy…" he continued to hum quietly. It was a song that always comforted him even when he was on the verge of tears.

After about fifteen minutes sitting in the same position, Mikey went to the kitchen and filled three glasses with orange juice. Even though the girls said they wanted nothing, Mikey still felt they should try to drink something. It was the least that he could do at that time to distract himself as well. He returned to the living room and gave each girl a glass which they accepted without a fuss. He did not know what to say, but told them that no matter what, he was there for them. Hetty smiled when he said that but did not bother to reply.

Two hours had passed, and Mikey was getting bored sitting there doing nothing. He told the girls that he was going to his garden and then get a bath. He told them to call him if they needed anything. With that, he went outside to his garden. While tending to his plants, his mind ran on Mrs. Andrews. He could not pretend that he was overwhelmingly affected as he was when Mr. Andrews passed away. Instead, he felt a sense of remorse that he was not closer to her. He could not understand why she was like that with him. He was not too keen on returning to look for her in the hospital and thought of a million excuses that he could give to Aunt Rose when next they planned to visit. Yet, he felt that he owed it to the girls to be there for them since he had people like Ms. Andrea and Mr. Gosine as his support during his darkest moments.

After spending time going through his plants, he eventually went to have his bath in the tiny shower on the outside of his room. By the time he had finished dressing, he heard Aunt Rose's car pull into the driveway. He closed his room door and met her by her car. As promised, she brought dinner, and Mikey assisted her with taking it to the kitchen. Aunt Rose went to the living room to check on the girls, who, by then, had fallen asleep with the empty glasses on the floor. She took them up and placed them in the kitchen sink. "How are they?" she asked Mikey who was dishing out the food. "They are not taking it well, but I guess they will try to deal with it as best as they can," he replied. Aunt Rose helped Mikey with the food and then placed it on the table. Mikey then told her that he would be going to his room to eat. "To your room?" she asked. "Yes, that is where I have been eating for the past few months; that is where Ms. D told me to eat," said Mikey. "Really?" replied Aunt Rose. "Well today you will eat here at the table with the rest of us so go sit there," she said sternly. Mikey followed her instructions without a murmur. Hetty and Cindy joined them and barely ate anything on their plates. Aunt Rose did not fuss because she knew that they were feeling distraught.

Once dinner was finished, Mikey helped with the cleaning of the kitchen while the girls went to get ready for bed. After that, Mikey left Aunt Rose, who by then was showing signs of fatigue. He bid her good night, and he walked out in the direction of his room. For a moment he stood in the garden looking up at the stars which were shining in all their glory. "What a beautiful sight!" he whispered to himself. For a while he stood transfixed by the splendor of nature, forgetting everything and just absorbing the peace that engulfed him in that space, in that moment. He sat on the small bench and closed his eyes. He said a small prayer asking God to watch over Mrs. Andrews and the girls and to make life comfortable for them all. When he was finished with his prayer, he went to his room and did an hour of studying before he finally turned off the lamp and got into his bed. Within five minutes he was out like a light, leaving the cares of the world behind at that time.

"Code Blue! Code Blue!" were the words blasting through the lobby. "Paging Doctor Burns! Doctor Burns please report to Ward 20!" As the four of them stepped off the elevator the next morning, they were greeted with those words coming over the Public Address system. The girls and Aunt Rose rushed to the Nurses Station indicating that they were there to see

Mrs. Andrews. "Please have seat. "We are dealing with an emergency at this time and will call you shortly," said the Nurse. "We heard it is Room 20. Is it my mother?" Cindy asked in a fearful voice. "I am unable to give you any information currently. I understand your concerns. Once there is word as to what is happening, the patient's relatives will be informed. For now, please excuse me. I must urgently get back to what I am doing." replied the Nurse. Without another word, they all walked towards the sitting area and sat anxiously awaiting some sort of information.

All this time, they observed nurses hustling back and forth but no one said anything to them. It was not until forty minutes had passed did a nurse come to the Waiting area and asked for the relatives of Diana Andrews. They all flew up from their seats as though it was a synchronized movement. "Yes," said Aunt Rose, "We are her family." "Hello, I am Nurse Walters. Please come with me," said the nurse in a gentle tone.

They followed her along the corridor and were told to wait outside the area of Room 20. They milled around in that area for about five minutes before Nurse Walters returned with Doctor Burns, whom they all remembered. "Hello everyone," he said with that fatherly smile. "Your mum gave us a bit of a worry there a while ago, but we have been able to stabilize her. Our tests have confirmed that she has a blockage in her heart. We would have to treat that urgently since it is having other side effects on her. Our concern is her blood pressure at this time because she could have gotten a stroke. We are going to monitor her closely, but we need to discuss surgery to deal with the blockage. I will need to give you the details and explain what must be done when you come tomorrow. For now, you can visit her but do not ask her any questions and do not spend too much time because she will need to get as much rest as possible. Please meet me tomorrow at 10am. You can ask for my office at the Receptionist's Desk when you arrive. Take care now and do not worry. She is well cared for." With that, he took his leave and the four of them proceeded to Mrs. Andrews' bedside.

Surprisingly when they entered the room, Mrs. Andrews was awake, eyes staring vacantly at everything and yet, at nothing. As soon as she spotted her children, her gaze remained fixed on them. Cindy was the first to hug her, followed by Hetty and Aunt Rose. Mikey stood by her bedside and simply said, "Hello Ms. D. Good to see you." For a moment she stared at Mikey and then shook her head in acknowledgement of his greeting. In a timid voice, she said to them all, "I need to say this to you all. I feel weak currently. If anything should happen to me, Rose please take care of these children. They are good children who must know that I love them."

She turned her head and stared at Mikey once again. The words that flowed from her lips shocked all who were around her bed. "Mikey, I know that I have been hard on you. When my husband passed away, I felt like a weight was on me and I lashed out at you. I said hurtful things to you and for that I am sorry. I realized that no matter what I said you never allowed it to get to you. You even continued to keep up your grades. Continue to do well. Mr. Andrews, your dad, believed in you," she said as tears flowed down her sunken cheek. With that, Mikey stepped forward and squeezed her hand. He then excused himself and went outside to wait for the others.

As he sat there, he could not help the tears that flowed as his mind ran back over some of the things that Mrs. Andrews had done and told him. Had it not been for Mr. Trim's caring and guidance, he may have succumbed to her cruelty. Mr. Trim had continued to remind him that his success lay in his own hands and that he could either choose to embrace it or lose it. He had chosen to embrace it and no hurtful words from Mrs. Andrews could have stopped him. When he heard those words coming out of her mouth, he felt a sense of victory over the situation. She had realized that none of her words were having a negative effect on him. Mikey sat with his head towards the ceiling and a smile slowly crept across his face. He remained in that position until he saw the girls and Aunt Rose walking towards him.

Mikey rose to meet them and without a word, they all walked out of the hospital and headed towards the car park. Aunt Rose dabbed her eyes from time to time with a worn-out tissue and tried her best to keep her chin up. The girls, however, were teary-eyed and Mikey did not say a thing because he felt that they needed to deal with their emotions on their own. He was there to support them in any way. They soon got to the car and Aunt Rose drove out of the compound.

On the way, she stopped at the Supermarket to get items for lunch. Mikey went in to help her while the girls remained in the car. In about fifteen minutes they were back on the road and heading towards the house. When they were finally inside and about to settle down, the house phone rang. Mikey answered in a low tone of voice. "Hello, is this the Andrews residence?" asked the voice on the other end of the phone. "Yes, it is," replied Mikey. "This is Nurse Prime from the General Hospital. Please hold for Dr. Burns. Mikey began to cold sweat as he waited for Dr. Burns to come on the line. Soon enough he heard Dr. Burns' voice on the other end. "Hello. To whom am I speaking?" he asked. "This is Mikey," he said as he waited anxiously for what was to be said. "Oh Mikey, good. Thus is Dr. Burns. I believe that you and the girls should return to the hospital as soon as possible. I will meet with you when you get here. Just ask Nurse Prime at the desk to call me when you get in. Uh, Mikey, please try to be calm in talking to the girls. I would not want them too flustered." With that, they both ended the conversation. Mikey stood there with his eyes closed. He took a deep breath and went to speak to Aunt Rose.

Aunt Rose herself was a bundle of nerves and even dropped the pot when she heard what Mikey had to say. The girls were on the couch when Mikey broke the news that they had to return to the hospital. Cindy began to get an anxiety attack and Mikey had to give her a glass of water. Hetty began pacing the floor wondering aloud what could have happened to her mother. Aunt Rose wasted no time in getting the car on the road. As they drove to the hospital, Aunt Rose told them to say a prayer and leave it in God's hands.

They were lucky to get a parking spot near to the entrance and they soon rushed inside the hospital and to the receptionist's desk where they asked for nurse Prime. She was in the room at the back of the desk. When they identified who they were, she scurried off to get Dr. Burns. In about three minutes he was there with them filling them in on what was taking place. "I am sorry to say, but your mum is not improving. Her condition is getting worse, and I am not sure how much longer she will be with us. Given her extremely weakened state, it would be risky for us to do surgery at this time. As much as I hate to say it, there is not much more that we can do. It was important for you to be here in her last moments and if you wish to call a priest or religious person you can do so. We will continue to monitor her," he explained in the gentlest tone. After answering a few questions from the girls and Aunt Rose, he left and the four of them moved swiftly to Mrs. Andrews' bedside for the second time that day.

On approaching her, they all noticed that there were more tubes attached to her. The person lying on the bed looked more comatose than before. Cindy and Hetty rushed to either side of their mother and caressed her hands. Tears flowed freely and the girls kissed her and told her that they loved her. For a moment she opened her eyes and looked at her daughters and as she recognized them, she smiled. Due to her weakening state, she could no longer talk and express her thoughts. Instead, she gave each girl a slight squeeze of her hand before she let out a gasp and closed her eyes.

The monitor immediately began beeping and the medical team came rushing through the door. Cindy and Hetty were still holding Diana's hand even when the nurses arrived. Diana's vitals were checked, and the doctor was summoned. When he got there, he bent his head and looked at the girls for a few seconds. From looking at them, he knew that they knew. Their mother had passed away while holding their hands. He instructed the nurse what to write with respect to the time of death. With that, he walked over to the girls and expressed his sympathy. So too, did the two nurses who were in the room. The medical team left the family in the room for a while to pay their respects to the deceased. By now, even Aunt Rose was awash with tears. "How could you leave us mummy? Come back please!" wailed Hetty. Mikey stood looking at what transpired before him, and he felt heart-broken when he looked at his sisters. What could he do to ease their pain? Just as he did when his mum died, they, too, would have to walk through that pain.

They knew that they could count on him for support. Mikey too found himself wiping away the tears and he stepped aside to the window.

After twenty minutes or so by their mother's bedside, the girls began to gather her belongings from the ward. Mikey assisted with the packing because they were in no frame of mind to do that. In the meantime, Aunt Rose went to the Reception Desk to get directives as to what they needed to do. The girls and Mikey met her at the desk and listened to what they needed to do next. With that, they left the hospital and proceeded to their home.

Diana's funeral was held three days after her death. There were about thirty persons at the church, some of whom were the children's classmates and teachers. After the burial in the churchyard, fewer yet came to the house. Mr. Trim had attended the funeral and had spoken with Mikey. He had offered his condolences and told him that they would speak further when he returned to school.

For the rest of that evening, the house was quiet. Both girls had retreated to their room and Aunt Rose sat quietly in the kitchen having a cup of green tea. Her mind seemed to be far off, and Mikey seized the opportunity to slip quietly out of the house and go to his room. He sat heavily on his small bed, feeling a sense of exhaustion for the first time since Mrs. Andrews had fallen ill. He was so busy supporting the girls that he did not notice the toll that it was taking on his body and his mind. He realized that he needed time alone and he embraced this moment. There he sat absorbing the peace and quiet, smiling when he heard the occasional chirp from the beds as they perched in the trees, preparing for slumber. In that moment, he deliberately blocked out any thoughts about what was going to happen next. He simply wanted to sit in the peace that surrounded him and clear his mind. Tomorrow is another day. With that, he laid on the bed and closed his eyes. He did not even notice when he fell asleep. He dreamt as though Ms. Andrea was standing beside his bed, telling him to be strong. Her hand was outstretched towards him and as he was about to hold her hand to get off the bed, he fell onto the floor. He soon realized that it was a dream. He had made up his mind there and then that he would try to communicate with her soon. He then went back to sleep and did so peacefully until the next morning. When he got up the next morning, he got himself together, had a bath and took a seat on the bench in the garden. He was now rested and able to spend time thinking before he faced the girls and Aunt Rose. He took the time to do some introspection with respect to how he felt, and he recognized that Mrs. Andrews,' despite how she treated him, would still miss her. Who would take care of them now since she had managed the household and took care of their transport to and from school? Would it be Aunt Rose?

What was about to happen? Things would change for sure, but to what extent? This was the conversation that they would all need to have that morning and somehow, he was anxiously looking forward to it.

Mikey went into the house and noticed that Aunt Rose was already preparing breakfast. Hetty was already downstairs helping to set the table, and she greeted Mikey as he entered the kitchen. He assisted Aunt Rose with the cleaning up while she cooked the food. By the time the food was finished and placed on the table, Cindy came down looking quite teary-eyed. Mikey gave her a hug when he saw her. Without a word, she sat at the table and Hetty and Aunt Rose soon joined her. As he would usually do, Mikey took his plate and cup and headed towards the door to go to his room where he would have his breakfast. When Aunt Rose saw that, she asked him if he was not going to eat with them. In response to her question, he mentioned that Mrs. Andrews had instructed him not to have breakfast at her table and since then he has been having breakfast in his room. She then got up, walked to Mikey, and guided him to the table. At that moment, he knew that old things were going to pass away and that they were now on the verge of a new day. What was to come, he did not know, but, with guidance, he was ready to move forward.

CHAPTER 5

Arise From the Ashes to Success

"You are my inspiration."

(Eight years later)

Shouts of joy filled the hall as the graduating class moved forward dressed in their black robes, waiting patiently to hear their names called and to walk across the stage to receive their scrolls. The noise for each graduate was deafening and when the name Mike Clary was called, it was no different.

"Mike Clary, First-Class Honors in Accounting with a minor in Law!" boomed the voice of the announcer. There was a cheer-leading squad for this young man who strode gracefully and confidently across the stage to receive his degree. From a corner in the middle of the crowd, his adopted sisters, Aunt Rose, Mr. Gosine, Mr. Trim and Ms. Andrea all stood clapping vigorously as he received his scroll. Each of them had tears pouring down their faces for they could not contain their joy and their pride in his accomplishment.

As he stepped down from the stage to rejoin his graduating mates, he lifted his scroll and acknowledged his small cheering party. His chest heaved with pride and he, too, could not help but beam through the tears that ran down his face. This was the symbol of victory over struggle. In that moment he reminisced about the journey to get to where he had reached.

He recalled that after Mrs. Andrews' death, Aunt Rose had moved in with him and the girls. Life at home had returned to some normalcy and he studied hard enough to pass the national examination. He had done so well that he was awarded a Scholarship. Mr. Trim, who had mentored him over the years, was so filled with pride on hearing the news. From there, he went on to the university to study Accounting and decided to minor in Law. The years spent were not easy because he had to assist in the home as well.

Cindy was not successful in the examination and chose to pursue a vocational path that would see her doing Nail Technology at one of the Vocational Schools. Hetty was studying Information Technology and was doing quite well. Even though he had won the scholarship, he kept his garden going and sold his produce on weekends. That money he continued to bank and use for his personal needs. He did not want to be a burden on Aunt Rose who did her best to make things comfortable around the home. Whatever money was left from the Insurance of both Mr. and Mrs. Andrews, was being used sparingly to manage the household.

During that time, he was also able to contact Ms. Andrea, who by then, had indicated that she was finished with the job that she was doing and was returning home. She had informed him that she would meet up with him once she got in. However, he had only heard from her once after that and the short conversation did not reveal whether she had returned. He had maintained contact with Mr. Gosine even though he never let him know how his adopted mother had treated him.

Mikey's mind was jolted back to the present when he heard, "Graduating class of 2016! Go forward! Create your niche in this world! Good luck to each of you!" With that the graduands rose and threw their caps into the air, hugging each other, giving best wishes. As they dispersed and went to their families, Mikey walked briskly towards the area where his family was seated. When they saw him coming, they jumped up from their seats and Hetty did a happy dance. His eyes almost popped out of his head when he saw Ms. Andrea. He embraced her so hard, lifting her off the ground and spinning her around. When he saw Mr. Gosine, he gave him such a bear hug, resting his head on his shoulders while the tears poured. Mr. Gosine patted him on his back, struggling to keep his emotion in check, he whispered to him, "You have done what I knew you could do. I am so immensely proud of you Mikey." Mikey wiped his eyes and noticed Mr. Trim standing there. Mr. Trim walked towards him and the two embraced each other as a father would do with his son. All Mikey could say to him was, "I kicked the pebbles to the side all the time. Thank you for your guidance." "I knew you would Mikey. I knew you were a conqueror," replied Mr. Trim choking with emotion. Mikey then opened his arms wide and beckoned to his two sisters. The three of them hugged each other so tightly while the flood of tears could not be stemmed. "So proud of you, so, so proud," said Hetty. "You are my inspiration." "I am sure that dad is looking down filled with pride as well. He loved you so much," chimed Cindy. After three minutes, they separated, wiping their eyes. He finally turned to Aunt Rose, who by now, was with a handkerchief mopping her eyes. "Thank you for taking over things at home. You were able to help all of us cope with the situation at home. That enabled me to focus on my work," he said while gently embracing her, placing a kiss on her wrinkled cheek.

As he wiped his eyes, he said, "Well, you all have hugged every ounce of my energy, and I believe all the water in my body has gone by now. I am famished. Where are we going to eat?" They all laughed. Mr. Trim indicated that he had to go but he would be in touch. Mr. Gosine indicated that he too had to get back to the Orphanage and that the emotions of the day had filled him. They took their leave and Andrea offered to take the family to dinner at a small restaurant in the area.

The girls piled into their car with Aunt Rose and Mikey went with Andrea. Mikey intended to do some catching up with her on the way. Before Andrea could even put the vehicle in drive, Mikey began his volley of questions. "How have you been?" he began. Without waiting for her to respond, he continued, "How long have you been back? Are you living in the same place? Will you be going back to work at the same place?" "Whoooa! Hold up!" replied Andrea laughingly. "You are going like a freight train there. I will let you know all that has been happening. Take a deep breath and relax. We have enough time to chat. Let us just enjoy this moment. Saying that I am proud of you is not even really expressing the depth of my happiness and my admiration for you Mikey. You are a conqueror and that is the best word that I can use to describe the journey of your life from the time I met you as a toddler and now you are a young man. You did not allow your circumstances to hold you hostage. Instead, you rose from the ashes, and you succeeded. Today, you were my son on that stage. Your mum is having a happy dance in heaven. You are an example for the children at the orphanage and for many others who have been in similar circumstances." Mikey smiled as he looked through the window at the scenery which flitted past his eyes.

His mind ran back to his time at the orphanage and how much he wanted to leave and go to a home where he would have family and love. He allowed his mind to journey from that time up to the present moment and it was then that his success truly sunk in. He closed his eyes and pictured his birth mother and the letter that she had left for him. He still had that letter, and he decided that he would frame it. It was his mother's last message to him. He somehow felt as though she was near, and he said to Andrea, "Ms. Andrea, it feels as though my mum is here with me right now. I can see her warm smile letting me know that she loves me. I recall even when she was doped out in the drug house, she would always find the strength to protect me if anyone came around me with foolishness. No one could touch her Mikey; no sir! She protected me tooth and nail. I always read her letter from time to time, and it gives me courage to go on." He paused for a while and then he said, "I did it mama! Your little boy did it!" Ms. Andrea then reached over and patted him on his shoulder.

On arriving at the car park at the Starlight restaurant, Mikey realized that the girls and Aunt Rose had not yet arrived, so they decided to wait in the vehicle until they got there. Andrea used that moment to update Mikey on her life.

She took a deep breath and said in a low tone, "You must have been wondering why you were not hearing from me for a while. It was not deliberate but I, myself, had some health challenges and I needed time to recuperate. I had gotten a bout of pneumonia, and it was bad. I was in the hospital for some months and then I had to go to another facility to convalesce. Contracting such illnesses was a risk with the job that I was doing. Since then, I do experience short breath from time to time. Despite that though, you were always on my mind, and I used to wonder what was happening on your end. I guess just wanting to see you again gave me the motivation to fight the sick days and here I am today. In there as well, was a lot of prayer for my health. Given the length of time that I was away from the job, I decided to retire on medical grounds. I could not endure the hustle and bustle anymore with the job and while I did love the environment, I needed to be back home. One of the first things I did was call the house number that your deceased dad had given to me and your Aunt Rose answered. I explained who I was, and she then told me that you were preparing for your graduation. It was then that we planned for me to attend and surprise you. I am so happy that I was back in time to witness this milestone in your life. I will always remember your journey from the day that we got that call to come for your mum to where you are today. Thank you for having me be a part of your journey Mikey. You were placed in this world for purpose, and you are on your way to fulfilling that."

There was an awkward silence when she had finished and without a word, Mikey leaned over and hugged her. "It is I who must thank you Ms. Andrea," he said quietly. You were my support during those days. You never gave up on me even when I was at the Orphanage. You treated me like your own and for that I will always be grateful. Many days when I wanted to give up, your face, your smile would be in front of me and the little boy you rescued with his mum, that little boy has always thanked God for you. You could have dropped me there and left that night, but you stayed, you took me home. You did not need to do all of that, but something made you stick with me. To this day, you are still stuck with me it seems." With that, they both went into a fit of laughter and then they saw Aunt Rose's car pull into the car park.

The hostess met them at the door and asked whether they had reservations to which they replied in the negative. "Do not worry," she said with a smile, "someone had just cancelled so you can get that slot." She ushered them to their table and indicated that their assigned server would be with them shortly. In that time, they all chatted with each other and even Aunt Rose was poking jokes at Cindy. The atmosphere was filled with gaiety, and they all reveled in it since it had been a while since they had not been in that mood. Mikey's success was enough to create such a feeling of euphoria among the siblings that for that moment in time, their pain was eased.

Andrea sat looking at the camaraderie among the three of them and she smiled, happy that Mikey had a family. "So, what are your plans now Mikey?" she interjected. "For now, I will continue with my small garden and sell my produce. However, I intend to send out my resume to as many firms as possible and I will be doing job searches. Hopefully, I can get a job that will entail the use of figures for that is my passion," he replied.

As soon as he finished speaking, the server came to the table and took their orders. Within twenty minutes the dishes arrived with steaming hot food. They inhaled the spicy aroma of the food and could not wait to eat. It was Aunt Rose who said to them, "Let us bless the meal before we dig in." She prayed and then they began to eat. Mikey was taking his time enjoying every mouthful of his beef lasagna and garlic rolls. With every bite he smiled and looked around the table. He was in a happy place at that time. He felt a sense of contentment that he could not explain. This was his family. After the struggles over the years, he finally had people whom he could call family.

After the meal was finished, they had dessert. Following that, they ordered a bottle of champagne to toast Mikey's success. "Cheers!" They all shouted around the table. Even the other guests clapped when they observed what was taking place. When the server returned with the bill, she informed them that dessert was on the house in honor of Mikey's success. They all chuckled for they could not believe it. The bill was then presented to them, and the server left to return. Andrea informed them that she would pay the bill. However, Aunt Rose insisted that they would give the tip. After payment was made, they remained for about a half an hour, chatting about things in general before they made their way to the vehicles.

This time, Mikey went with Aunt Rose and the girls since Andrea had to go in the opposite direction to get to her residence. They said their goodbyes and Andrea promised Mikey that she would stay in touch. As she drove off, they entered their vehicle and Aunt Rose put the car in gear and drove cautiously out of the car park.

In twenty minutes, they pulled into their driveway, and they proceeded to their rooms. Mikey had not moved back into the house even though he was given the opportunity to do so. He enjoyed his independence in that room and had simply become a creature of habit. After taking his shower, he changed into his night clothes and instead of going to bed, he went over to the house and called his sisters to the sitting room where he encouraged them to play a few card games. The laughter and the noise that they made the house feel alive again. It seemed like ages since there was any cheerfulness in the house. Aunt Rose sat sipping a cup of hot tea and watching one of her favorite soap operas. After an hour of games, the siblings were ready for bed. Aunt Rose was nodding away on the chair and Mikey took the cup from her and led her up the stairs to her room. He then said good night to the girls and went to his room. In a few minutes, the exhaustion of the day stepped in, and he was out like a light on his bed.

Mikey woke up the next morning excited that he would start to take driving lessons that day. He felt it was necessary since it was a burden for Aunt Rose to do all the driving. For him, this was a step towards his independence. From his savings, he had already paid to get his Learner's permit. With that in hand, he enrolled in Jackson's Driving School which was near to where they lived. He did not tell the girls nor Aunt Rose that he was learning to drive. This was supposed to be a complete surprise for them. He smiled thinking about how they would react when they realized that he could drive.

After doing his chores, he dressed and went to the driving school. He had told his family that he was going out to do some business and he would be back. The only thing he prayed for was that they did not see him while he was practicing. He had already taken the written test and had passed it with ease. Now it was the practical and he hoped that he would not make a fool of himself. His driving instructor, Tilly Brown, was a lanky guy who walked with a limp. He made Mikey feel extremely comfortable behind the wheel and he patiently pointed out the controls on the car and their function. Mikey was advised with respect to what he needed to do and had to go through all the paces adjusting his seat as well like mirrors, putting on the seat belt, putting on the lights at various degrees of brightness, sounding the horn, putting on the indicator lights, pressing the brakes and even putting on the radio. He was then taken outside of the car after he was told to open the bonnet. Tilly took the time to show him the inside of the car and explained the function of the radiator, the engine and where the oil stick was located. Tilly informed him that their Driving School was a thorough one and on the first day he would not necessarily be driving. He even went as far as to show Mikey how to change a tire. This he did before the day's lesson ended. Mikey laughed to himself on his way home because he really thought that he would be on the road that day. In any case, he was happy with the approach of the school because they made sure that he was well prepared as a driver and that he understood the responsibility when the vehicle was put in motion. At the end of the lesson, Tilly offered to give him a lift and he decided to drop off close to his home. He did not want to risk being seen by his sisters. The very thought made his smile even more and he walked with a bounce in his step.

Later that day, he got a call from a company inviting him for an interview. He was chatting with Aunt Rose in the kitchen when the house phone rang. On answering, the caller had asked to speak with Mr. Mike Clary. "This is him," Mikey replied. "Mr. Clary, I am calling you from Kramer's Real Estate Agency. My name is Sheena White. Your resume was recently passed to us as part of the process where the resumes of recent university graduates are passed to us for consideration for any openings. We noted that you do have a degree in Accounting and Law, and we wondered if you would be interested in being interviewed for a real estate agent's position. It may not be the normal accounting and law, but those qualifications would certainly be a good fit for an Entry Level Real Estate Agent position. Do you think this is something that you would want to explore?" asked the voice on the other end of the line.

Mikey stood speechless for a moment and in the shortest time he said, "Sure, why not? It would be a start, and it would keep me occupied until an accounting position opens for me. In any case, I would be interested in knowing what the world of Real Estate entails. It is not something that I thought about before." "Great!" replied Sheena, "Would you be able to come in to meet with us on Friday at 9:00 am?" Mikey did not hesitate to reply in the affirmative since he really did not have anything planned. Having agreed with the time, he hung up and proceeded to give Aunt Rose feedback from the conversation. "That is excellent Mikey!" said Aunt Rose excitedly, "You will soon be a working man! God bless you, my boy!" She patted him on his back. She continued, "You will have to go check to make sure that you have the right clothes to wear. You would want to impress them on that day even when you do not have a clue what you are getting into." With that, he smiled and went out the door to his room. He had one day to prepare himself and he took Aunt Rose's advice to look his best. He looked in the cracked mirror that hung on his wall and he realized that he needed to go to the barber. "Wow! Is that how I look?" he asked himself. "A haircut is overdue." He made a promise to himself that would be on his bucket list of things to get done the next day.

He also realized that he needed to get himself some clothes since he would soon be entering the world of work, and this would be a bit different to when he worked at the diner. He reminisced a bit about those days and could not help but smile when he thought of the tips he had made and how that became the basis for his savings. He realized, too, that he would need to open a Bank Account, and this was what he also needed to add to his list of things to do.

Mikey spent the rest of the day tending to his plants and taking care of the small garden. He washed down the driveway and called Aunt Rose to move the car so that he could clean up the garage as well. When she came out to move the car, she said, "Mikey, I was thinking it is time for you to learn to drive. We would need another driver in the family so that I can get an ease with the driving." Mikey replied, "Yeah. I gave that some thought Aunt Rose. We will see how things go."

Later that evening when the girls returned home, he suggested that they could all go to the Drive-In cinema which was about half an hour away. He told them that it was his treat. They left home to get to the drive-in on time for the 6:00 pm show. It was the first time that Mikey had gone to a cinema and a drive-in one at that. He gave Aunt Rose the money to pay and they got a good park. The evening was cool, and they took advantage of that by opening their doors. Mikey and Cindy went to the cafeteria and purchased popcorn and drinks before the movie began. Armed with their refreshments, the two soon returned to the car just in time for the start of the movie, Jaws.

On the way home, Mikey informed his sisters about the upcoming interview. "That is great news Mikey!" said Hetty excitedly. "Look who will be a working man just now. Proud of you bro!" said Hetty, giving him a high five as she spoke. Mikey giggled in the back seat. He simply imagined how they would react when he got his Driver's License. "Thanks, Hetty and Cindy," he said quietly.

On the day of the interview, Mikey got up early and prepared himself. He was nervous but was able to contain his anxiety. He had never been on an interview, and this was his first. "Just go and be yourself," said Cindy as she wished him the best on her way out of the house.

He went to the kitchen but could only drink a glass of orange juice. He looked at the clock and realized that it was 7:30am. He knew that time did not wait for anyone and if he had to get to the venue on time, he needed to leave home by at least 8:15am for the latest. Aunt Rose had volunteered to take him, and she did not drive fast. As such, he had to factor the speed at which she drove as well as the traffic in the area. He washed the wares and hustled to his room to get ready.

It took him at least twenty minutes to get prepared and when he looked at himself in the mirror, he was impressed. His hair was well groomed, and he was happy that he had gone to the barber the day before. His new shirt and shoes looked immaculate. To top off his outfit, he had a slim black tie which he took a while to fix, and which required Aunt Rose's assistance. He was soon ready to leave the house, and he said a little prayer that all would go well. On the way to the venue, Aunt Rose said a prayer for him as well and gave him a few tips on how to conduct himself in the interview. She had recalled some of the strategies that she had used in her younger days in the world of work. Mikey smiled and graciously thanked her for her advice. The traffic was light, and they were able to get to the venue with almost fifteen minutes to spare. Mikey took advantage of that and decided to go in and relax. He thanked Aunt Rose who insisted that she would return to pick him up at a time when she felt that the interview would be completed. "Good luck, Mikey." said Aunt Rose as Mikey exited the vehicle.

As Mikey walked towards the building, the sun's rays embraced him with a warmth that gave him a positive vibe. He checked in with the security officer who guided him to his destination. He sat in the lobby and waited for another ten minutes before he was greeted by Sheena White, who came out of the adjoining conference room. Sheena was of medium height, with a round face and a bubbly personality. She welcomed Mikey and made him feel comfortable.

"Hello Mikey. How are you today?" asked Sheena in a very pleasant voice. "I am as good as can be," replied Mikey with a smile. Sheena smiled and responded, "Welcome to Kramer's Real Estate Agency. We are ready to have a chat with you, so please follow me," she said. Mikey followed her into the large conference room where two other persons were seated with heads bent reading the documents in front of them. He was introduced to the first person, Ms. Smith, and as he was about to be introduced to the second interviewer, he almost collapsed when he realized that the second person was no other than Bob Kramer. "Hello Mikey," he said. "It has been a few years since I have seen you. Please have a seat." He tried his best to sit at ease while taking deep breaths to calm his nerves. He smiled and looked at the three persons with an aura of confidence. His mind was now racing thinking that when he had received the call inviting him to the interview, he never really gave thought to who may have owned the company. Now that he was here, he realized that the owner was Bob Kramer whom he had met at the diner and who had organized the restoration work for the orphanage. The panel soon began the interview, and Mikey did his best to respond.

After forty minutes, he emerged from the room walking more assuredly than when he had gone in. It was over and he was happy. As far as he was concerned, whichever way it turned out, he would be fine for it was not like this was the dream job that he so needed. For him, it was a steppingstone and an experience to prepare him for other interviews. He was happy that he went through this process so he would know what to expect in any other interview. Sheena escorted him to the door and reminded him that he would hear from them in a few days.

With that, he took his leave of the Kramer building and walked towards the car park where he searched for Aunt Rose's vehicle. He walked towards the same area where she had dropped him off and he realized that she had never left but was parked there reading a book. He walked towards the car and before he got in, he walked to the driver's side of the car, pushed his head through the window and gave her a quick peck on her cheek. This caught her by surprise, and she responded with a peal of laughter. "What was that for?" she asked. "Taking the time to wait for me. You could have gone to do your own business, but you opted to wait for me. Thank you, Aunt Rose," he said to her. "How did it go?" she asked. "Well for one I was taken by surprise when I saw who the owner was. It was Mr. Kramer whom I met when I was at the orphanage. I did not think about the name of the agency when I got the call. However, the interview itself went well. I was made to feel comfortable, and I was able to answer all that was asked of me. Mr. Kramer smiled throughout the interview. When they asked what salary I was looking at, I simply said just pay me the best that you can for I do not yet have experience. Mr. Kramer then said that is a smart answer. I laughed because what I really wanted to say to Aunt Rose was pay me top dollar," he said with a big laugh at the end. They both laughed as Aunt Rose pulled out of the car park.

As they drove on the way home, Mikey went into a quiet mood, and he turned and asked Aunt Rose to stop off by the cemetery. "The cemetery?" she asked in a puzzled tone. "Yes, please if you don't mind," he replied. "I want to visit dad and Ms. Diana." Without questioning him any further, Aunt Rose drove to the cemetery after they got some flowers. She then accompanied him to the graves.

On getting to Mr. Andrews' resting place, Mikey knelt at the headstone and placed a vase with a single red rose next to it. He then whispered a prayer and said in an inaudible voice, "Dad, I did it! I did my best to make you proud of me. Thanks for taking me in as your son. You did well by me. My achievements are in your honor. I love you." He then got up and walked to Mrs. Andrews' grave which was next to her husband's. He also placed a vase with a single red rose next to the headstone. He knelt and said quietly, "Ms. Diana, I feel a bit awkward coming to visit you. After how you treated me, it might have been easier for me to forget all about you. Yet, despite that, I knew deep inside of me that I cared for you and wanted you to simply give me a mother's love. All I wanted was to hear you say, I love you Mikey. Those words never came from your lips, but one thing I must say is that you motivated me enough to succeed so that I could get away from your cruel treatment. Sadly, you died before I could leave your house. That is now in the past though. Aunt Rose has taken care of us, and she does her best to make a home with love. I needed to come here to let you know that the boy you thought was a fool; the boy you thought would turn out to be nothing, has achieved his degree. I did it Ms. D. For what it is worth, I did it mum." With that, he turned, wiping away the tears that trickled down his cheek and walked slowly to meet Aunt Rose who had moved away to give him his privacy.

"Are you ok?" she asked as he approached her. "Yeah, yes Aunt Rose, I am good," he replied. He placed his hand around her shoulder, and they strolled towards the car without looking back.

Four weeks after the interview, Mikey received another call from the Real Estate Agency, this time informing him that he was successful in attaining one of the Entry Level Real Estate positions. He was on cloud nine when he got the news and hopped around the house after hanging up the phone. So ecstatic was he that he did not notice Cindy had come in behind him and he bumped into her. "What's gotten into you?" she asked while spinning him out of her path. "I got the job! I got the job!" he replied with all the gusto he could muster. Cindy screamed with delight and they both hugged and jumped around the kitchen. Aunt Rose and Hetty rushed in behind them wondering what the cause of the excitement could be. "Mikey got the job!" shouted Cindy all out of breath. This time Aunt Rose and Hetty joined the crazy hugging and dancing until they finally exhausted themselves and fell on the chairs.

"Congratulations Mikey!" said Aunt Rose. "I knew you would do it." "My brother is now a working man. This is great news, and I am so happy for you Mikey!" said Hetty, her face all lit up like a Christmas tree. "When do you start?" asked Hetty. "I start on Monday coming," Mikey responded. Aunt Rose interjected and said, "Well, today is Wednesday. You have a few days to get yourself together. I will cook your favorite lasagna dish to celebrate Mikey!" She then moved to get the utensils and begin the preparations. "Thanks guys. I appreciate you all," said Mikey. He then offered to assist Aunt Rose with the preparations, while the girls set the table.

The four of them celebrated that evening with lasagna, garlic bread, salad, and a bottle of non-alcoholic wine. After they were finished with the scrumptious meal, the girls cleaned up the kitchen while Aunt Rose and Mikey retired to the living room where they watched a Game show on television. The girls then joined them bringing with them a pack of cards. Soon enough, a card game was played until they were all sleepy. They all rose from the chairs and moved groggily towards their beds.

Mikey retired to his small room outside and sat for a while on the bench in the garden looking up at the stars. He felt mixed emotions as his mind raced back to his birth mother and to his adopted father who were now both deceased. "I hope you are both looking down on me," he said to himself. "I will make you both proud of me." With that, he shuffled towards his room and fell asleep in the shortest time.

The next morning, Mikey went for his driving lesson indicating that he was going out to get some stuff done. He had been progressing well since he had driving lessons three times a week. His driving test was on Friday of that week, and he really wanted to do well. He was hoping that all would go well so that he could get driving out of the way before he started the new job. That day his instructor told him that he was doing well and that he could not see why he could not ace the test. "I will do my best tomorrow," he replied to Mr. Brown, his instructor.

On Friday morning, Mikey once again indicated that he was going out to get some items for his garden and left the house. His driving test was scheduled for 9:00 am and he arrived by 8:30 am at the test site. He had enough time to relax and watch other people being taken on their road tests. He became a bit anxious but with Tilly Brown's encouragement, he pulled himself together and eagerly stepped forward when his name was called. After thirty minutes of maneuvers at the site and on the road, Mikey was finished. He had to wait another twenty minutes before he was given the results. At the end of that time there, he was informed that he had succeeded in the exams. His instructor patted him on his back, and he went to the office to do the administrative process to have his Driver's license issued to him. Mikey looked at the license and could not help the broad smile that spread across his face. "I cannot wait to see the look on their faces at home," he said to himself. He then left the driving site and went to purchase his garden supplies before he returned home.

That evening when everyone was at home, he asked them all to step outside and without any of them noticing, he took the car keys from the hook where Aunt Rose usually hung them. "What is it Mikey?" asked Aunt Rose who stood on the side with the girls. Without a word, Mikey walked to the driver's side and opened the door. He then sat, adjusted his seat, and started the ignition. "What on earth are you doing?" asked Cindy. "Do you even have a Driver's License?" asked Hetty. Mikey only smiled when he heard these questions. He then drove the car out of the driveway and went down the block before he returned to the yard. His sisters and Aunt Rose were by now laughing hysterically when they realized that he could indeed drive. When he got out of the car, he pulled out his license and showed it to them. Shouts of laughter once again erupted from them. It was Hetty who composed herself first and asked, "Mikey when on earth did you do all of this?" He shook his head, laughed, and said, "Aha! Too many questions. All you need to know is that there is now another driver in the family. Aunt Rose you do not have to do all the running around. You now have some help even though the help is still green on the road." She then hugged him and told him that he needed to be careful on the road and that driving was a serious responsibility. They then retreated to the house and Mikey was teased by his sisters for the rest of the evening.

The following Monday, Mikey reported for work at 9am at Kramer's Real Estate Agency. He was given a warm welcome by the receptionist and escorted to meet Sheena, whom he had met previously. She shook his hands and ushered him to an area which consisted of six cubicles arranged in a circular design. She led him to a cubicle which was furthest from the door but from which he had a clear view of the city's harbor. Sheena asked him to place his belongings on his desk and then she took him on a tour of the building while simultaneously introducing him to the other staff members who were present at the time. After about fifteen minutes, Mikey returned to his workspace and was allowed time to settle himself. She then brought the employee administrative documents for him to fill out and then the Information Technology personnel arrived to set him up with his computer credentials.

Sheena had advised him that a meeting would be held that morning at 10:00 am and he looked forward to that. She then returned to his cubicle to give him a company mobile phone to be used when he was out in the field. He was also provided with the policy document that governed the use of the mobile phone. This he sat reading until he was informed that the meeting was about to begin, and he was directed to the Conference Room. Seated at the head of the table was none other than Mr. Kramer as well as two other senior Real Estate personnel. Mr. Kramer introduced himself to the six persons sitting in the room and welcomed them all on board. He chatted about the company and its objectives for that year. He then indicated that the two persons seated with him would each be responsible for mentoring two new persons. He was about to indicate who the third person would be when the door was opened and in came a young man about five feet eight inches tall, sporting a dreadlocks hairstyle. The hairstyle framed a face which Mikey recognized immediately.

He had entered, apologizing as he hastened to the table and sat with a broad smile on his face. Mikey shook his head and snickered to himself as he recognized who it was. "Chad Homer," he said quietly to himself. Mikey remembered Chad, his friend from the orphanage. Chad had left the orphanage before him and when he was adopted, they lost touch with each other. "Mikey and Gina will work with Mr. Chad Homer here who came in fashionably late to the meeting," continued Mr. Kramer as he looked across the table at Chad. "I do hope that our new agents would understand the importance of being on time since that is critical in this line of work," he continued. The meeting went on for about ten more minutes before Mr. Kramer ended it and allowed the new hires to meet with their mentors.

Mikey and Gina sat waiting for Chad to come over to them and when he arrived, he said in a loud voice, "Mike Clary, where have you been man? It is great to see you!" They hugged each other, exchanging compliments and then Chad moved on to shake Gina's hands. "Welcome Miss Gina," he said, "Nice to have you on board." Gina was of medium height, hair neatly tied in a bun and sporting a navy-blue pant suit. She smiled as Chad shook her hand and replied, "Happy to be here." Chad then proceeded to speak to both about the basics of the real estate business and informed them that in the initial period, they would meet daily to discuss matters and that he would be taking them out when he had to meet with clients. Since it was their first day, he decided that he would meet with each of them to get to know them better.

He had a meeting with Gina first and after about twenty minutes he met with Mikey. Once again, he shook Mikey's hand and said, "Well, well, well, look who is getting into real estate. How have you been Mikey? Our meeting up like this could only be fate. After I left the orphanage, I really did not hear from or about you. I had my share of difficulties but that is another story for another time. Tell me about you. I am excited to know how you have been doing. You look well. You have gotten taller. I almost did not recognize you."

I recognized you as soon as you entered the room though," replied Mikey with a laugh. He then proceeded to summarize his life from the time he left the orphanage. He made sure that he omitted the rough times with Diana and stuck to the positives that occurred. "I have had my share of ups and downs as well, but I am still standing," he said as he finished speaking. "So, what have you been up to Chad?" he asked.

"Well, for starters I live with a lovely young lady who was my high school sweetheart. Jenny and I have had our rough patches, and we have still managed to stay together in clear weather and bad. She wants to get married, but I am not so sure that I am ready for that yet," he said with a shrug and a smile. "Oh, I see," replied Mikey. "I guess you would when you are ready then." Chad informed him that they would meet the next day to learn more about the business of real estate and how to attract and retain clients. "I only handle million-dollar property sales, so you got to stick close to me to understand the tricks of the trade. I will leave you alone to do some reading about the company and get yourself settled. If you have any questions on the administrative side you can check with Sheena," said Chad as he sauntered off to his cubicle.

Mikey spent the rest of the day reading up on the company and even meeting with his team member, Gina, who was also getting herself acquainted with the company. The difference with them was that she had always wanted to get into the Real Estate business while for Mikey this was a filler until an accounting job became available. She was excited about it while he was not too sure how to feel until he got into it.

That evening when he left work, he had decided that he would keep an open mind about the job. It did involve money and figures and that was his passion. On his arrival at home, he had to field a load of questions from the girls and Aunt Rose. He told them that he was tired and needed to get a few minutes rest before he gave them an overview of his first day. At dinner that evening, Mikey gave his siblings and Aunt Rose an account of his first day starting with the meeting and the surprise encounter with Chad. He ended by informing them that he was interested in what the field of real estate would be about. With that said, he changed the topic and informed Aunt Rose that he would like to use the car to go to work the next day. "Well, that would be a great help if you can use the car to do some errands after work as well," said Aunt Rose. "That would not be a problem," he replied. After dinner was finished and the kitchen cleaned, Mikey went to his room early. He felt that he needed to get his clothes ready for the next day and get as much rest as possible so that he could leave the following morning.

CHAPTER 6

Changing Lanes

"Find your passion."

The next morning, Mikey woke up at around 6:00 am and got ready for work. At around 7:30 am, he had already made breakfast for everyone and was ready to get on the road. He wanted to leave early to avoid being in the traffic and to get accustomed to the route. This was going to be the first day that he would be driving, and he knew that leaving early would be a smart thing to do.

When he pulled out of the garage, Aunt Rose and the girls were there to see him off. "Take your time on the road and do not forget to pick up the stuff at the grocery on your way back home," said Aunt Rose encouragingly. "Don't worry, I will not forget," he replied.

On his way to work, there was little traffic that morning and Mikey gave thanks. He remembered all his driving instructions and was happy to be able to be alone at this time to do his thing on his own. He felt a sense of accomplishment when he pulled into the car park at his workplace. He had taken about half an hour to get to work, and he was happy. "Wow!" he said to himself, as he rested his head on the headrest. He had arrived at around 8:15 am and was pleased with himself for getting there without any issues and having enough time to get to his cubicle and relax. He spent about fifteen minutes in the car just relaxing before he strolled into the building.

On his arrival, he was greeted by security and informed that a security swipe would need to be issued to him that day. He thanked the officer and made his way to his desk. The office was empty at that time, and he made his way to the kitchen to get himself a cup of coffee since the office was quite cold. He made a mental note to walk with an extra sweater. He had time to finish his coffee and return to his cubicle before other workers began filling in through the door. "Morning Mikey. How are you today?" Gina asked upon her arrival. "Not bad and yourself?" he asked. "I am quite good. Ready for today and what it will bring," she replied.

At around 9:30 am, they had a meeting with Chad that morning. He had greeted them both and told them to meet in the training room. Chad used a PowerPoint presentation to explain the basics of the Real Estate business and to advise on some of the procedures used in engaging clients. He indicated that the Real Estate agent needed to know everything about a property and that he needed to be well prepared to field any questions from the clients. He also spoke about Dress Code and personal appearance, etiquette and setting times with the clients. He went on to speak about negotiating deals and that is what struck Mikey's interest. He had never really given that any thought. However, Chad also mentioned that they would not be doing negotiations for a while since they needed to write some levels of Examinations to be considered as certified Agents. "Look at what I do, listen to how I speak with my clients and just be observant," he said to both.

He went on to say to them, "In here, we are competitive since we are paid commissions based on what is sold. Our teams try to outdo each other in terms of the highest volume of sales per quarter. One of the important things is trust and integrity with the client." Chad went on to give more tips and advice based on the questions directed to him by Mikey and Gina. After two hours, they had enough information to pique their interest.

That day he had a new client to chat with over the phone and he invited them to sit in and listen to how he would engage the person. Mikey looked on at his friend Chad and was impressed with the smooth way he dealt with the client. In the end the client had agreed to a meeting time the following day and Chad was happy when the call ended. "That, my dear colleagues, was step one of the engagement," he said with a smile. "You make it look so easy," said Gina. "Don't be fooled," Chad retorted. "There are times when there are some difficult clients, so be prepared for them all."

Mikey spent the rest of the day completing more administrative matters and even got his Security swipe issued. At five that evening, he left the building and began walking towards the road when he remembered that he had driven to work. "My goodness, I forgot that I drove today," he laughed to himself. He sauntered across to the car park and started up Aunt Rose's car. He also checked the list of items that he was supposed to get at the supermarket that was close to home. Mikey pulled out and made his way to the main road that he would follow to his home. The traffic was not bad again and he was happy.

When he got home that evening, only Aunt Rose was there to greet him because the girls had not yet arrived home. She smiled broadly when she saw him alight and took out the bags with the grocery items. "Well done, Mikey!" she said ecstatically, "You can now do several errands once you get accustomed to the routes. How was the traffic?" "It was not bad, Aunt Rose," he replied with a smile. She helped him with the bags, and he left her to prepare dinner while he went to get a little rest. After about an hour, he joined the rest of the family for dinner and spent time giving them an account of what took place that day.

The next day at work, Mikey and Gina went out with Chad to meet a client. Chad had informed the client that they were in training and were there to get experience. Chad did all the talking and engaging of the client.

Mikey and Gina observed how he spoke to the client and how knowledgeable he was about the property that he was showing that day. Mikey's interest peaked when he heard the price that was being negotiated for the property. His Mathematical brain went into gear when he heard the figures being discussed, but he said nothing. He was there to observe and that is what he did. When they got back to the office and Chad held a feedback session with them, he was able to ask questions and make comments about the current prices of properties in that area. "Great observation Mikey!" said Chad. Gina was also able to provide feedback about what transpired that day. Chad seemed pleased with how they both paid attention and gave relevant feedback. "Wow! You two learn quickly!" he said with a smile.

That evening before they left work, Chad informed them that as part of their training, they would be accompanying him to Open House get-togethers. "At the Open-House get togethers you will meet many influential folks based on the value of the properties that are on the listing. I have one coming up next week and I will let you know ahead of time. You will see how to engage with the high- rollers," said Chad with his signature smile.

As they were about to leave the office that evening, Chad invited Mikey to have a cocktail with him since it was Friday evening. "Oh Chad, I would love to, but I promised my aunt that I would take her somewhere this evening," replied Mikey. "No problem, we can take a rain check on that," said Chad. With that they gave each other a high-five and left for their vehicles.

Mikey arrived home close to 6:00 pm and met Aunt Rose already preparing dinner. "Wow! You are early Aunt Rose. Do you still wish to go to the store?" "No thanks Mikey. I changed my mind and decided to use what we had in the pantry," she replied. He then said, "Well, let us go for a drive and do something this evening with the girls when they get in." "Sounds great to me," she replied and continued with what she was doing.

After dinner that evening, they all piled into the car and Mikey drove off. The girls chatted non-stop and even complimented Mikey on his driving. They went to a small mall in their area and spent about an hour there.

Following that, they got ice cream and returned home too tired to even watch a show on the television. Mikey felt exhausted and did not take long to fall asleep.

During the following week, Chad took Mikey and Gina to their first Open-House in the affluent Crystal Vale area where the properties were worth millions of dollars. As Chad drove his sleek Porsche through the neighborhood, Mikey marveled at the landscaping and the architectural designs of the homes. He could not help but stare at the many houses that stood behind high concrete walls and remote gates. He wondered himself if he would ever be able to afford such luxury at any point in his life. His mind soon snapped back to reality when he realized that Chad had turned up a long driveway with a canopy of palm trees. Gina, who sat in the front seat, said, "Wow! This is fascinating Chad! Who owns this property?" "This property," Chad replied, "is currently owned by a high- profile person, whose name I would not disclose. Let that be one of your principles. Keep your client's details concealed. If he comes around, you will surely know who it is. He has it on the market since he is desirous of moving to another area. I want you all to pay attention to how I greet the guests who will be coming for the viewing." Around 10am the first guest arrived and was introduced to the team. Chad was very suave in how he engaged the man and his wife. Mikey was impressed with how effortlessly he was able to give all the details about the property and even make suggestions as to how the space could be used based on what the guests would have disclosed to him. Mikey and Gina stood within earshot but did not intrude upon their space.

The gentleman's wife liked the property, but he had some concerns which he raised with Chad. Mikey heard Chad, for the first-time, state that he would discuss with the owner of the property and give the guest some feedback. Chad would have made a note in his diary. The final matter discussed was the price and Chad indicated that it was on the market for two million. Mikey noted that the couple did not bat an eyelid but asked what was the lowest the owner would be willing to go. Chad was able to answer that question and a few more before they made their exit.

By 11:00 am, three guests were shown around the property. Chad would have indicated that since it was a weekday, showings were by appointment only. "On weekends we have a bit more of a party style and mingling with some of the other agents," he mentioned. Chad had completed the rounds with the guests when he noticed a sleek gray Mercedes Benz pull into the driveway and a tall guy emerged. He disappeared through the grove of trees leading to the trees and soon appeared in the doorway. Up close, he was about 6 ft. 11 in., and seemed to weigh about 250 lbs. His bald head gleamed in the light, and he had a most enamoring smile on his face.

As he walked uprightly into the room, he attracted everyone's attention. Chad moved swiftly across the floor to greet him, and they hugged each other as familiar buddies would. "Hey Dave, welcome man!" said Chad. "Welcome as always to our Open House." Chad turned to Mikey and Gina and made the introductions. "Meet Mikey and Gina, my two new associates who are, at this time, shadowing me until they can do this on their own." He turned to his two teammates and said, "Colleagues, I want you to meet my legal advisor, Dave Connor, owner of Connor and Associates Law firm. Dave usually gives me advice when I am about to close on some of my deals. He is here today to have a view of the property so that he can advise accordingly. He had never guided me wrong before. He can be your go-to man when you are doing this single-handedly." "Pleased to meet you both, Mikey and Gina, Dave replied. "When the time comes, you can call on me like Chad does." "Mikey did some Law in his studies as well so, both of you can knock heads together," said Chad chirpily. Mikey was surprised that Chad knew this, and he simply smiled. "That is excellent Mikey. You can put your knowledge to work here as you progress in the field," replied Dave. Chad and Dave excused themselves and went to another area of the building to chat privately.

After about twenty minutes, Dave took his leave and Chad indicated that they needed to wrap up since all the scheduled guests had already turned up and the one for the afternoon had been cancelled.

Chad offered to take them both to lunch that day, and they opted to eat at a small downtown restaurant that served fish lunches that Chad deemed as downright delicious. The food lived up to Chad's expectations and both Mikey and Gina gave it high praises. "Thanks for lunch Chad. I owe you one," said Mikey with a raucous laugh. The three of them returned to the office that day feeling quite filled.

Before leaving the office that day, Mikey was given the opportunity to call and engage a potential client. This was done under Chad's watchful eyes. After five minutes, Mikey was able to schedule an appointment with the potential client. His teammate, Gina, was also able to schedule an appointment with another client. They both felt elated at the end of the evening. "Today was very productive," said Mikey. "Yeah!" Gina exclaimed. "This is just the start. You have much more to learn especially if you meet a challenging client," retorted Chad. "So far you are both doing well," he continued. They gave each other high-fives and left the office for the evening.

On his drive home, Mikey felt a sense of accomplishment and said to himself, "This Real Estate business has potential. I realize that I can still use my accounting and legal skills in this field. Who knows? Maybe if I push hard enough, I can do the exams and elevate myself. Hmmm. Time will tell." So lost in thought was he that he did not realize that the car in front of him had stopped suddenly causing him to apply his brakes hard enough to avoid a collision. He was a bit shaken but was able to maintain his composure. He thanked God that he did not hit the car in front of him and drove with greater caution than before. This was enough for him to re-focus. As he drove at a leisurely pace on the rest of the way home, he sang a little ditty, "Yeah! Yeah! I can do this! I know I can! Yeah, yeah!"

CHAPTER 7

Navigating the Complexities of Love

"An angry face does not make money."

(Six years later)

Mikey stood at the bar having a glass of club soda with a twist of lemon. Now and again, he would take a bite from the trays of hors d'oeuvres that were being passed around for guests. He was an invited guest at a banquet thrown by the law firm of Harris and White. He sat on the bar stool looking at the wealthy gentlemen dressed in black suits and ties. Every one of them seemed to be accompanied by a beautiful lady by their side. "Seems that I am the odd one out here. Everyone is paired off. Had I known better I may have invited a female friend," he chuckled to himself as he gazed around. "I guess this is how the wealthy do it when it comes to banquets. I am glad that I came early so that I would not look like the odd duck walking through that door," he chuckled to himself as he took another sip from his glass.

As he sat taking in the glitz and glamor on parade in front of him, he pondered on how he had gotten there. Farah Harris was a lawyer who would interact with them from time to time. Her firm was celebrating its tenth anniversary with a banquet, and she had issued invitations to a few of the agents at the Agency; himself and Chad included. Unfortunately, Gina was no longer with the agency because she had gotten married and moved on to another city. She had a baby girl within that time, and she had decided that she wanted to stay at home for a short while with her daughter. Her husband was a banker who could take care of the finances while she charted a different path.

As such, it was Mikey and Chad who had become the team and what a team it was! In every quarter, they were the top crew at the agency. Mikey had learned how to utilize his training in the field of Accountancy and Law, and he was raking in good commissions. During his tenure at the agency, he had written some of the real estate examinations and had also done well. He needed to write the examination to run his own agency, but he decided that was not on his agenda at that time. He recognized that he still needed to know more before he could take on such responsibility. His focus now was to become one of the best in the business and Chad was an excellent mentor showing him the ropes.

He reminisced for a moment about his time at the orphanage when he and Chad were the friends who would stick together. "Who would have thought that we would end up working together and that he would be my mentor? You just never know how life will turn out," he said to himself. As he was about to pop a shrimp cup into his mouth, he heard a familiar baritone voice behind him saying, "Well, hello there Mikey!" He turned around to see Dave Connor standing behind him and smiling. From the time that Chad had introduced Dave to the team a few years before, he was the go-to person when they had to close deals. Dave said, "How are things going? As I entered, I saw you across the room and decided to make a beeline in your direction." Mikey spun around and both he and Dave shook hands. "Dave it is so good to see you! I was wondering when you and Chad would get here. I feel like a fish out of water for I do not know many of these folks here," he said quietly.

Dave laughed and said, "This is a fantastic opportunity for you to practice your engagement skills for you never know who your next big client may be. They may not come to you, but nothing stops you from going to them and making their acquaintance. Look for a loophole and capitalize on it."

Mikey replied, "Chad is usually the one to make the initial engagement. I am not certain that I am that comfortable yet. Where is Chad? I thought that he would be here by now." Dave laughed and said, "Chad is a gem, but he can be on the wild side as you very well know. He is my close friend but for some reason one woman cannot satisfy him. You know while he does not play with his job outside of that he has a large appetite for females and seems to be a sucker for punishment at home. He called me to say that he and his lady had a disagreement and from the sound of things, he may not attend. He is in the doghouse." Mikey snickered and shook his head saying, "Wow! One day he will come into his own, I guess. He will be alright." They both paused for a moment scanning the room.

"Well, it seems like you are stuck with me tonight so let us not waste the opportunity for you to meet potential clients," Dave said with an encouraging smile. "Who knows? I can get you hitched with some beautiful young lady tonight," he continued as he smiled broadly at Mikey. "Yeah right," replied Mikey as he scoffed at the idea. "I have yet to see a single woman here. Everyone is well paired off. "Oh, ye of little faith," jeered Dave. "The same way you came without someone, is it not possible that a young lady may do the same? Just relax and go with the flow. Come let us go mix and mingle." "After you then," said Mikey as he began to walk alongside Dave.

He observed how well-known Dave was. He made sure to introduce Mikey to the persons with whom he spoke. He observed how he engaged with those whom he met for the first time. He even allowed Mikey to initiate conversation with some of the unfamiliar folk who were at the banquet. He was enjoying himself and even said to Dave, "I am getting better at this. For a while I thought it would be difficult but thank you for throwing me in the water." "No worries there," replied Dave.

After about thirty minutes of mingling, the guests were asked to take their places at the beautifully decorated dinner tables. When everyone was seated, the two principal lawyers from Harris and White went to the podium to start the formal part of the evening's function. After about forty-five minutes of speeches and distribution of awards, the formal dinner began. Mikey and Dave sat at the same table and had their dinner with some of the other agents from Mikey's agency. There was little being discussed while they savored the scrumptious dinner. When Mikey was finished, he told Dave that he would go to the dessert table. Dave had opted out of dessert, so Mikey walked over on his own.

The dessert table was laden with cakes of all kinds. There was a frosted chocolate cake which Mikey wanted, and he noted too, that there was only one more slice. "Aha, they saved the best for last," he said as he moved quickly to the side to get a small plate and fork. After he lifted the last piece onto his plate, he was about to have his first bite when he heard an angelic sounding voice saying, "Are you really going to eat the last piece of that cake and leave a girl hungry?" When he heard the voice, he was wondering if someone was speaking to him. He slowly turned around, only to realize that apart from himself and the young woman who was now positioned in front of him, there was no one else at the table.

She was Malaysian with long dark hair, light brown complexion, and a curvy athletic body. Staring at him with green eyes, she smiled broadly showing a set of pearly white teeth. She said, "As soon as you pick your bottom jaw up off the floor, you can decide if you will leave a girl hungry. She then extended her arm and said in the softest voice, "Hi there, I'm Aisha." As though struck by lightning, Mikey moved robotically, setting the fork on the plate and shook hands with her. He made a conscious note of how soft and tiny her hands felt in the palm of his big hand. "Hi, I am Mike Clary. Everyone calls me Mikey. Pleasure to meet you. Here, you can have the last slice of cake. No problem," he said shyly, while moving to hand over the plate to her. "My goodness," she replied, "A man who gives up his last piece of cake for a lady is a true gentleman indeed. How about we share it?" she smiled encouragingly while looking at him with her doe-shaped eyes. "That is a great idea," he responded. "You take the first bite," he said as he lifted the fork to her thin pink lips. "My goodness, this cake is so moist, just as I imagined it," she said after swallowing slowly. "Thanks for sharing your cake with me Mikey, but I must excuse myself before your better half gets the wrong idea." Before I could even respond she disappeared among the throng of invited guests, who, by now, were finished with their dinner and were warming up on the dance floor.

Mikey stood staring at the guests trying to see if he could recognize the young woman who had appeared and disappeared in the twinkling of an eye. As he stood there, Dave sauntered towards him saying, "For a moment I thought you disappeared without a trace. Did something happen? You look like you saw a ghost." Mikey seemed a little frustrated as he stood there pointing in the direction of the guests. "Did you see…?" he started saying before he stopped short. "See what?" replied Dave. Mikey decided to say nothing in case he looked foolish and simply muttered, "No, nothing man." "Hmm," replied Dave. "I was chatting with the Pattersons for a while after you left the table. Let's get a refill at the bar before we leave here. I socialized enough for the night." With that being said, the two men walked towards the bar and gave the bartender their orders. They then held up their glasses and gave a toast. Half an hour later, Mikey was ready to call it a night. "I am turning in for the night. I had a full day, and I still have a twenty- minute drive ahead of me," said Mikey. "Ok Cinderella. I guess you got to get in before the clock strikes midnight," said Dave jokingly. "Be careful on the road Mikey. See you around," he said as he patted Mikey on his back. "Thanks Dave, get home safely yourself," he said as he walked quickly, making long strides as he exited the front entrance of the building.

Mikey walked to his black Jaguar motorcar and sat behind the steering wheel. It was not the most modern vehicle, but it was a step up from Aunt Rose's old car. After two years of driving her vehicle, Mikey felt the time had come to upgrade and purchase his own vehicle given the nature of the job that he did. His sisters, by then, had also got their driver's licenses and it was always a battle for the use of the car. Aunt Rose had stopped driving due to her failing health and most times the girls had to run the errands. It was only fitting that he got his own. To top it off, he had also purchased a property which was on the market, about three blocks away from the family home. It was a modest four-bedroom house with enough space for him to have his kitchen garden. He had fallen in love with the house when he first saw it on the listing. He had utilized his savings to acquire it and made some renovations before he moved in. He had invited Aunt Rose to come live with him, but she had declined stating that she was too old to make such a move, and she was comfortable where she was. She had given Mikey her blessing and promised him that she would visit. She kept her word in that regard. From time to time, she and the girls would visit and help Mikey to clean up and even cook. They would all hang out and enjoy each other's company.

After moving, Mikey had also invited Andrea to come over. On the one occasion that she did, Mikey was taken aback by her appearance. The once strong, beautiful woman was now walking around with a stick. Her face was now creased with lines and her bent walk told a tale of her battle with her spinal issues. She now lived with a family member who took care of her needs. When Mikey had seen her, he hugged her as though he did not want to let go. "Do you want to live with me Ms. Andrea? I can get a live-in nurse to take care of your needs," he said. "Ah Mikey! You have always been a young man who genuinely cared. There was something about you that first time I met you as a toddler. This is life you know. One minute we are up and the next we are down. I take this in stride. My cousin is taking care of me so no need to worry. I am so proud of how your life's journey has been. Your mother would have been so proud of you. Do you remember the letter that she wrote to you?" she said. With that question being asked, he held her by the arm and walked her to the living room where he stood in front of a document that was framed and placed at the center of a space saver. There, inside a gold frame, was the letter that his mother had written to him and which he had kept among his prized possessions.

Andrea was overcome by emotion and embraced Mikey. "You actually kept this letter all these years!" she said as she struggled to hold back the tears. "I recalled when your mum got ill, and we found that letter in your bag. Wow! She is surely smiling down on you." "At times I wish that she had been here still. I would have taken care of my mum no matter what," Mikey responded to her at the time.

When that flashback ended, Mikey started the ignition, placed the car in drive and began his journey home. "Life has surely had its twists and turns, and I thank God for the precious people who stood by me over the years," he said to himself. After twenty minutes of driving, he pulled into his garage and headed up to his room.

The next morning, Mikey got up around 6:00 am feeling a bit ill. He was not a habitual drinker, and he realized that this was the "morning after" feeling. He was grateful that he did not have to go into the office that day because he had a house viewing with some potential buyers that morning at 10:00 am. He dragged himself out of his bed and walked lazily to the bathroom and then to the kitchen where he proceeded to make himself a cup of coffee. "Boy, it is times like these that a man really needs a significant other," he uttered groggily as he put the kettle to boil. It was then his mind ran back on the Malaysian beauty who had crossed his path and disappeared. "Ah mystery woman Aisha! Where have you disappeared? It would be nice to meet you again, but for now I need to clear my head," he said to himself.

While waiting for his coffee to brew, he called to check in with Aunt Rose, who would usually be up at that time. He told her about his night out and how he was feeling. She advised him to get some coffee and some rest and that should do the trick. He then hung up the phone, set his alarm for the next hour and went back to bed. When the alarm did go off, he realized that it was almost 8:00 am. He felt more composed and prepared himself for the day ahead.

At 9:00 am, he rolled out of the garage allowing the fresh air to hit his face as he began the journey to his destination. Half an hour after, he pulled into the driveway of the property that was to be viewed that day. He did not waste time entering the house, ensuring that all was set for the potential buyers. He always made it his business to be punctual all the time and make his final checks. This was no exception. He turned on taps; he scanned each room, double- checking to make sure that the rooms were in order; he went out onto the back veranda and looked out at the grounds which were cut two days before. He had finished scanning the property when his phone rang. He noticed that it was Dave who was calling. Simultaneously, he observed that his clients were making their way up the driveway. He hastily answered the phone as he began making his way to the Ground Floor. "Hi, Dave!" he answered quickly. "Hi, Mikey. How are you today? Did you get home all right?" asked Dave. "Yes, I got home fine but awoke with a bit of a hangover. Nothing that some coffee and rest did not take care of," replied Mikey. The conversation was interrupted by the ringing of the doorbell. "Did I call at an inconvenient time? I failed to ask you, and I am hearing a doorbell behind you," said Dave. "Yeah, you know I always got time for you, but my potential clients have arrived five minutes earlier than the scheduled time and are now at the door. Would you be available in about forty minutes' time? There is a possibility that the viewing may be completed within that time. I can call you as soon as I am finished," replied Mikey. "Do not worry about it. I do not have court this morning so you can feel free to call me as soon as you are finished. I do hope that you nail this one," said Dave encouragingly as he hung up. Mikey rushed to the door where he met his clients.

There at the door stood a couple from China, Ling Peng, a banker, his wife Sue, a Software Engineer, and their two-year-old daughter, Zang. They loved the view of the ocean, the spacious backyard, the huge pool and outdoor spa, the beautiful marble kitchen as well as the six bedrooms with the self-contained bathrooms sitting on an acre of land. Sue was mesmerized with the view which spilled from the open-plan kitchen onto the deck of the pool. Ling then began to discuss price with Mikey and was happy when he learned that the asking price of eight million was negotiable. Mikey was able to get from them the price that they were willing to pay and promised to contact Ling by the next day once he chatted with the seller. Almost fifty minutes after their arrival, the Peng's were driving back down the driveway.

Mikey went out onto the back veranda from where he made a call to Dave, "Hi Dave, I am all yours now. Just finished doing a viewing and the clients are willing to purchase. However, the asking price is eight million and he is willing to pay 7.5 million immediately. I know that the seller was not willing to negotiate so I believe that I will need your advice on this one as I always lean on your expertise." Dave did not hesitate to ask Dave a few questions before he provided his advice. When he was through giving the advice, he said to Mikey, "My reason for calling you earlier is that I have an address for you. Do you have a pen nearby?" Mikey quickly pulled his pen from his pocket, grabbed his diary, and wrote as Dave dictated, "72 Laurelwood Drive, Building Six, 5th floor. Ask for Miss Khan since she will be expecting you. Remember dude that an angry face does not make money." "Yes Dave. You said it about a million times. How can I forget?" replied Mikey on the other end of the phone before he ended the call.

Dave had always looked out for him, and Chad and he had come to love him as much as Chad. He was always ready to give his advice when called upon or through lucrative deals their way. This time seemed no different from the rest.

He scheduled that visit for the next day since there was one more viewing at noon that day. After that, he intended to go into the office to complete some work before he left for the day. "I really am not in the frame of mind to meet with anyone else for today. My head is hurting slightly so after office it will be homeward bound for me. Laurelwood Drive will see me tomorrow," he said as he drove to the office that afternoon.

After an hour of meeting up with Chad and discussing what took place with the viewing, Chad patted him on the back and told him that he was proud of his progress. "Wow! I do hope that you are able to close that deal. See how it goes after you speak to the seller," said Chad as he walked out the office. Mikey then left about fifteen minutes after and headed straight to Aunt Rose's house because he felt the need for her pampering and some family time with his sisters."

Your destination is on the right," said the voice coming over the Waze app linked by Bluetooth inside of the vehicle. After driving for about forty minutes and singing as though he was Centre stage at a concert, Mikey pulled close to the curb trying to ascertain which of the tall brown stone buildings was Number Six. He sat there gazing up at the row of buildings and noted that Building Six was near an entrance displaying several signs. He drove around that building and found a park. As he got out of his car, he took a panoramic view of the area with its tree-lined landscaping and quiet surroundings. He walked towards the building which had Number 6 attached to its exterior.

Mikey walked through the large polished, double mahogany door into the lobby of the building and looked around for the bank of elevators. He observed where they were and took the first available elevator, pressing the button for the fifth floor. As the elevator door opened, he walked directly to the receptionist who was seated behind a semi-circular mahogany enclosure surrounded by glass. "Hello, good morning. I am Michael Clary, and I have a 10:30 am appointment with Miss Khan," he said with a smile. "Yes Mr. Clary, Miss Khan is expecting you. Please sign in to the Visitors' Log and then you will follow me," said the Receptionist in a most welcoming voice. When he had finished signing the logbook, she ushered him down a corridor to a large conference room. She asked him if he needed any refreshments, and he opted for a bottle of water. She then informed him that Miss Khan would be with him shortly as she exited the room, closing the door quietly behind her.

Mikey sat looking over the room, which was simply, but tastefully outfitted and decorated. He looked on at the television as he awaited Miss Khan's arrival. He was a bit engrossed in a newscaster's report on the television that he did not hear when the door was opened. The voice behind him startled him and as he turned around, he almost fell off the chair. "Sorry to keep you waiting Mr. Clary. I was closing off a critical matter that had just come to my attention," said the person standing before him. There, in the flesh, was Aisha. "I see we meet again," she continued.

He was at a loss for words and began to stutter, "Ahmm, nice to, ahmm, nice meeting you again, Miss Khan." He rose to shake her hand and then she took a seat opposite him. "Yes, I am Ms. Khan. However, you can continue to call me, Aisha. How have you been?" she continued in a very matter-of-fact tone. Mikey finally found his tongue and replied, "I have been doing well thanks. I was given this address and asked to meet with Miss Khan.

I did not know who it was and was curious as to who it was and what was the nature of the meeting," he said as quickly as he could. He did not want her to see him sweating beads as he looked upon her face. Here at last and quite unexpectedly, he was sitting in the presence of the woman who had magically appeared and disappeared at the banquet; the woman who would have occupied his thoughts since then. Now that he was in her presence, he was getting cold feet and opted to stick to the formal side of the conversation. In any case, she made it easy for him to do so for she was very business-like and formal in her attitude.

Flipping through some paperwork in front of her she slid a file over to him and said, "Our law firm has a client from Saudi Arabia who is interested in the Crown Jewel property. Would you happen to have that listing?" "I am not familiar with that property so I will have to say that we do not have that listing," Mikey replied. "Well, it is pretty new and at this time, Dave has suggested that you be the preferred agent," she stated. "He always makes referrals to this law firm and so we trust his word. Will you be up for the challenge and how long do you think it will take to flip this property?" "To be honest," he said, "I will have to peruse the file thoroughly before I can give you an answer. I can do so tonight and give you a call tomorrow if that is acceptable to you." "Sure, that would be excellent," she stated. "Ok then Mikey, that concludes our business here today. It is certainly nice meeting up with you again." she said as she gathered her files and stood up, looking at him with a smile etched across her face.

Mikey swallowed hard and for a moment stood wondering what to do next for he did not want to just end the interaction like a puff of air. "Should I ask her out? What would she think?" were some of the thoughts that raced through his mind. At last, he found his tongue and said, "Is it possible to have a contact number for you? Would I be able to call you outside of office hours to discuss this project?" She extended her hand to give him a farewell and said to him curtly, "We will stick to office hours, for now, until we dive further into the matter at hand. As such, you can get me on the office line. My secretary will be advised to make your calls a priority. Enjoy the rest of your day, Mikey." She then escorted him to the elevators and waved him goodbye as the elevator door closed.

As he exited the building, he had such mixed emotions that he hustled to his car and simply sat there not knowing what to think. "Geez! I messed up big time! I looked like a fool asking her for her number," he said to himself as he pounded on the car's dashboard. "Oh no! Oh no! Oh no! I messed up! What would she think of me? Probably thinking she would not want to deal with this idiot anymore." Mikey sat with his eyes closed for a few more minutes. He then took a huge breath before he put his vehicle in drive to join the slow-moving traffic on the road. He switched to a radio station that had some comedy and soon enough he was laughing, doing his best to drown out his underlying emotions. Based on how he was feeling, he decided to work from home for the rest of the day.

After locking his front door, he changed into more comfortable wear and sat on his bed. He then proceeded to peruse the twenty-five-page document in the file while sipping on a glass of orange juice. The more he read, the more excited he got and before he knew it, he had opened his computer and began crunching numbers. "What is this! If I get this sale, the commission will be a game changer!" he said to himself excitedly. "Why did Dave recommend me for this? This is mega! Thank you, God! Thank you, Dave!" He was now sitting on the edge of his bed, all semblance of tiredness gone for the moment.

He then placed his computer on the bedside table and decided to finally take a nap. He slept fitfully for about an hour and upon awakening, he then propped himself on his pillows as he played back the day's events in his mind. He marveled at how his day had progressed and how he had finally met up with Aisha. He was still puzzled by her formal approach with him but was grateful that he would still get to see her again. "Next time I will be brave enough to ask her out. She did not even want to give me her number," he said to himself. He then got up lazily and went to make a cup of coffee.

He returned to his bedroom to pick up the file and on his way to his office to study, he noticed that something had fallen on the floor. He stooped to pick it up and noticed that it was a small white business card. His first thought was that someone had forgotten a card in the file or had used the card as a place marker. Upon closer examination, Mikey could not believe what he saw. There on the card were written Aisha's name and contact numbers. He also realized that a note was scribbled at the bottom in black ink. What he saw made him throw back his head and laugh for a few seconds. Then he looked once more at the note which read: "You might want to call this number after work." Mikey felt like a child in a candy store, unable to contain his emotions. He threw up his hands and punched the air, while saying to himself, "Yes! There is a God! Ok Ms. Khan! You like being a mystery woman!"

He sat for a moment contemplating the events of the day and understood why Aisha did not give him her number directly. It appeared to him that she was one who separated business from personal life and was careful not to mix the two. After that discovery, Mikey seemed to have gotten an adrenaline rush. He went to his study and in about an hour, he was able to finish quite a bit of work before he wrapped up for the day. He then went to his small gym and exercised for another hour before he had a shower. As he sat drying his hair, he realized that he had not really had a proper meal that day. The way things had gone that day was enough to make him forget about food. He contemplated what he would have for dinner that evening and remembered that he had some of Aunt Rose's leftover spaghetti and meatballs in the fridge and he had a pack of garlic bread rolls. After getting himself dressed, he warmed up the food and proceeded to sit at the dining table where he devoured the delicious meal.

He then switched on the television and sipped on a passion fruit smoothie which he had chilling in the fridge. In his hand, he had the card with Aisha's contact details. He turned it over a couple of times contemplating whether to give her a call that evening. He certainly did not want to come across as being desperate for her friendship and yet, he pondered on the risk of losing out on time to get to speak with her. "Hmm. I better flip a coin," he said to himself. He placed the card on the small glass table at the side of the couch and listened to the news for a while. Approximately fifteen minutes after, without an ounce of hesitation, he grabbed the card and dialed the mobile number on it.

The phone rang about four times and as he was about to hang up, he heard a soft voice on the other end saying, "Hello, Khan's residence. How may I help you?" On hearing the voice, Mikey paused for a moment, stuttering for a bit as he replied, "Ahmm..hi Aisha. This is Mike Clary." Oh, hi Mikey. Nice to hear from you. I was wondering if you had seen the card," she replied with a laugh. "I did see the card and the note I might add and felt that I should obey instructions," he retorted. "Obey instructions! That is a good one. I did not realize I had given you any," she once again replied. "Well, let us just say it was quiet coercion," he said with a laugh. "So how are you doing today?" He continued, trying to keep his voice as controlled as possible without her realizing that he was really a bundle of nerves at the end of the line.

"I am doing just fine, thank you," she responded. "I was wondering if you would call at all," she said with a chuckle. "Well, since you did not state a specific time to call, I decided to take my time," he stated casually. "Oh, so no time instructions. Next time I would know better," she laughed. He liked the sound of her angelic voice and could not help but smile while chatting with her. Before long, he was feeling more comfortable, and the conversation went on for about forty minutes. "It would certainly be nice to get to know more about you. That is, if you will allow me to," he said fleetingly.

"You wish to know all about me?" she said sarcastically. "Well, let us pause for a moment and first speak about the guy who wakes up every morning at 5am and has morning devotions for twenty minutes. The guy who then runs on his treadmill for about an hour, after which he cools down and sips on a cup of coffee while catching up with the news. Do you recognize who I am speaking about?" she said, pausing for effect. "Wow! Continue! This is interesting!" he said, sitting up on his sofa. "Let's see," she continued. "This guy then showers and dresses and in about fifteen minutes, he is out the door. Before reaching his office, he always stops at Remy's Coffee Shop, which is a block away from his office. Do you recognize him?"

"I am speechless! You must have paid your PI a tidy sum for that kind of in- depth information," he said with some degree of unease. "Were you spying on me all along? Did you install cameras at my house? How did you know so many details about me? This is worrisome though." "Relax Mikey," she said. "My PI is the best. In fact, you know him quite well." "I do?" Mikey questioned. "Who is he?" "Well since I need to put your mind at ease, I will tell you. He is my father," she said in a calm voice. "Your father?" he replied in a puzzled tone of voice. "How would your father know such details about me? Who is he?" Aisha paused for a bit before she answered him. "My father happens to be a man who holds you in high esteem. His name is….." As she was about to state his name, someone was ringing her doorbell. "I will have to call you back if that is fine with you. The delivery guy is at the front door."

During the few minutes that he was awaiting her call, Mikey could not keep quiet. He paced the floor, running his hand over his hair. "Who was Aisha's father? Who would know me so well? He did not know anyone with the surname, Khan. This woman is really a mystery!" He went to the kitchen to top up his glass and in about ten minutes, he heard his phone ringing. He scrambled up the phone as if his life depended on the call. "Hello?" he said, doing his best to remain calm. "Hi Mikey, how are you doing?" said the voice on the other end. It was Aunt Rose calling to check up on him. "Hey Aunt Rose, I am a bit busy right now. Could I get back to you in about an hour? I am handling a matter that came up," he said as quickly and calmly as he could. As soon as she hung up, he sat back sipping on his drink and watching the clock.

It was not until half an hour after that Aisha's call came in. He exhaled, grateful to hear her voice on the other end. He did his best to contain his anxiety. "Hi there," she said on the other end. "Hi. Is everything ok?" he asked. "Sure, I am good. I decided to take care of something in the kitchen before I called back," she replied. "Now, where were we? Oh, yes, I was telling you that my father knows you well. In fact, you were both at the banquet when I met you." "Seriously?" he replied. "Who was it then? I do not know anyone with the surname, Khan." "He does not have my surname. So let me take you out of your pain. My father is Dave Connor!" she stated in a very business-like manner.

"What!" Mikey shouted as he slid off the sofa onto the floor. "Dave has a daughter. I never knew he had children! Wow! This is a shocker!" "The truth is he's not my biological father," she said hastily. "Bob and my mum met each other some years ago while he lived in Malaysia. When they met, I was three years old and fatherless. She was a single mother who worked in a law firm as a secretary. By the time they met, my biological father had left her without a trace. My mum searched for him everywhere she thought he would be. However, after a year of futile searching, she gave up. Bob had come to Malaysia to do some work in the law firm where my mum worked and soon enough, they fell in love with each other. After a year of courting, they got married and returned to this country. Bob decided that he would adopt me since he had no children at the time. It was decided that I would keep my father's surname until I was old enough to decide what I wanted. That is Aisha Khan, in a nutshell. I said enough for today about me. I am sorry that I sprung this on you, but I am a kind of direct, no beating around the bush kinda gal."

Following that, they spent a few more minutes chatting about things in general. Mikey, however, needed time to process what he had heard. His head was spinning now, and he felt tired. He was thankful when she said that she was tired and suggested that they should both retire for the evening. They both promised to keep in touch. After he hung up, he sat on the floor with his knees propped and his head resting on them. As he digested the information, he was now able to put the pieces together and realized how he was recommended for the life-changing business deal.

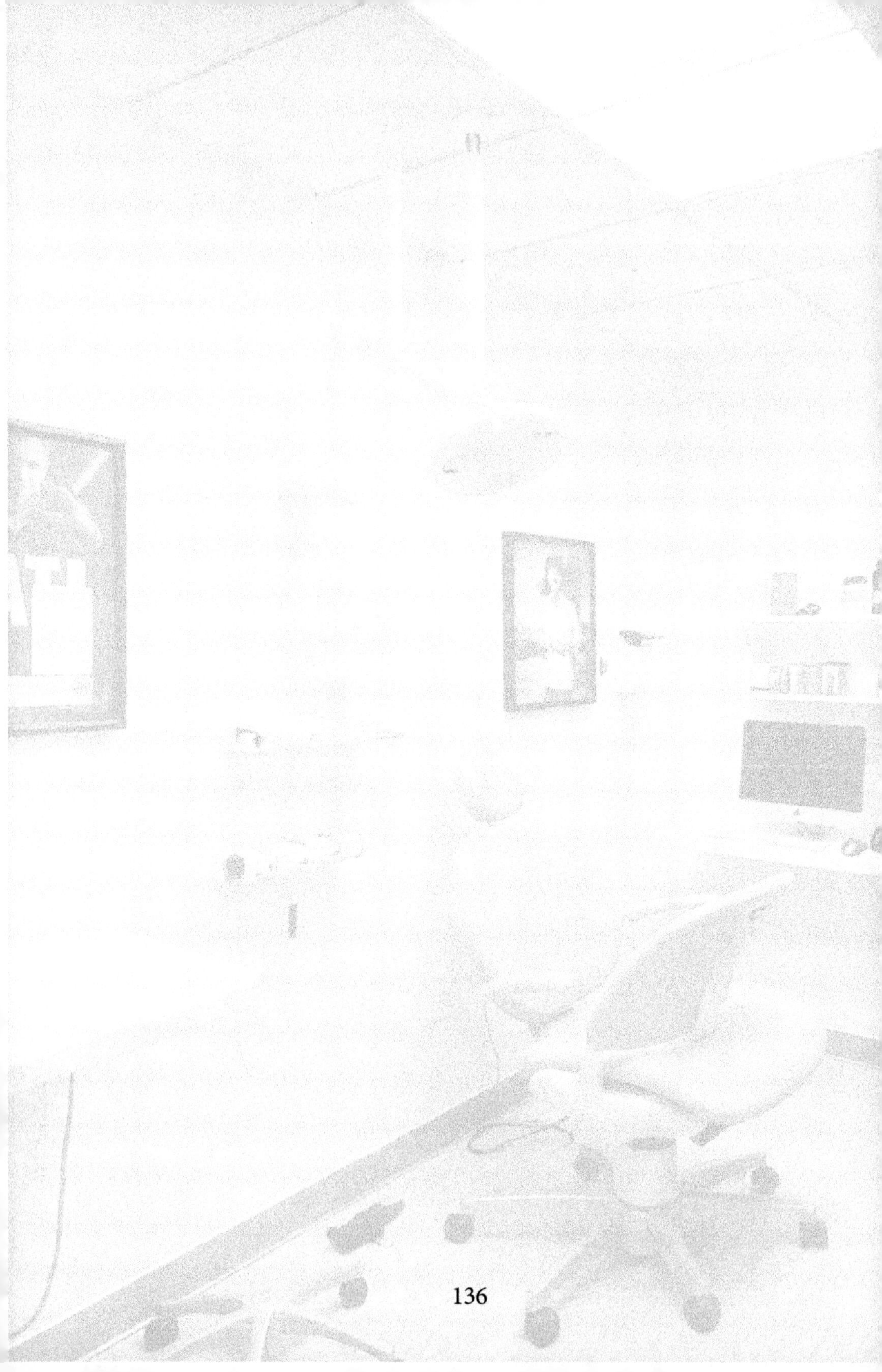

Chapter 8

Loving Larger than Life

"We have one life to live; make it count and be a blessing to others."

Mikey awoke the next morning feeling a sense of warmth, not only from the sun's beams which drenched his room with its radiance, but also from the feeling which somehow filled his being. He got up that next morning and laid awake in his bed reminiscing about his chat with Aisha. He realized that he was indeed exhausted after hearing what she had to say and now that he was rested, he sat deciphering all that they had discussed. What a shocker for him to realize the connection between Dave and Aisha. He smiled thinking about it all. "Small world indeed," he said, nodding his head. He wondered if he should mention this to Dave. After contemplating, he decided that he would keep his personal life private and if Dave approached him about it then he would have something to say. For now, he opted to be quiet.

He remembered the luxury property that was now his to manage and he realized that he needed to call Dave to first thank him and then to discuss some legal aspects with him. Having remembered that, he flew out of his bed with a burst of energy and began his morning preparations. Before long, he was ready and set out from his home. As he proceeded out of his driveway, his mobile rang, and he pressed the button to accept the call on his dashboard. "Mikey!" said the person on the other end, "Aunt Rose fell and hurt herself! You got to get here now!" Upon recognizing Hetty's voice, he did not hesitate to make a detour. He got to the house within two minutes of receiving the call. As soon as he got to the door, Hetty opened it, and he rushed in. There, on the floor, was Aunt Rose lying down and moaning. Mikey quickly helped his sisters to lift her and place her on the couch. "Call the ambulance!" shouted Mikey. Cindy was about to call the ambulance when Aunt Rose said feebly, "No! Call Dr Prince instead. He is my physician. His number is on the kitchen calendar." With that, Cindy dashed to the kitchen, found the number, and called Dr. Prince. "He will be here in fifteen minutes," she said quite out of breath. In the time being, Mikey ensured that she was comfortable by propping her up on some pillows before he questioned her. She indicated that her leg was paining where she had hit it. "How did you manage to fall?" he asked. "I was just walking to the kitchen when I suddenly felt dizzy and the next thing I was on the floor," she replied. "You must be careful though. We will have to find out about that dizzy spell when Dr. Prince gets here. Why is he taking so long?" "Dr. Prince said fifteen minutes Mikey. We need to be patient," said Cindy. The three of them sat in the living room awaiting Dr. Prince's arrival.

After what seemed like an eternity, Dr. Prince was knocking at the door. Without a moment's hesitation, Hetty rushed to open the door. Upon entering he went straight to Aunt Rose who was still groaning in pain. Dr. Prince proceeded to diagnose her situation before he eventually called Mikey to the side. "Your aunt has high extremely low blood pressure which, more than likely, was the cause of her dizzy spell. Right now, she is in pain because she hit her leg when she fell. Given her age, I would want to have an x-ray and blood tests done to make sure that all is well. I also work at the St. Lucy Private Hospital as well so you can bring her there for that to be done.

I will be there around 11:00 am. In the meantime, I will give her an injection and medication for the pain. That will give her some time to rest," he said in a hushed tone.

When Mikey heard this, he said, "Aunt Rose has been our caretaker for the past number of years. She did not want to go to the hospital and asked us to call you. Based on what you recommended, I will take her to the hospital you recommended for the x-ray and tests today. The sooner we get the results we will know what we are dealing with." Dr. Prince gave Aunt Rose an injection. "That would keep her sedated for a while," he said as he was finished with her. He also advised Mikey to call and make the appointment to see him later that morning at the St. Lucy Private Hospital which was about a half an hour's drive from the house.

After Dr. Prince left the house, Mikey and his sisters made sure that Aunt Rose was quite comfortable on the sofa which expanded like a bed. They gave her coffee and light toast with cheese because she did not want to eat anything else. Once she had that, she fell asleep. Mikey sat next to her on the bed, stroking her white hair, while the girls tidied the kitchen. As he did so, his mind raced back to how she entered their lives and how well she had treated them over the years. "I will make sure you get the best care, Aunt Rose," he whispered and as she slept, he kissed her lightly on the forehead.

Mikey looked at his watch and noted that it was almost 9:00 am. He called into work and left a message to inform Chad that he had a family emergency. Even though he was now a certified agent, he still consulted with Chad at the office. He then made the call to the St. Lucy Private Hospital to make the appointment to see Dr. Prince that morning. By then, Hetty had to leave for work and Cindy decided to take a day off to help with Aunt Rose. Mikey had checked his day's schedule and realized that he had a viewing at ten that morning. He did not usually like cancelling a viewing but that morning he called the client and re-scheduled it for the next day. The client was very understanding and even mentioned that the next day would be perfect. With that being done, he was able to clear his calendar for the rest of the day and focus on Aunt Rose.

At around ten, Aunt Rose had awakened, and Mikey and Cindy had informed her about what was taking place. She felt a bit tired but did not fuss about the tests that were to be done. They went in Mikey's vehicle and on the way, she was having her laughs with them. "Mikey, you were to call me back last night. Do not have an old woman waiting up for your calls when I could be in my bed snoring," she joked. "Ahhh, about that Aunt Rose, I got caught up in a matter and by the time I was finished, it would have been too late to call you, Sorry about that," he said with a smile. For a fleeting moment, his mind ran on Aisha but then he decided that he must stay focused on the matter at hand. They were soon at the hospital. Mikey dropped off Aunt Rose and Cindy at the Reception area after which he proceeded to park the vehicle.

After doing her triage, the attending nurse then ushered them to a room where Dr. Prince was waiting. "Aunt Rose how are you feeling right now?" he asked. "Like a ton of bricks fell on me," she said. "Well, let us make sure that ton of bricks did not damage you. All we will do today is do an x-ray in your leg and take a little blood to test. Are you fine with that?" he asked. She nodded her head in response to the question. Soon enough he called for an attendant to take her in a wheelchair to the x-ray room. After about fifteen minutes in there, she was then taken to another room where she they drew blood from her.

When this was done, Dr. Prince once again saw her and informed her that he would be in touch with her later that evening once he got the results of the tests. In the meantime, he instructed her to get as much rest as possible. Aunt Rose then left the hospital with Mikey and Cindy for the drive back home. On the way home she fell asleep, and the two siblings decided that they would not awaken her until they got home. They spent the time chatting about things in general until they got home.

Mikey spent the rest of the day at the house with Aunt Rose and Cindy and took the time to check on the garden and his old room. His previous herb garden was now dried up since no one was watering or tending to the plants. He realized that there was need for some general sprucing up and made a mental note that he would either go over there a little more to assist with the upkeep of the yard or get someone to do a general cleaning at intervals. He was focused on his property now and work and had little time to be at his siblings' house to do much. He did a bit of cleaning up before he re-entered the house.

By the evening time, Aunt Rose sat chatting with them because the painkillers had worked well to reduce her discomfort. "Thank you all," she said to Mikey and Cindy. "You all sacrificed your day's work to be with me and I am grateful. I just felt giddy for a moment and the next thing I knew I was on the floor. I doubt that I have any broken bones, but Dr. Prince needed to be sure. Maybe if I feel better, I can make your favorite lasagna." "That is not happening today, Aunt Rose," replied Mikey. "You are going to remain just where you are, and we will manage things. You have done so much for us that what we are doing is our way of saying thanks." "I agree," chimed Cindy. "When Hetty gets in, she and I will make a lasagna, and we will see how well we can match yours." They all chuckled and when Hetty did get in, she was given the update. "No way you are going in that kitchen Aunt Rose! At least not today! Please relax and let us take care of you." she said as she placed her arms around Aunt Rose and gave her a tender kiss on her forehead. Aunt Rose's response was a tear that trickled down her face. "Ok then," said Mikey. "If we continue to shower her with love, when will she eat?" They all laughed, and the girls made their way to the kitchen to prepare the lasagna. Mikey sat chatting with her making sure from time to time to prop up her pillows and get her water or whatever she needed.

By 7:00 pm, Mikey was on his way to his house having been satisfied that all was well with Aunt Rose and the girls. By the time he had left Aunt Rose was already in deep slumber having enjoyed the lasagna and having taken her medication. He had left instructions that they were to call him any time of the night if anything went wrong. When he got inside his house, he showered and was about to watch a movie when he decided to check his messages. He had not really checked his phone for the day and was surprised to see that he had missed a call from Aisha. With Aunt Rose not being well, that had occupied his time. He decided that he would give her a quick call and so he checked the time and realized that it was 8:15 pm.

After about four rings, Aisha answered the phone. Her voice on the other end made Mikey smile and he said, "Hi there. Sorry I missed your call today, but my aunt had a medical emergency and that was my focus for the day. How are you doing?" "I am not bad. I had called earlier to find out what progress you had made with the listing but from what you just said, you did not do much," replied Aisha. "Correct!" said Mikey. "It is one of my priorities for tomorrow though. My Aunt sacrificed a lot for us and when we had no one she stepped in without being asked. How could I not sacrifice for her? No amount of money in the world can replace my aunt. Sorry if I come across as aggressive but once she is in danger, she is my priority then." "Ah I see that you are a man who takes care of his family in a very enthusiastic way," she said. "I will make a note of that." "Listen, I am not doing what I do for anyone to agree or disagree. I do what I must do by my family and that is all there is to it."

"So, how is your aunt doing now, asked Aisha?" "I left her sleeping comfortably but my sisters know that if anything happens, they are to call me immediately anytime." "You have sisters?" Aisha asked. "Yes, Hetty and Cindy. They became my sisters when I was adopted into their family," Mikey replied. "One day I will tell you my life story which, in some parts, may be like yours. However, this evening is not the time since I am really feeling drained. I am now realizing that my energy is spent, and I am not the best company right now. Please forgive me. Could I make it up to you by taking you to dinner tomorrow night? In any case, it will be Friday so you can go home later without thinking of work the next day." With Aisha having accepted his dinner invitation, Mikey ended the call and switched to a movie. When morning dawned, he realized that the movie was watching him all night since he had slipped into a sound sleep from which he had arisen at around 5:00 am the next day.

That Friday morning was a hectic one for Mikey. He got to the office earlier than usual and took care of administrative matters. He then went out to do a viewing with the client he had canceled the day before. The viewing was a potential success, and he was hoping that all would go well.

At around 10:00 am, he gave Dave a call to discuss some legal aspects of the Crown Jewel property. "Hey Mikey! I have not heard from you in some days now. What's up buddy?" said Dave. "Hi Dave. Just wanted to say thanks for the referral to Ms. Khan for me to manage the Crown Jewel property. She indicated that their firm had a client from Saudi Arabia who would be interested so I needed to run something by you before I proceeded with the call today. Can we meet for about fifteen minutes this morning? I do not know if you can spare me that time," replied Mikey. "Sure Mikey. I do not have a full calendar today, but I am signing off on some documents here now. Let us meet at Café Blue for about 10:30 if that works for you," said Dave. "That suits me fine," said Mikey. Mikey smiled as he recalled how he referred to Aisha by her formal name. He decided that he would raise the matter of Aisha once he saw that the timing was right. At 10:40am there was Dave, striding into the café where they had agreed to meet.

Mikey was already seated, and they both shook hands and sat to converse. "Dave man, let me start by saying a huge thanks for this referral. I could not understand why you felt that I was the person to execute this mega deal, but I am willing to give it my all and I am humbled at the same time," said Mikey in a humble tone of voice. "Look Mikey, you have paid your dues. I have watched your progress from the time you entered the field, and I noticed that there was something about you that stood out. You learn quickly and your values are on point. You have enormous potential, and I felt why not recommend him for something that is outside of his comfort zone. As such, when Ms. Khan informed me about the property, I did not have to think about which agent I could recommend to her," replied Dave with a smile across his face.

"If I get this deal completed, this will be a huge inspiration for me. I am thinking of one day opening my own Agency so who knows? I just needed to get some idea about some legal matters with this," said Mikey. "Sure, no problem, Mikey," responded Dave. They spent the next half an hour discussing what Mikey needed to know. At the end of the conversation, they parted ways without any mention of the name Aisha nor of Dave being her father. It was very formal, and Mikey opted to keep it that way for now.

He then left and made a call to the potential Saudi Arabian client. This was going to be a game changer and after arranging to meet the client the next day, he went back to the office to arrange an Open House at another location with the administrative team.

That day flowed well for him and by evening he was on his way to Aunt Rose to check up on her. He made a call to Dr. Prince to find out about the test results. "Hey Mikey, I was just about to call you," said Dr. Prince. "I just received the test result, and the strong lady has no broken bones. However, her blood tests showed that she has a slight infection which can be cleared up with some antibiotics. I will come across to the house at around 5:30 pm this evening and will give you the necessary prescription for her course of medicine." "No problem, Dr. Prince. We will look out for you," replied Mikey. He smiled as he recalled the words "strong lady."

That evening, Dr. Prince came by and provided her with an update on her health. Aunt Rose was happy to know that she could go about her business with some degree of caution. She had mentioned that the pain in her leg was decreasing and the blue spot on her leg was clearing up. When the doctor departed, Mikey stayed for another twenty minutes before he left the house. The girls were home by then and he informed them that he had a dinner date. This brought some banter between himself and his siblings who wanted to know who the person was who had caught their brother's attention. "It is too early in the game to jump to conclusions," said Mikey with a laugh. "This is just two friends having a casual evening out. Stop reading more into this." With that he kissed them all and took off.

By 6:30 pm, he left home to pick up Aisha at her home. Because he was using Waze for directions, the twenty-minute drive would ensure that he was on time to pick her up at 7:00 pm. He could not help but look at himself in the rear-view mirror for he made sure to get a quick haircut and shave that day. His cologne was carefully applied, and he exuded a sense of confidence as he sat behind the wheel. On arriving at Aisha's residence, he parked in front of her house and proceeded to ring the doorbell. After a minute, the door was slowly opened and there in front of him stood a woman so beautifully dressed in a fitted emerald, green dress that hugged every curve of her body. So stunned was Mikey that he had to blink about three times and seemed at a loss for words. "Hi, Aisha. You look stunning this evening," he managed to say awkwardly. She smiled and said cheekily," You look dapper yourself. In fact, I smelled you before I saw you. That is one heck of a fantastic cologne. I trust you have good taste in everything."

She turned to lock her door. He then escorted her to the car and made sure that she was comfortably seated before he went to the driver's side. "Wow! We do have a gentleman here," she said with a smile. With that he smiled and drove out of her driveway. On the way, they chatted about work and other general matters but nothing of any particular interest. Mikey was in a great mood for he thought to himself that here he was in the presence of the woman who had invaded his thoughts after the banquet. "Maybe I need to pinch myself," he chuckled. "What is so funny?" asked Aisha. "Oh, nothing much. Just a memory that floated across my mind," he replied. He had stopped at a traffic light and took the opportunity to look at the beauty that was seated next to him. She had also turned her head, and their eyes connected. They both laughed shyly as they looked at each other. The connection was broken when the light changed, and Mikey drove off.

After a twenty-minute commute, Mikey pulled into the car park of the restaurant. From the outside he could see that the place was filled with several persons who were lined up waiting on tables to become available. "Oh dear," he said, "we would have a wait. Do you mind if we go to another restaurant which is about another fifteen minutes' drive? I am sorry about this, but I would not want you to wait too long before we can dine. Is that alright with you?" "Mikey, it is Friday, and I am in no rush. The night is completely in your hands so feel free to do what you think is best," Aisha replied with a smile. This made him feel more relaxed and he then drove off to another restaurant.

On arrival at the Hub restaurant, they were lucky to be seated within ten minutes. As they walked in, Mikey noticed that several guys turned to admire Aisha as she swayed past their tables. He could not help but smile because he felt like he had won the lotto just being in her company. They were soon seated, and they each began the evening with a glass of Merlot. Mikey had come to appreciate a glass of wine intermittently and this was one such occasion where he would have a glass of wine. The waiter brought the menu and after they made their choices, they settled down to chat. He took the opportunity to inform her that he had been in contact with the Saudi Arabian client and that a meeting was arranged for the next day. "I do hope that all will go well. I believe that if my father has faith in you then I should too," Aisha replied with a smile. Her smile was infectious, warm, and inviting. For him, this was what the doctor ordered. The conversation was easy and relaxed between them both, all formalities would have disappeared that night and they were simply two persons enjoying each other's company.

When the food arrived, Aisha opted to bless the meal before both began savoring the delicious tasting meal. "I do hope the food is as good as I would have heard," said Mikey between bites. "Mmmmm," said Aisha, "The aroma is great and so is the taste." They finished their meal in silence, exchanging friendly glances with each other from time to time. The table was soon cleared, and the dessert menu was brought to them. "Honestly, I am filled to capacity, but you can select whatever you wish," said Mikey. "No way. I have no more room, so I will pass on dessert," she said lazily. The waiter then cleared the remaining wares and instead, brought them each a glass of tea which they had ordered.

As the evening progressed, a live band struck up some music and the restaurant area were transformed into a lively place with many of the guests leaving their tables to go to the dance area where they did their fancy footwork. Mikey stretched out his hand and said to her, "May I have this dance milady?" With that she laughed and said, "I thought you would never ask." They both enjoyed the tunes played by the band and they both proved to be smooth dancers. When the slow music was played Aisha placed her head on Mikey's shoulder and they danced as though drifting off when one of Whitney Houston's selection was played. When the tune was finished, they returned to their seats and spent the rest of the time chatting and looking at the other patrons until they both grew weary.

At around 11pm, they made their way to the car which was parked not too far from the entrance. Before he drove off, Mikey asked her what she would like to do, and she indicated that she did not mind going home because she was getting sleepy. He was silently happy since he had to meet with the Saudi client the next day. On the way home they sang along with the music being played on the radio and soon realized that they had similar musical interests. "Perhaps I will take you to a concert one of these days," said Mikey. "I will hold you to that," Aisha replied. When Mikey got to Aisha's home, he parked and walked her to the door. "Thank you for a lovely evening, Mikey. It was certainly relaxing," said Aisha. "I do hope this will not be the last of such evenings," he replied. "You were certainly great company." They hugged each other, and she went inside. Mikey trotted back to his car and made his way home feeling elated. "Ok Mikey," he said to himself. "I think I like her vibe." With that, he chuckled to himself and drove on to his home.

He showered, got into his bed, and put on a movie. He was wrapped in his comforter, his mind replaying the events of the evening and in no time at all he was dozing off, completely unaware of what was taking place on the screen.

Mikey got up the next morning feeling well-rested. He felt that this was the best sleep that he had gotten in a while. Even though it was Saturday morning, he had a number of things to get done. He got his daily routine going and made a call to check up on Aunt Rose. He told her that he would pass in and inquire of her what she would like to have. He then checked his diary to confirm his time with his client for that day. He was happy that it was at 11:00 am that day so he had sufficient time to do his errands.

Within an hour he was at Aunt Rose's home, and he was happy to see that she was feeling much better. His sisters had been ensuring that she was well taken care of. "How was your date Mikey?" inquired Cindy. "Boy, you don't forget anything do you?" he responded with a laugh. "It was a pleasant evening," he replied.

Cindy shot back with a volley of questions, "That is all you have to say? Did you like the girl? Do you think you will take her out again? When will we meet her?" "Hey what do you think this is? Stop speeding sis. Life must be taken one day at a time you hear me. Relax yourself. This was just one evening out with a young lady whose company I enjoyed a lot," he responded with a laugh. "Stop reading more into it and let things flow." He then spent time chatting with Aunt Rose in the living room.

While he was there, his phone rang. On the other end, he did not really make out the voice that was asking for Mike Clary. "This is Mike Clary. To whom am I speaking?" "Hi Mr. Clary. I am Andrea's caretaker, Jody. I was given your number by Andrea who had insisted that should anything go wrong with her, that you were to be contacted. I am sorry to inform you that she has taken a turn for the worse and it was important for you to be contacted. I can email you the directions to get here to my home since it is her wish that she does not want to go to the hospital."

Mikey dropped to the chair as though he had seen a ghost. "What is it Mikey?" asked Hetty who was standing near to him. "Ms. Andrea," he replied. "Ms. Andrea is very ill and has sent for me." The tears rolled uncontrollably from his eyes as his mind traveled back to that moment in time when he had met her. "Hold on Ms. Andrea. I am coming to you." "Where does she live?" asked Cindy, who had overheard the conversation. He looked at her and said, "Port Town. It will take me two hours to drive. I must meet a client at eleven this morning so once I am through with him, I am going there directly." "Would you like one of us to come with you?" asked Cindy. "No thanks sis. This is something that I must process on my own. The drive will give me time to think as well. I will keep you updated on what takes place. Love you all," he said as he rushed out the door. On the way to his vehicle, he thought that he did not say that often to his family and Ms. Andrea's illness was a grim reminder that no one would be around forever.

He returned to his house and quickly packed a small bag because he did not know what he would encounter on his trip there. On hustling out of the house to meet with the client, he began to breathe better when he realized that he still had half an hour before the appointed time. He utilized that time to make sure that all the logistics for the viewing were in place.

At exactly 11:00 am, he saw the sleek, black Mercedes Benz pulling up the driveway. He did not wait for the bell to be rung, but instead, opened the teak door and waited for the client to walk towards the front door. Dressed in his white flowing robe, the client looked resplendent as he made his way towards him with a smile. "Good morning and welcome Sheik Ahamad! I am Mike Clary!" He greeted his client with a firm handshake. "Good morning Mr. Clary. Pleased to meet you," the Sheik replied in a pleasant voice. "We would have been speaking through your representative and it is indeed a pleasure to meet you in person. Please feel free to call me Mikey. Can I get you anything to drink before we start the viewing?" said Mikey in a most hospitable manner. "No thank you Mikey. That was gracious of you, but I had a late breakfast, so I am quite filled. I would not want to ruin my appetite for my wife's lunch," he said with a mischievous laugh. "Very well then," retorted Mikey, "Let us get started."

The viewing took about two hours with Mikey being able to answer all of what was asked. He had done his preparation thoroughly and had even anticipated some of the questions that were posed. The client was impressed with what he saw and when it was time to ask about the price, Mikey was able to mention the figure without hesitation. Sheik Ahamad did not seem to blink an eye when he heard the asking price. "What will be the lowest that the seller is willing to go?" he asked. Mikey had already known but decided to stall the response by doing as though he needed to find out from the seller. He excused himself and walked away to make a call. The call was in fact placed to Aisha. He spoke with her a bit, updating her on his current situation and told her that he was going to get back to his client. "You are a cheeky one," she said and hung up with a laugh. Mikey returned to the Sheik and informed him of the revised price. The Sheik asked a few more questions and then told him that before the end of the day, he would give him an answer. Mikey walked him to the door and waited for the car to go out of sight before he moved from the door.

He wondered what the answer might be but did not hesitate in getting to his vehicle to begin his journey to Ms. Andrea. "On my way to you Ms. Andrea. Hang in there," he said as he pulled out from the driveway. He did not even stop to get lunch for he was simply focused on getting to Port Town as quickly as he could but at the same time, within the speed limit. On his way, Mikey said a prayer for Ms. Andrea and asked God to sustain her until he got to her. "She was there for me when my mama was ill. She could have left me alone, God, but she stayed with me. She was with me even when I was at the orphanage.

Ms. Andrea was like a mama to me over the years. Even though we may have lost touch at times, she was never far from my thoughts. I cannot leave her alone now Lord. I ask for your mercies on this journey," he said as he ended his prayer.

He took off his music in the car and took the time to enjoy the peace and take time to process what it would mean to have no more Ms. Andrea to update about his life. The clear road enabled him to get to Port Town in less than the estimated two hours.

Using the app in the vehicle, he was able to find Ms. Andrea's location quite easily. The neighborhood did not appear to be an upscale one but had modestly built homes with neat little gardens lining the driveways. Where Ms. Andrea was located had a tree in the center of the lawn, laden with beautiful white roses. He pulled into the driveway and parked. He quickly got out of the car and stopped to pick one of the flowers. With the flower hidden behind his back, he rang the doorbell at least three times before it was answered by a medium-sized woman with gray hair, a lovely smile and wearing a long red and white cotton dress.

Before he could say a word, she said, "Mikey?" He smiled as he replied, "Yes ma'am. I am here to see Ms. Andrea. I suppose you are Jody." "Yes, I am Jody. I spoke to you over the phone. Come on in. Andrea really spoke about how well- mannered you are. She is not doing too well, but I am sure your presence here would mean so much to her. Follow me young man."

Mikey stepped gingerly behind Jody not knowing what to expect but hoping for the best. Jody ushered him to a room in the house where Andrea lay on a queen-sized bed. She was propped up on two pillows and her eyes stared vacantly at him. His heart immediately became full, and he did not want to break down in front of her. Instead, he pulled himself together and gave her his best smile while he walked up to her and kissed her on the cheek and forehead. "Ms. Andrea, I am here," he said affectionately. He pulled out the rose and placed it on the table at the side of her bed. Her face lit up with a smile and she stretched forth her hand to him. Without a moment's hesitation, he held her hand and she pulled him towards her in the deepest embrace ever. When Jody saw this, she smiled and left the room.

Mikey and Andrea held their embrace for almost three minutes. No words needed to be said and yet, so much was spoken. Their hearts beat together for that moment and became one with the universe. It was then that the tears flowed from them both. The embrace was broken when Andrea patted him on his back and told him to take a seat on the chair next to the bed. "Mikey! Mikey! Mikey! Words cannot express how happy I am to see you here right now. I will be honest with you. I am going down. I feel weaker by the moment, and I know that I will soon cross over to the other side." She paused for a while to breathe while he gently rubbed her hand.

She continued by saying, "From the day that I met you I knew that was God. Even though I could not take you, you became my own. I watched you grow into one of the finest young men on this earth and I am happy." This time she paused to smile and said, "To say that you made me proud would not be expressing the depth of love and appreciation I have for you. The little scared boy has beaten the odds as I always thought he would. We have only one life to live Mike; so, make it count. Be a blessing to someone in your life. You have had so many folks inject love into yours that they outnumbered the ones who treated you badly. They were like pebbles remember?" He nodded as he recalled those words from his past teacher.

"My only regret is that I will not see you marry," said Andrea as she began coughing. Mikey immediately got the glass of water near to the bedside and offered her some. After a few moments, she continued, "That will be one lucky gal because she will be getting a husband with a heart of gold. Let your life lessons stay with you, and I want to bless you as you move forward. I have left a little something for you in my Will. It is not much, but all I ask is that you use some of it and use the rest to bless someone less fortunate. Do not worry about my funeral expenses for those who have been taken care of. I told Jody that I asked God to keep me long enough to see you again. He has answered my prayer, and I am happy. I love you Mikey."

Andrea looked at Mikey with such a beautiful smile and closed her eyes. A calm came across her face and her grip on Mikey's hand decreased. "Ms. Andrea!" he shouted to her. "Do not worry Mikey," she said, "I am still here." "I needed to shut my mouth there," she joked as she coughed. He grabbed the glass of water that was on the nearby table and put it to her lips.

"It is I, who must thank you," said Mikey as soon as he replaced the glass on the table. "I often sit, and wonder what my life would have been like without you being there? I do not know if I could ever repay you, but all I could have done was do my best to show you that your time with me was not in vain. Yes, I was blessed to have had people like you, Mr. Gosine, and Mr. Trim in my corner. I say a silent prayer for all of you daily. I will continue your good work and will do what you have asked. I met a young lady who has the potential to be my future wife. I really do not know if it will reach that but so far, I like her a lot. One thing I will promise you is that if ever I have a daughter, she will be called Andrea. Thank you for taking a chance on me. I love you with my whole heart."

As he said those words, he bent his head on her chest and allowed the tears to flow. He felt her weakening hands stroking his head and he felt a peace within his bosom as she did so. As he raised his head, he realized that her hand was no longer stroking his head, her head had slumped to the side and her chest was no longer moving. In that moment, he knew. Strangely enough, as he sat there holding on to her hand, he felt at peace. A few minutes after, he called Jody into the room to let her know that the inevitable had taken place.

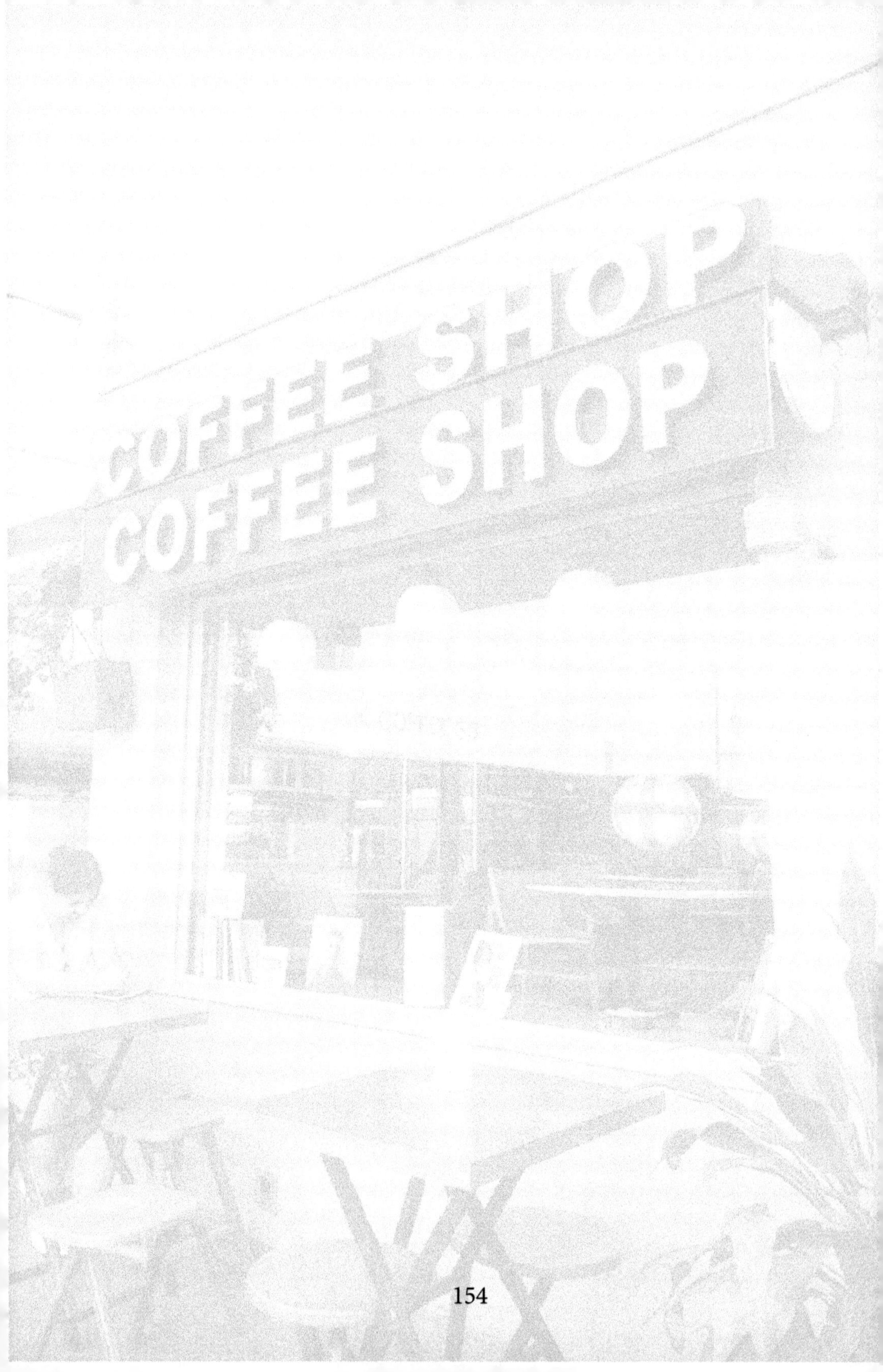
COFFEE SHOP
COFFEE SHOP

CHAPTER 9

Stolen Heart

"You stole my heart like no one else."

(Six months later)

"That new chicken bagel was mouth-watering," said Aisha as she sat in the coffee shop with Mikey. "You simply love any bagel, chicken or otherwise," he replied cheekily. She gave him a playful thump on his shoulder as they both sat in their usual corner of the Coffee Shop near to Mikey's office. They had been meeting at the Coffee Shop for the past six months and were now having a serious affair. Their communication had increased over time, not only through Coffee Shop meetings but several phone calls during the day and each night.

Mikey had even taken Aisha one evening to meet his family. They both sat reminiscing on how that went, and he could not help but laugh when he remembered Cindy's thumb-up sign which she gave to him when they were leaving the house. Aisha had blended well with the girls and Aunt Rose said that she "loved her vibe." "Now that you have met my family, when will you be telling Dave about this hot love affair? I hate pretending behind the man's back especially since he was so instrumental in getting me that deal which turned out to be a success for me. That sale was epic, and I met with Dave to thank him. You would not believe how much I wanted to tell him about us but decided against it at that moment," said Mikey. "So how did you refer to me when you were speaking to him? I can imagine you biting your tongue each time you wanted to say that you spoke to Aisha but had to slow down and say Ms. Khan," she provoked him. "Well, that is true, and it needs to be corrected. Now let us decide finally, who will tell Dave?" he said in a serious tone.

They both looked at each other and then Aisha said, "Let us tell him together." He looked at her with a frown which eventually morphed into a smile. "Hmmm. Not a bad idea but we have to plan how we will execute that. Let us decide on a time. Will it be this evening after work or tomorrow?" he asked.

They both agreed that Aisha would organize the meeting for that evening after work. When they went their separate ways that morning, Mikey felt nervous all day for he wondered how Dave would react to the news that he had been dating his daughter for the past few months and nothing was said to him. Since he had to deal with Ms. Andrea's funeral and his emotions after, he really did not give much thought to anything else.

He realized that his emotions were still raw when he remembered Andrea. After six months he still could not believe that she was gone, and many times found himself taking up his phone to call her. He had taken time away from work for two weeks to deal with her death. He had limited his interaction with people for that period. Aside from Aunt Rose and the girls who had allowed him his space to grieve, the only other person who interacted with him was Aisha. She, too, had respected his need to be by himself and made it her business not to contact him. She knew that when he was ready, he would communicate. Mikey was grateful for their understanding and took that time to do some self-reflection and soul-searching. He remembered Andrea's last conversation with him and remained committed to doing some good deed for someone someday.

At the end of his two weeks hiatus, the first person he would have called was Aisha. He recalled how much he had missed her and made a promise to himself to spend more time with her. He kept his promise and was happy with the connection that they had. That day was going to be the day that they would tell Dave about their relationship, and he did not know what he was going to say. Yet, he looked forward to the meeting and what would transpire at the meeting.

At 5:00 pm, Mikey drove to the agreed location where he met Aisha, who had arrived before him. Mikey looked at her to get some indication as to whether Dave was there already. She read his face and said, "No, he has not yet arrived. He called already to say that he would be fifteen minutes late.

Do not worry about it. Just relax and let me handle things." "Ok captain. This is your show," replied Mikey with some degree of anxiety. He ordered a rum and coke which he slowly sipped hoping that it would calm his nerves. Both he and Aisha chatted about nothing until they noticed Dave's car pulling into the parking lot. "Well, this is it. After today, Dave will either continue to be my friend or he will think the worst of me," he said with a nervous chuckle. Aisha placed her hand on his hand and gave him the reassurance that all would be well.

Soon enough Dave strolled into the restaurant and was ushered to their table. He was all smiles as he hugged Aisha and Shook hands with Mikey. "I am here at your call Ms. Khan," he said with a laugh. "I am assuming that you have a new deal to discuss with me since I see that Mikey is also here."

"Sure, it is a deal but of a different kind," said Aisha. "Listen Dave, you know that I am not one to beat around the bush so first, Mikey here is aware that you are my father. I would have indicated this to him for some time now. Secondly, dad, we have been dating for a while now and we believe that the time has come to be open about it; particularly with you. It is not that we have been trying to be deceptive, but we really needed to find out if we were compatible before we said anything. If this comes as a shock to you, I do apologize."

During that time, Mikey quietly sipped on his drink wishing that the floor would open and whisk him away. He did not make eye contact with Dave, who sat transfixed with a smile on his face. When Aisha was finished, he looked at them both for a few seconds before he burst out laughing. "What is wrong?" asked Aisha. "Did I say something stupid?"

"Listen to me my dear daughter," replied Dave. "You have been the ones who were in the dark. I was aware of your little meetings; dates as you called them. In fact, I was at one of the locations where you had dinner, and I decided not to interrupt you. You are old enough to make your choices in life. I must say that in this case, you have chosen wisely, for this young man here is one whom I have admired from the day that I was introduced to him. You have my blessing. I do hope that your relationship will be a positive one." He then turned to Mikey and said, "Mikey I have known you for some time and we have been friends. However, you are to take care of my beloved daughter. If not, that will certainly be the first time that we would have grounds for a disagreement." said, he patted Mikey on his back.

Half an hour after, Dave left Aisha and Mikey at the restaurant indicating that he had a critical meeting to attend. After his departure, both Aisha and Mikey sat speechless looking at each other. They were both relieved that their secret was now open, and both sat holding each other's hands in silence.

"Hip! Hip! Hooray!" shouted the ten guests in unison. They were gathered in Mikey's backyard to celebrate his engagement to Aisha. This was exactly three months after their meeting with Dave. Aisha was ecstatic and did not hesitate to accept Mikey's marriage proposal. His sisters were delighted that they would soon have another sister in the family and Aunt Rose could not contain her excitement. They had met Aisha a few times when Mikey checked on them and they had taken a liking to her.

On the other hand, Mikey met Aisha's mother for the first time soon after their chat with Dave. She was warm and embracing and Mikey too had a pleasant evening with her. She had told him that evening, "You must be special Mikey. I have never seen my daughter take a liking to anyone before. She has her heart set on you." With that she had given him a smile and a gentle squeeze on his shoulder. Mikey found himself blushing and he also noted Aisha's stunning beauty would have been inherited from her mother.

During the engagement event, Dave asked Mikey to go somewhere private where they could have a small chat. They retired to the study area to have their conversation. "Well Mikey," started Dave, "you are going to be the son-in-law very soon. I always thought about what that day would be like when I must give my baby girl over to her future husband. Truth be told, I am elated that it is you. However, I have a confession to make. Years ago, when you were at the Orphanage, I came in periodically to the diner where you did your work rotation. I was not a regular customer, but each time that I entered there I noticed how hard you worked and your complete work ethic. You would have served me as well as other people and you would have been very friendly. I happened to be there the day when the old lady came in and you helped her out. Do you remember that?" "Oh boy! Yes. I remember this lady who would come in regularly. I cannot remember her name right now, but yes," responded Mikey.

"Well, it was since then I observed how you worked, and I would get updates about you from my other friend, Mr. Kramer, who would also keep me informed about your progress whenever we would meet up. For several years, I did not hear much more about you. When Chad came to work at Kramer's Real Estate Agency and he said that he knew you, further inquiries were made as to what you were doing then. Chad was unable to say but I put out my feelers and noticed how well you had done for yourself. Luckily, Kramer was doing a new project and had to hire a few folks. That is when a call was made to you and to a couple other folks who would have graduated as well. However, no matter how much I knew you, you had to prove that you were suitable and that you did. Your being hired by Kramer's had nothing to do with me. I just needed to get that clear. Anyway, I was the one who set the wheels in motion for you to meet up with Aisha, who happens to be my stepdaughter. When you saw her at the Banquet and could not find her after, all added to the mystery, and I smiled but held my tongue. The meeting of the two minds came together with the Saudi client. I would have watched you grow in the business gradually, taking your time to learn the technical aspects. I am proud of what you have achieved. However, today, I want you to know that you proved to be the type of man that would be able to support my daughter and take care of a family. I must admit that I am ill. I have been diagnosed with a terminal disease and it is only a matter of time. As such, it is important for me to ask that the wedding be held a little earlier than you two may have planned. I have not yet told Aisha about my illness, but I intend to do so this week. I need you to be there for her. I have had a good life and although I may not look ill, I am. I know this is a lot for you to digest so I will leave you now and rejoin the others. I just needed you to know the truth before you got married." Dave quickly got up, patted Mikey on his back and strutted out of the room in his usual elegant style, leaving Mikey sitting at the table trying to come to terms with all that he had just heard.

After sitting for half an hour, rubbing his head several times, he leaned back on a cushion trying to make up his mind how he would move forward. To think that this entire affair was a set-up was something that he felt uneasy about. Aisha had revealed some of it to him before, but he did not realize that Dave, too, had a hand in it. "Should I even go forward with this marriage?" he asked himself softly. "I do not want anyone planning my life for me. Yet, I know deep down that I love Aisha. Should I dissolve this before it goes further? To think that I am now being asked to push up the wedding seems like some kind of hijacking taking place here. Has Dave been controlling this aspect of my life, and I did not know? I need time to think about this. This is where I miss Ms. Andrea. She would have guided me as to what I could do," he continued talking to himself.

He eventually decided to go back to his guests and make some excuse to leave. As soon as he returned to the gathering, Aisha came towards him and held his hand. He was not in the mood to talk with her, and he gave her the excuse that he was feeling a bit nauseous and needed to retire to his room. He had asked her if she did not mind letting Dave give her a lift home when she was ready to leave. She had given him a puzzled look and assured him that she would be able to do so. With that he had given her a kiss on her cheek and walked over to his aunt and sisters. He had kissed Aunt Rose and his sisters informing them that he was not feeling too well but that they should continue to enjoy themselves. He then left the room and went to his bedroom where he locked the door and sat in the dark for quite some time before he fell asleep.

The ferocious clapping of the thunder and the raindrops pounding as though a volley of stones was unleashed against his bedroom windowpane gave Mikey every reason to dive back under his cover. That Sunday morning was going to be one to stay inside and so he did by simply lying late in his bed. The weather reflected his messed-up mood, and he took the time to do some meditation and introspection.

As he laid in bed, he decided to apply his critical thinking skills to his situation. He looked at the fact that when he saw Aisha, no one had forced him to become interested in her. There were a few single ladies at the banquet, and he did not have to think about Aisha. He recalled that Dave did not say anything to him about her over time and as such, it was all on him to make his decision about her. When they met to discuss the Saudi client, once again no one had forced his interest even though it was a setup for them to meet. He then asked himself why he loved her. With that question, he shouted, "For so many reasons!" He then realized that without Dave he may still be working and not even thinking of a lady in his life. Dave was how I would meet my future wife. He decided to look at it from another perspective and not take it as though Dave was controlling his life. The final decision to have a relationship with Aisha had all to do with himself and Aisha's interaction and really nothing to do with Dave. He realized that like his work, Dave was instrumental in assisting him with a lot. He suddenly realized he owed Dave a debt of gratitude rather than a debt of disgust. He made up his mind that he needed to have a chat with Dave, on his own terms.

He then pulled his cover back over his head and went back to sleep for about an hour. He was awakened by his phone ringing on his bedside table.

"Yeah, hello?" he said sleepily. "Mikey are you alright?" said the voice on the other end. "Hey Aunt Rose, I am fine. I decided to take advantage of the rainy morning," he replied with a slight laugh. "Ok then. We were worried about you leaving the party last night. You did not look too well so we did not bother to disturb you. We noticed that, not long after, Aisha left with her father as well. Did something happen?" she asked. "No, Aunt Rose dear. You worry too much. I drank a little and you know I am not a big alcohol drinker. It took a toll on me, giving me some nausea, so I had to get my rest. I am feeling much better this morning. Now that you have called, I will get up and get a cup of hot chocolate. Did you and the girls get home all right?" he asked. "Yes, we are fine. I think we will do some soup today. Right for this weather. If you wish you can come by and get a bowl," she replied. "That is enticing! Once the weather is fine around lunch time, sure," he said. After hanging up, he got out of his bed, had a bath, and then went to the kitchen. He was sitting drinking his cup of hot chocolate when his phone rang again.

Aisha's voice on the other end sent a warmth through his body. "Hey Mikey, how are you feeling this morning?" she blurted out. "I have seen better days, but not as bad as last night. I was able to get up and get myself together and now I am having a cup of hot chocolate. How are you doing? I gather you got home safely with Dave," he replied. "Yes, I did," she replied. "Last night you did not look like yourself after both of you had a chat. I noticed that you returned and said that you were feeling nauseous. You were, but it had nothing to do with the drink. Do you care to tell me the real source of your nausea?" she pressed him. "Listen Aisha, I am good.

We can meet up later this evening if you are free. Given that it is a rainy morning, we can spend some time here, at my home, eating popcorn and playing some Scrabble. "Ok. No problem. I will get to your house around 6pm if that time works for you," she said. "Great! See you later my dear," he said to her. He hung up the phone and smiled realizing that Aisha was able to sense when something was off with him. She did not accept the excuse that it was the drink that made him feel sick. He recognized that somehow, she felt that something had gone awry between himself and Dave. "Yeah, Aisha dear. We are going to have a heart-to-heart talk later," he said to himself as he blew the steam coming from his cup.

The rest of the morning was spent doing his chores and then he settled to do some reading. The rain continued relentlessly and soon enough he began to wonder if it was a small storm in their area. He had not seen rain like that in a long while and he was happy that he did not have to go out that day.

Closer to twelve that day, the rain finally eased a bit and, as he promised Aunt Rose, he drove over to have lunch with her and his sisters. Mikey returned to his house around 2:00 pm and missed getting drenched when the rain pick began pounding away once again. He closed his front door and retired to his study where he began to do some reading. He felt it was important for him to keep up with Real Estate trends and spent quite a bit of time reading. For some odd reason, his mind ran on his biological mother, and he smiled as he looked up at her last letter to him which he had framed and placed in his study. "This is all for you, mama," he said to himself. "Your little boy is now a man, and he intends to continue to make you proud. I love you mama." He was surprised to find that a tear had rolled down his cheek. He slowly wiped it away and continued his reading.

At around 4:00 pm he began preparing for the evening with Aisha. He checked the pantry to make sure that he had popcorn and a few other snacks. It was a cold, wet day so he felt like he could make broth as well. He felt that he had everything covered for his guest and finally hopped into his bed to get a nap.

By half past five that evening he was ready for his guest, and he fiddled around the house making sure that the cushions were in order and the magazines were neat. Finally, at close to 6:00 pm, he heard Aisha's Audi rumbling up his driveway. He grabbed an umbrella and went out to meet her by her car. Upon her exit from her car, he placed his arm around her shoulder and guided her to his front door. When they got inside, he brought her a towel to dry herself in case she had gotten wet.

He then invited her to the living room where he sat with her on the sofa.

"Welcome again to my humble abode," he said to her, "Thank you. It is beautiful and cozy," she replied. "Make yourself at home. Would you like a glass of wine to start off the evening or would you prefer hot chocolate for the weather?" asked Mikey. "For now, just some water would do. We have the rest of the evening for me to decide on wine or hot chocolate," she replied. "Your wish is my command," Mikey said with a smile and a bow.

When he returned with the water, he noticed that she had kicked off her sandals and her feet were curled up on the sofa. Something about that image set the scene for a heart-to-heart discussion. He believed that before any socializing took place, they needed to have that discourse.

He had placed a bowl of Cashew nuts on the table and a bowl of seedless grapes. He then settled himself next to her on the sofa. He looked at her and smiled as he said, "This morning you felt that something had gone awry with Dave and me, so you did not believe that I was truly ill. What gave you that impression?" Before she answered, she popped a grape in her mouth and waited a few seconds as she savored the juicy fruit. "I know you by now. I can pick up that something was wrong but, like the gentleman that you are, you prefer to move away from the scene and deal with your issues on your own. So, you can start by telling me exactly what transpired between you and Dave," said Aisha.

"Well now that you have opened that window of conversation, I will let you know what has been on my mind," said Mikey. "After speaking with Dave, I felt that our getting together was a setup and to be honest, I felt sick to my stomach about it. You had a part to play in it and so I thought that the best way to deal with this is to have a face-to-face conversation with you. When you called, I grasped the opportunity to meet with you and to handle this immediately," he said with a straight face. He then went on to tell her most of what Dave revealed to him. However, he made sure not to tell her anything about his health. He felt that part was for Dave to do for himself.

"What was interesting as well, was that he asked me to move up the wedding date earlier for personal reasons. He will have to tell you what those reasons are. After the conversation, I will be honest with you, I pondered whether there would still be a wedding," he said as he looked her in the eyes. Aisha did not wince for a moment but slowly chewed on her grapes as Mikey spoke. "When I first met you, you knew a lot about me. Now hearing Dave speak about this made me feel as though this was a well-orchestrated plan and that I was being led like a lamb. Now that you are here, I would deeply appreciate it if you can clear up this entire situation."

Aisha then placed the bowl of grapes on the table and sat up straight looking at Mikey. "When I first heard about you, it was when my father was telling my mother about you. I happened to have been within earshot of him telling her about this young man whom he knew about from the orphanage; a young man whom he had closely followed his progress and who had impressed him with the way he dealt with the odds in his life. He was telling my mother that this young man reminded him about himself for he too, had been a product of an orphanage. That side of his life I never really knew for he, in fact, is my step- father. To hear him talk that day, I was intrigued because I had never known him to be so bowled over by many people.

I recalled that evening that I finally entered the kitchen and asked him, "Who is this person you seem to have taken a liking to dad?" "He had replied with a smile, and I recalled him saying that he was mentoring two young men with the Kramer Agency, and it would be nice to invite them both to the banquet and that I could meet up with the one who so reminded him of himself.

It was a conversation in passing and nothing that I gave thought to before the banquet. On the evening of the event, I was assisting with the guests and quickly asked my father who this person was. He gave a quick description as to who you were and that was when I decided to make a fleeting appearance to simply see for myself who you were. I was bold enough to strike up a conversation and simply get back out of sight.

I did not think my disappearing act worked because I did not hear my father mention anything about you after that. It was not until the Saudi matter reared its head that I heard your name mentioned once again. This time it was a suggestion as to which agent should be asked to oversee the project.

On hearing your name, I did a double-take and would have asked him to tell me more about you since he was the one recommending you for the job. It was then he gave me some interesting tidbits concerning yourself and I stored them away. When you came to meet Ms. Khan, you had no clue that it was me, but I knew that it was you by then." "Yeah, when you were so formal," Mikey interjected. Aisha snickered and continued, "Well, I did not know you formally and at work I had to keep things business-like. As I got to know you better, I realized that I was falling for you. You did not see it and it was best to hide how I felt. Throughout our interactions, I saw your heart, I saw how you dealt with people, I saw how you cared for others and that bowled me over completely. So here I am Mike Clary, guilty of loving you, guilty of caring enough not because of my father, but simply because you stole my heart in a way no one else has. If you have a problem with that, you can call off the wedding and I will be out of your life in a flash. Just remember that no one is forcing you to marry me."

Mikey sat looking at Aisha for about five minutes without saying a word. In that moment her realized this was the woman he wanted in his life; his feelings for her at that moment had only deepened. He then got up and sat behind her, wrapped his arms around her shoulders and cuddled her as she reclined against him. In the background, soft love tunes piped from the radio as they sat listening to the rain keeping its own tempo. He turned her around and kissed her gently on her lips, savoring the sweet taste of her mouth. She responded passionately to his kiss and soon enough they were both yearning for each other. Mikey held her hand and guided her to the bedroom where they made love; forgetting the world and all its cares.

CHAPTER 10

Shifting Winds

"Making sense of it all"

When Mikey woke up the next morning, the rain had subsided, and he got up realizing that Aisha was lying there staring at him. "Good morning beautiful," he said to her. "Good morning my love," she responded. "I can get accustomed to this," he said playfully. "Really? To which part I wonder?" she replied in jest. "To all of it," he said as he planted a kiss on her mouth. "Are you busy this morning though? I do believe that we need to talk about the wedding."

"I am not, but, firstly, I will need to get my bag from the car. I packed a bag just in case the rain caught me here. Other things caught me instead and you certainly do not expect me to stay like this," she said looking at him with a smirk on her face. "Ahhh! It would certainly be a sight to see you running out to your car as you are. My neighbors will have a fit," said Mikey as he playfully hopped out of the bed. She threw a pillow after him as he scampered to the bathroom.

Soon enough, he took her car keys and went to retrieve her overnight bag. She was already in the bathroom by the time he returned. He placed the bag on the chair in his bedroom and he proceeded to the kitchen to prepare breakfast. By the time she was dressed and came downstairs, he was waiting for her at the table. The aroma of the bacon and eggs wafted through the house, and she smiled as she sat down. "I can sign up for this Chef Mikey," she said after swallowing a mouthful of the food. "You are a very good cook," she complimented him. Mikey smiled and poured her coffee and sat back sipping on his hot chocolate. "I am not much of a coffee drinker, but I can brew a good pot. Hope it is good enough for you," he said.

After breakfast, they tidied the kitchen together and then sat on the sofa to talk. Mikey said to her, "I am happy that you came over and explained your side of the matter to me. For a moment I thought it was a setup but now I realize that I was wrong in my thinking, and I apologize for that. In my conversation with Dave, he too, explained how he had gotten to know me and so on. In that conversation, though, he asked that we move up the date for the wedding. He also mentioned that it was for personal reasons, and he would talk to you about it. Did you two have that conversation?"

"Since he dropped me off at my place that night, I have not heard from him. I must check my mum so I will pass there on my way home," she responded. "No problem. Could we then decide what is the earliest time that we can have the wedding? I do not wish for anything lavish since I am a simple guy and prefer a small gathering in an intimate setting like a garden. How do you feel about that?" She held his hand and said, "We are like two peas in a pod in that regard. If it was up to me, we can call a priest right now and have him pronounce us as man and wife. Sadly, though, you do not have a dog or cat that can witness," she replied as they both laughed.

"Well, what about the next three months then? We were planning for the end of the year. Would you be able to get your stuff together by then? I believe that if we are having a small gathering then that should be manageable. Let me get my sisters to do the organizing if that is fine with you. We can tell them what we want, and they can do the running back and forth. You nor

I will have the time, and they would surely love that. What say you?" he asked. "That is a yes, for me! It will certainly leave me with time to focus on my dress and whatever else that I must get done," she replied. "Now can we select a date?" he asked as he placed the calendar in front of them both.

After some discussion, a date was decided, and they agreed to confirm with the parish priest before telling anyone else. Mikey opted to speak with Father Brown that week and they both agreed that they wanted their nuptials at a venue where there was a beautiful garden. Aisha left Mikey's home around eleven that morning and informed him that she would check in with Dave later that day. Once she had departed his home, Mikey got dressed and went over to his siblings and Aunt Rose. On getting there, he observed that the heavy rain had caused the drain to flood a bit at the side of the house. He went immediately to the tool shed at the back of the house and spent about half an hour clearing the drain and the backyard before he went inside.

"I knew I heard you come but I was wondering where you were," said Hetty as he entered the house. "Yeah, I was just clearing the drain at the side there. How are you all? He then went to Aunt Rose who was seated in the Living Room and kissed her on the cheek. "Hey Cindy, where are you? Come let us chat!" he said. Once they were all seated, he updated them on the proposed plan for the wedding and their involvement. His sisters were excited about the proposal and Cindy immediately jumped up and got her diary to begin writing the logistics. They all confirmed that they were available for the proposed date and began throwing out ideas with respect to the venue. "If you want a garden wedding, why not use the venue at the Smithson Lodge?" asked Aunt Rose. They all paused for a moment and Mikey was the first to say, "Aunt Rose, you are a genius! I never gave that place a thought.

We can all go over there and have a view of the place before we decide." "Yes, the setting there is beautiful, and I do know the daughter of the owner. I did some work for her before. I can give her a call tomorrow and get more information from her," Hetty replied. "Well, once all the plans get started, we would need to meet for updates once per week, for the time is not far off. In addition to that, we will have to get our clothes for the wedding as well. I do not intend to wear any old thing to my brother's wedding. Aunt Rose, you are going to be the mother-giver, so you must look extra special," said Cindy as she giggled.

"You can let me know what Aunt Rose must get and I will give you the money for all that she needs. You girls too, can tell me if you need anything as well. It is not every day that we have a wedding here," Mikey said laughing. After chatting, they decided to take a drive over to the Smithson Lodge to get a feel for the place. They all bundled into Mikey's car, with Aunt Rose in the front. They noted that the venue was a forty-minute drive from their house.

The Smithson Lodge was well hidden within a grove of oak trees. One got the impression that this was some sort of fairy-tale location. The sprawling mansion stood on an acre of land and from the road one could see a partial view of a beautiful garden. Not much more could be seen from the road and that was a good thing in Mikey's mind. He wanted an intimate setting and once he was able to view the place, he would make a firm decision. However, for now, he liked what he was seeing. "I think you can also get the house for the day of the wedding so that the wedding party can get dressed there. If that is the case then it will save you so much time and effort. All you would have to do is get your caterer, decorator, and music," said Hetty. "Do not forget, the priest too," said Cindy. "Which priest would be doing the wedding?"

Mikey replied, "I will be speaking to Father Brown this week. Once he is available, I will have him do the ceremony." "Who will be the Chief Bridesmaid?" asked Hetty. "Hmm, I do not think we got that far in our plans, but I will leave that for Aisha to decide. She does not have sisters, so I cannot say if she even wants any bridesmaids to start with," responded Mikey. "Do not forget that most of your planning will be based on the number of guests you intend to invite from both sides. "As much as you both want a small wedding, it will all depend on who you invite," said Aunt Rose in her counseling tone. "We will keep that in mind," Mikey replied soberly. They then turned the car around and proceeded to get some items in the grocery store before returning to the house. Mikey helped with the cooking and sat playing a game of cards before he left for his home. On the way home, his mind was swirling with so many thoughts and he realized that he needed some time to himself. Instead of going directly to his house, he headed towards Lake Cyrie, which was about a twenty-minute drive from where he lived. He needed to just sit there, relax, and get his thoughts together.

He parked his vehicle and walked slowly to the perimeter of the lake. The recent rain had caused the lake to become quite swollen and he ventured cautiously to a bench under a tree. The water was calm and several times he spotted a fish or two jumping in the water. Luckily, he was the only person there at that time and he embraced the moment by closing his eyes, inhaling the fresh air, and exhaling his stress. With his eyes closed, he sat in a meditative mood and said a prayer asking God for guidance in all that he was about to undertake. As he sat there, his mind resurrected some things from his past and he thought of Mr. Gosine. It was a while since he had touched base with him, and he felt that he needed to reach out to him. As his eyes opened, he felt at peace with himself and his surroundings and as if an answer to his prayer, a beautiful double rainbow emerged across the lake.

During the next two days, Mikey was so preoccupied with work, personal matters, and the wedding, that he barely noticed that Aisha had not spoken to him much for those two days. When he had called her the Sunday night, she did not answer her phone, and he felt that she was tired and needed her space. On Monday, he had called her, but she was busy in the office, and she had promised to call him that night. While she did call, she mentioned that she was not in a talking mood and simply needed time to clear her head. Mikey had decided that he would not force her into talking, and on Tuesday, he simply thought that he would wait for her to call whenever she was ready.

Around 5:00 am on Wednesday morning, her phone call awakened him and all she said to him was, "Can we meet at our usual place this morning for the same time?" "Sure. Are you alright?" he replied. "We will chat when we meet," she responded and hung up the phone. He pondered for a while as to what could be the cause of her strange behavior but decided that there was nothing he could do then and went fitfully back to sleep.

Around 8:00 am that morning they met for breakfast. They each ordered their usual fare and sat looking at each other. "I know you would have been wondering why I was behaving out of the ordinary," Aisha said as Mikey sat with his arms folded staring at her soberly. She continued, "I visited my mother yesterday and had that talk with my father." Tears began rolling down her cheeks and Mikey held her hand. "What is it Aisha? What did Dave tell you that has you in such a funk?" He passed her a tissue and she wiped her eyes. She then said slowly, "Dave has Stage 4 Cancer. His doctors have given him a brief time before the inevitable happens. He withheld this information from the family for he did not want us to be alarmed. However, now that the wedding is being planned, he wants to ensure that he can walk me down the aisle."

On hearing this news, Mikey sat at the edge of his seat in shock. "So, this was the reason he asked us to mention the time for the ceremony. How could that be? Dave looks great! I could never believe that he was ill in any way. Are you sure about this?" She nodded her head without saying anything.

As they sat holding hands, the waitress arrived with their meal. They both asked her to pack their food to go since they had both lost their appetite. They sat in silence drinking their beverages and thinking of Dave's situation. Aisha had informed Mikey that she would be unable to work that day and that she was returning home. Mikey informed her that he had two clients that day and once he was through with them; he would contact her. He paid the bill, and they went their separate ways.

Mikey sat at his desk that morning and was lost in thought. How could Dave be ill? Was there a misdiagnosis? The man looked fit and walked with his usual stride. Nothing indicated that he was ill except his absence of late from around his office. He really noticed that he was not coming around as often as he did, but never gave it a thought. He felt that Dave had a lot on his hands and that was the reason. Little did he know the facts. Mikey shook his head in disbelief and sat staring at the computer until an alert went off on his phone, reminding him that he needed to get going if he was to be on time for his appointment.

He managed to get to the location about five minutes ahead of time and found his client waiting for him. "Hello, Mrs. Black," he said as chirpily as he could under the circumstances. His emotions were on the brink of overpowering him, but he kept himself in check. He felt that after all that Dave had instilled in him, he would honor him in the way he conducted his work. He moved forward to shake hands with Mrs. Black and proceeded to show her the property. After an hour and a half, Mikey was finished with her, and he drove to his next showing that morning. In another two hours, he was wrapped up with his appointments for the day.

He called his administrative staff and informed them that he would not be in for the rest of the day. He then called Aisha and informed her that he was on his way to her house. She was not her usual self, for obvious reasons and he needed to be there for her. He also needed to visit Dave and to have a chat with him. That was overdue and it was even more urgent now.

Mikey got to Aisha's residence in no time and upon entering her home, he embraced her. They were locked in that embrace for a while as she held onto him and wept uncontrollably. It would seem as though Mikey's presence was what she was waiting on to simply release her pent-up emotions. He, too, had tears streaming down his face as he held her. When the tears seemed to have been exhausted, they both sat in silence on her sofa. After what seemed like half an hour, she turned to Mikey and asked, "Do you need anything to drink? I really do not have much since I had postponed going to the supermarket." "Hey, do not worry about me," he replied comfortingly, "All I want you to do at this time is relax. You have some rough days ahead and I will be there every step of the way.

I just want you to know that. Once we have water that will be fine." With that they both gave a short laugh. Mikey then went to her kitchen and searched for what there was to make dinner. The result was a mouth-watering spaghetti and meatballs dish which they both ate slowly. "Your aunt surely showed you how to cook. That was quite tasty," said Aisha as he took up the wares. "Well, I am a good student, and she is a great teacher," he said with a smile. After cleaning up the kitchen, he spent another two hours with her before he left for his house. By then she was more composed, and they talked through their plans for the wedding. Mikey would have given her the ideas which he had discussed with his family, to which she readily agreed. "I trust your sisters would do a great job and I am grateful to them for making my burden light," said Aisha.

After saying their goodbyes, Mikey decided to drive over to Dave's residence. It was time for him to have that talk with Dave. He had listened to Dave. Now was time for the tables to be turned. He got out his phone and called Dave, who, fortunately, answered on the second ring. "Hey Dave!" said Mikey. "Hey buddy, what's up? Good to hear from you as always," replied Dave. "I am in your neighborhood now and wanted to quickly visit. Do you have time to spare for about ten minutes? I needed to run something by you," said Mikey without giving a hint of the real purpose for the visit. "Sure thing! You can pass by" replied Dave.

Within fifteen minutes, Mikey was pulling into Dave's driveway. He had no idea what he was going to say but all he knew was that something needed to be said and would be said. On getting to the door, Aisha's mum met him and gave him a hug. After exchanging pleasantries, she escorted him to the back porch where Dave was seated on a recliner. The sun was setting and from Dave's porch, the panoramic view of the city was nothing short of breath-taking.

He got up slowly to embrace Mikey and then eased back into his chair. He invited Mikey to sit on the next recliner. Within minutes, Aisha's mum brought in a tray with water and juices. She placed it on the table positioned between the chairs and then went back inside, leaving both men to themselves.

After chatting about the job and some of the matters on his slate, Mikey then said to Dave, "Well Dave, you would have met with me and asked me to consider moving up the wedding date. You never told me why you wanted us to do that, but in speaking with Aisha, I became aware of your health challenge. I understood then why you made such a request. I must say that such news has not been an easy pill to swallow and both Aisha and I have been struggling to come to terms with it. Nonetheless, I needed to chat with you given that you had your chat with me before. I needed to say thanks for all that you have done for me. At first, I thought this whole affair with Aisha was a setup on your part, but really, regardless of what you could have put in place, it was up to Aisha and me to determine whether we were interested in each other. No one could have done that for us. Fortunately, I fell in love with her and here we are planning to cement that love with wedding vows. What I wanted you to know, though, is that you did a lot for my career. Had you not been there for Chad, who introduced me to you, I am not sure how far along I may have gone. You set things in motion in your own way, and you left me to gain my experience. You have always been just a phone call away. Not once did I ever hear you tell me that you did not have time. Thanks for your mentorship.

I often ask myself if I would have made it this far without you. I doubt that very much. I may not be fully in the family yet, but I will never turn my back on you. You can count on me as much as your daughter can count on me. I just wanted you to know how much you mean to me and how much I have grown to love you as a person. For whatever time you have with us, know that Michael Clary will only be a call away. While Aisha is having a tough time processing this, we have agreed to move up the wedding date and it will be held next month. We are still confirming the venue and once that is settled, the rest will be overseen. It will certainly be an honor to call you, dad."

Mikey got up and walked over to Dave's chair where he bent to give the man a long embrace. By the time he got up from his knees, both their faces were awash with tears. In that moment, he realized that the towering stalwart of a man was now a human being shattered by his illness, stoic in his struggle with his pain, clinging to life as best as he could. Through all of that, there he sat, putting on his brave face, embracing all that was beautiful around him, doing his best to encourage those close to him to go on with their lives and not be worried. "Those were beautiful words coming from you Mikey. I know that I can leave this world knowing that my daughter will have the kind of husband who will be there for her in fair or foul weather. I thank you as well for acceding to my request. My strength may be failing but I will walk my daughter up the aisle. Let us not spend time on my illness but focus on what is beautiful. Let us enjoy the rest of this magnificent day," replied Dave.

They both sat there for another hour sipping their drinks, taking in the view, and meditating on whatever took center-stage in their minds.

CHAPTER 11

Love is Enough

"A man cannot move forward looking back."

The garden setting was picturesque. The lake formed the backdrop to the gazebo and the venue adorned in Baby Blue and white, lent to that enchanting ambience as the groom stood patiently waiting with Aunt Rose for his bride to walk down the aisle. He was nervous for the first time in a long while. Chad, his best-man, was whispering a few jokes in his ear and he did his best to laugh quietly. Aunt Rose looked at him with pride and one could see that she, too, was nervous and emotional. Mikey noticed that Aisha's mother was seated in the front row dressed in a burgundy dress that did justice to her beauty. She blew him a kiss as he stood there blushing.

As the guitarist struck up the first chord, all the fifty guests turned their attention to the entrance. In walked four bridesmaids, dressed in lovely champagne-colored dresses, accompanied by four groomsmen dressed in navy blue suits. Mikey recognized one of the bridesmaids as his sister and he chuckled a bit when she gave him a wink. His other sister was coordinating the activities, and he froze when he heard her asking the guests to stand for the bride's entrance. As the guitarist began to play the Bridal March, he observed that Dave had walked to the entrance. Within a few seconds, the most beautiful figure emerged, dressed in a resplendent white off-the shoulder wedding dress with a small train. From afar, she looked like a fairy without wings and as she took Dave's extended hand, she seemed to float down the aisle with every step.

Mikey could not believe his eyes. He was transfixed by the woman walking towards him; the woman with whom he would spend the rest of his life. He did his best to hold back the tear that was about to trickle down his face. His heart was filled, and he looked up, for a moment, at the sky and shook his head. Aisha took her time to glide up the aisle with her father at her side, as the guests stood waiting for her to get to the area where her intended husband was waiting nervously.

Despite his pain, Dave walked slowly, leaning on the stick he now used; his daughter entwined on his other arm. Father and daughter looked at each other and smiled. The pride on his face was priceless and her radiant smile was infectious. At that moment, there was a heavenly radiance that emanated around them both. Mikey observed that and smiled.

Upon the bride's arrival at the podium, Aunt Rose kissed Mikey and walked to her seat. Aisha then gave her bouquet to her best friend, Dr. Patty Patel, who was her chief bridesmaid. Father Brown then asked, "Who gives this woman to be married to this man?" "I give this woman," said Dave. He then carefully placed Aisha's hand in Mikey's and went to sit next to his wife. The service proceeded smoothly and after the vows were said and the Marriage Register was signed, Father Brown then turned to the congregation and said, "I now present to you, Mr., and Mrs. Clary. Please stand, as the newly minted husband and wife take their first walk down the aisle."

The guests gave thunderous applause as they stood. On their way down the aisle, the couple first stood where Aisha's parents were, and they both proceeded to hug them both. They then went to the other side of the aisle where they hugged Aunt Rose.

After that, they walked down the aisle cheered on by their guests. Among the guests, Mikey recognized Mr. Gosine and Mr. Trim, both of whom had aged by then. He paused by them both, bowed to them, and placed his free hand over his heart. It was his way of recognizing them for their input in his life.

As he and Aisha moved down the aisle, they sent kisses and stopped to hug some of their guests. At the end of the walkway, they both turned and blew kisses before they and their bridal party exited the area. The guests were then ushered to the reception area where they partook of cocktails while awaiting the bride and groom, who were in another area having their photo session. After forty- five minutes, the bridal party emerged, doing a small dance. This alerted the guests that the bride and groom were about to enter. Soon enough, they too entered, dancing on their way towards the reception table which was beautifully decorated in the blue and white theme.

Once they were seated, the reception got underway with toasts being done and speeches from friends and family. It was then time for Mikey to speak and he did so with much aplomb. "On behalf of my wife and I..." he said, beaming with pride. The guests clapped vigorously. "Yeah Mikey!" one guest shouted. He looked across at Aisha, who sat looking lovingly at her husband. He continued, "Today, we want to thank each of you for being here with us to celebrate. We are indeed indebted to some incredibly special people in this room, and they know who they are. Some of you have been there for me from the time I was little Mikey, the boy from the orphanage. Some of you have been there for me when I endured a rough patch in my life and taught me to kick the pebbles. Some of you have held my hand in so many ways and here I am today, the product of your investment in my life. Today, God has blessed me with the most beautiful woman who has now become my wife. Today, I also know that two special people are looking down on us right now: my mama and Ms. Andrea." With that, he paused for a moment and then looking up, he raised his glass towards heaven and spoke to the guests, "Ladies and gentlemen, let us give a toast in memory of my mama and Ms. Andrea."

Following that, food was served, and the rest of the evening was spent socializing with their guests. The couple went to each guest and shared tokens of appreciation, taking the time to chat with them and make the necessary introductions. Aunt Rose was in her glee as she sat around the table with Dave and his wife. Mikey and his sisters made sure that she was taken care of. It was then time for Mikey and Aisha to have their first dance. This was followed by the father and daughter dance. Despite his pain, Dave held his daughter and moved her slowly and gracefully across the floor. No one would believe that he was ill. Mikey then had his dance with Aunt Rose, who, surprisingly, was quite a smooth dancer. The dance floor was then opened for the guests, and they had fun. Chad, his best man, said to him, "Now that you have done this walk, I will do the same soon. It is time for me to settle down." Mikey smiled and hugged him saying, "You do that Chad, once you believe in your heart that you are ready." With that Chad left to chat with Dave.

Mikey then went to his two sisters, hugging and kissing them as they huddled together at one end of the reception hall. He thanked them for the splendid job that they did and even joked that he could put them in business. The three of them took to the dance floor and spent the rest of the evening enjoying the planned activities.

By 11:00 pm, the guests had departed, and Mr. and Mrs. Clary retired to their bridal suite to spend their first night as husband and wife.

(Two months later)

As Aisha and Mikey sat at the dining table having dinner around 7:00 pm that evening, her phone rang. Within seconds of her answering, Mikey heard her screaming, "No! No! No! Tell me it is not so! We are coming over!" As soon as Mikey heard those words, he knew. He held his wife as she slumped to the floor. "Dad is gone! Dad passed away a short while ago! Tell me this is not real Mikey! This hurts so much!" she wailed. As the tears flowed from her eyes, it was like déjà vu for him. He chose not to say much but held on to her, allowing her space to release her emotions.

As he sat holding her on the floor, his mind went back to the first time that he met Dave and the interactions with him over the years. He, too, became emotional and as he sat holding his wife, her body shaking with grief, he could not help the tears that poured down his face. They embraced each other for a while until they both seemed to have no more tears left. He kissed Aisha and gently said to her, "Let us get ready to go over to your mum." With that, he helped her up from the floor and they both got ready to leave the house.

On arriving at Dave's house, they noticed that the police and the District Medical Officer were already there as well as the funeral home's vehicle. Dave's body had not yet been removed and was still on his bed. The District Medical Officer had signed the documents stating the estimated time of death and its release to the funeral home. Aisha asked for a moment alone with her mother in the room. About fifteen minutes later, she opened the door, and the funeral home attendants did what they had to do before placing the body on the gurney to take it to the waiting vehicle. Aisha and her mother followed the attendants and looked on as they loaded the body in the vehicle. They both broke down in tears as the vehicle departed with Dave's body. Mikey held Aisha while her mother was held by one of her close friends.

The usual warm, inviting atmosphere in their home was now one of weeping and pain. The news had traveled quickly, and a few close friends began to arrive at the house. Among them was Chad, who stated that while he knew that Dave was ill, he did not realize he was terminal. "Not even at the wedding did I get the impression that he was close to the end," said Chad in a voice brimming with emotion. "I owe you so much Dave. You were my mentor." As he said those words, Chad found himself overwhelmed with tears and Mikey held on to him. He sunk his head into Mikey's shoulder and wept uncontrollably.

With emotions running high, Mikey realized that he had to be strong, not only for Aisha and her mother, but for the close friends who knew him and Dave. He seemed to be the one comforting everyone who dared to show their emotions that night.

It was not until midnight that he and Aisha departed for their home. On the way, they held hands as Mikey navigated the car with his other hand; little was said.

On getting home, they both got hot showers and were, understandably, too tired to chat. Within minutes they both sunk into deep slumber, shutting out the cares of the world knowing quite well that they would have to pick them up again in a few hours.

Three days after his death, Dave's funeral was held in the Cathedral. The church was packed to capacity as many of his friends and colleagues turned out to pay their respects. Aisha and her mum were inconsolable. In the eulogy, Aisha informed the congregation that Dave was not her biological father, but he was everything a father ought to be over the years. She spoke in glowing terms about his yearning to walk her up the aisle for her wedding. "He was in so much pain on my wedding day, but could anyone tell? No, this man lying there was determined to walk me up the aisle with a big smile on his face. Could anyone tell when he danced with me? No. That is who he was. Self-sacrificing, patient, loving, mentor to many. You earned your wings dad. Rest easy, until we meet again. I love you in life and in death." she said as her voice cracked and she returned to her seat.

After the service, Dave was buried in the family's burial plot in the church yard. Several of the congregation attended the repast at Dave's house while others said their goodbyes at the cemetery. At Dave's house, Mikey sat in a corner of the living room with Chad and their usual banter was absent. In its place were memories of Dave when they first met and his mentorship of them both over the years. Aisha walked over to them both to inquire if they had eaten. She then went to the kitchen to organize plates of food for them.

After consuming the food, Mikey suggested to Aisha that she could stay for the rest of the day with her mum if she wanted and he would return for her later that night. She, in turn, suggested that he return for her the next day since she did not want her mum to be by herself at that time. He agreed with her suggestion and noted that he still had to take Aunt Rose home.

Aunt Rose had insisted that she should attend the funeral, for she had grown fond of Dave and could not miss saying goodbye to him. She had been sitting on the back porch chatting with Aisha's mum when he went to inform her that he was ready to take her home.

On the way, they chatted about things in general and she reminded him that he needed to be there for Aisha as well as her mother. "You are one lucky guy. You started off with only your mum and now you have two sets of family who love you. What a blessing, Mr. Clary!" she said as she gave him a friendly poke to his side. He smiled but did not say anything in response. On arriving at Aunt Rose's home, he stopped to make sure that she was settled in and even spent a half an hour with his sisters. It was nice to connect and be Mikey, the brother at times.

On arriving at his home that evening, he showered and relaxed in front of the television. As he sat there, he realized that he could not focus on the movie. Instead, his mind reflected over his life right up to where he was today. Here was Mikey, the successful real estate agent, with a home and now a wife. He smiled as he thought of Aisha. In the two months that they were married, he felt like the luckiest man in the world. He and his wife had honest communication between themselves and complemented each other's personalities. He prayed that this would continue to be the story of his married life. He had heard many stories about marriage, but he was determined that he would work at his. "We ain't perfect, but we are perfect for each other. Thanks again, Dave. I will always remember you, my friend. In fact, I cannot forget you, even if I tried," he said to himself as he took a sip from his glass of fruit juice.

"I am looking forward to one more piece to complete my life story; being a father!" he said to himself loudly. With that, he pondered on how his life would change once children entered the picture. "Hmm, the pitter patter of little feet from one boy and one girl would be a game-changer and I look forward to that," he said to himself. He noted, too, that he was having this conversation with himself and not with Aisha. He had gotten so accustomed to her being around, that he somehow forgot how to be by himself. He chuckled with that thought.

As he sat there, pondering on his life, unexpectedly, a poem of sorts began to take shape in his head. After repeating the first few lines, he quickly grabbed his notepad and scribbled the words:

"He was only twelve years old;
life was cold and rough
Just like other kids he wanted to be loved.
But every day she said you not good enough.
So, he fought back the tears
and tried to build his heart back up.
Oh Mother, mother, if you could see me now
Oh Mother, mother, if you could see me now.

Chorus:
I finally found a way out of the past
A man cannot move forward looking back,
I know you will look down from above,
But I found a greater love, And it is enough."

He then began to hum a tune and realized that he had the making of a song right there. His song was one of triumph, rising out of that dark place particularly where he had been with Mrs. Andrews, whom he thought would have been a mother to him. Instead of love, she had given him the worst treatment of his life. He was surprised that the memory was still rooted within him and was happy to purge his emotions by writing those words of triumph. "I will never be a parent like you. It was hard for me to even call you mum. What I know is that I will shower my children with love," he said sadly. As he bit on his pen reviewing what he had written, he realized the trajectory of the song and he was anxious to complete it. Soon enough, tiredness overcame him, and he put down his notes for that evening and headed for his bed.

After napping for an hour, he got up feeling refreshed and did some exercises. He checked his schedule for the next day and noted that he had a full day of showings. He would inform Aisha when he spoke to her later and they would decide on a pick-up time. With that being done, he went to the back of his house to organize some gardening items. He realized that he needed to get back to his hobby, gardening. That is where he spent the rest of his evening before he showered and had a late dinner. By 10:00 pm he sat reading a novel, but made sure to call his wife. She, as expected, was exhausted and was about to tuck in. "I will pick you up around 4:00 pm since I have a full slate tomorrow. You relax and I will see you then. Call me if you need anything. I love you my darling," he said. "I love you too honey, sleep well," she replied as they both hung up their phones.

A few weeks after the funeral, Aisha and Mikey were sitting in the doctor's office. She had complained about not feeling well for some days and Mikey had suggested that she should visit the doctor. She had argued with him that it was the stress from her father's death and had insisted that all she needed was a vacation since she had not taken one in a while. Mikey, however, wanted to make sure that she was fine and had made the appointment with her best friend, Dr. Patel.

After welcoming them to her office, that morning, Dr. Patel asked, "So what brings you two lovebirds here? You look a bit flushed Aisha. Tell me what has been happening." Once Aisha gave her feedback about what she was experiencing, she told her to sit at the examination table where she did her usual checks. She then put her through a further battery of tests before she sat back down with the husband and wife.

"Ok. Now there is really no need for worry. The only thing you will have to do is prepare to welcome a little addition to your family. You are pregnant my friend! Congratulations to you both!" said Dr. Patel gleefully. "What!" exclaimed Mikey and Aisha at once as though on cue. They both looked at each other in shock before the revelation sunk into their minds. Mikey placed his arms around Aisha and said, "Honey, we are about to be parents. Wow! This must take time to soak in," he said. "I do not know what to say. I didn't even expect this," Aisha replied. "I am to become a mum. This is a shocker!"

"Well, for most first-time parents, the news is usually a shock indeed, but as the baby develops you will go through the stages of the pregnancy right up to delivery. It is normal and taking care of the expected mother and baby is key. In a few weeks you will need to return for an ultrasound to be done so that we can check to make sure all is well inside of there. For now, you know your status and you will need to start by getting some relaxation," said Dr. Patel.

On leaving the doctor's office, Mikey and Aisha picked up some food which they later ate on reaching home. After having lunch, they retired to the back porch where they sat in silence for a while, holding hands. Mikey then said to her, "I love you Aisha Clary and I am the happiest man alive right now knowing that you are going to be the mother of my children." "Children? How many children do you hope to have my dear husband? Let us see how this one goes before we talk about more," she said with a laugh. He got up and gave her a deep kiss before he went inside for drinks. As Aisha sat outside, she heard a shout from inside of the house, "Yes! I am going to be a father! Yes!"

Aisha just shook her head and smiled. He soon returned with a glass of cold fruit juice for his wife and himself. "Honey, I am so excited that I could call Aunt Rose and the girls and give them the news," he said. "Not so fast, mister," she replied. "Let us wait for the ultrasound before we say anything to anyone." "Ok my love. You know it will be hard for me to contain my excitement," he said with a chuckle.

They spent the rest of the evening relaxing on the back porch chatting about baby names for boys and girls; chatting about changes that they would have to make once the baby was born.

Several weeks later, they returned to Dr. Patel's office where the ultrasound was done. What they saw on the monitor was even more bewildering. Instead of one heartbeat, the machine was picking up two. "What a surprise! You have been blessed with twins!" said Dr. Patel excitedly. "Do you wish to know the gender of the twins?"

Mikey and Aisha looked at each other, too stunned to say a word just then. He got up slowly and rubbed his head, trying to digest the news that he had just heard. "At this time, we would prefer to wait for the surprise at delivery. I cannot believe it! I am going to be a father of twins!" he said to himself as he paced the floor. Aisha, however, was too stunned to say a word. She could not contain her emotions, and the tears flowed down her cheek. Mikey went to her and kissed her as he helped her to get up from the examination table. "This is beyond my expectations! My goodness!" she said. "Let us go home honey, I just need to get some sleep. I am so tired right now. I need time to really absorb this."

With that, he placed his arms around her, and they walked out of the doctor's office leaning on each other, smiles on their faces like kids in a candy shop.

CHAPTER 12

Unexpected Joy

"Joy is found in your bundles."

(Three years later)

"Happy birthday to you! Happy birthday Dave! Happy birthday David! Happy birthday to you!" shouted the gathering of friends and family at the birthday party for the identical twins. Mikey and Aisha beamed with pride as they held their sons who were not too keen on the birthday celebrations. They were now three years of age and, as usual, were bundles of energy.

Dave, who was the leader, wriggled in his father's arms trying to get back to his business of running around the house. David, however, was crying as Aisha held him, for he too, did not seem too keen on the birthday celebrations. Aisha said to them, "Eat one little piece for mummy and you will go back to what you were doing." This calmed them, and they grudgingly ate a small bite of cake before they were released from their parents' arms.

Aisha's mum, the doting grandmother, ran after them as they made their exit. Mikey and Aisha looked at them and laughed. "I believe that I need to have extra supplements to keep up with those two," he said to his wife. She shook her head and said, "Not just you. Parenting is really for the young, for that type of energy will keep you on your toes. Yet, it is a joy to have them around the house and for them to have you on your toes." She laughed and planted a kiss on his lips as she moved away from him and went to mingle with the guests. In the meantime, Mikey went to keep an eye on his sons.

He took a seat next to Aunt Rose, who, by now, was walking with the aid of a walking-stick. Despite that and her now fully gray head of hair, she was always happy to participate in any family events. Hetty had gotten married and had moved to the next town with her husband, while Cindy had remained at the house to take care of Aunt Rose. As a single woman, she seemed content doing what she loved and was not in any hurry to leave the home she grew up in. Mikey would usually take the twins over to visit her and Aunt Rose since they both loved having them around the house. Cindy enjoyed the aunt's role to the extent that she spoilt them once they were around her. This was evident by the peals of laughter which emanated from the house once the twins were there. Cindy had proven to be a major help to Mikey and Aisha when the twins were born.

In the first two years, as they grew accustomed to parenting two highly active boys, Cindy was there to assist. She had a natural knack for dealing with children and helped with taking care of the boys from the time they were released from the hospital. Mikey and Aisha, as first-time parents, had progressed from getting anxious when the boys got the flu, to calmly handling any bouts of childhood illnesses that may come their sons' way from time to time. The boys had proven to be resilient for, while they may keep them quiet for a day or two, in no time they would be back to their normal mischief around the house. Aisha and Mikey had agreed that if one were a boy, he would be named after her deceased father and if one were a girl, she would be named after his deceased mother, Sheila. However, since it turned out that there were no girls, he named the other twin, David. The boys brought much joy to their household and Mikey could not wait to be involved in their activities as they grew older.

One night, after tucking them in their beds, Mikey and Aisha were having a chat as they retired to their bedroom. "Honey," said Mikey, "It would be nice to try to have one more child so that the boys can have company. I do not think we should wait too long before we try for a girl this time. It would certainly be the icing on the cake to have a little girl. Hopefully, she would take some of the steam out of our two energy bundles. You know, it is often said that boys are for their mothers while girls are for their daddies. In fact, I love the glow that you get when you are pregnant. What do you say to that babe?" Aisha looked at him with a smirk on her face and said, "Michael Clary, please stop speeding and take it slow. I am in no hurry to get back into a labor ward anytime soon. That idea of another child will have to wait a bit longer. Have you forgotten some of the complications that I had while bearing our two busy bodies? If it is God's Will for us to have more children, then so be it but I am not rushing it." She cuddled next to him and turned off the night-light. In no time at all, they were both in deep slumber.

"Come here David! Do not climb on top of the cupboard!" shouted Aisha as she did a circuit around the house trying to hold the boys to give them their bath. "Catch me mama!" said David with much delight as he scampered to another part of the house trying to escape his mother's clutches. After ten minutes of running around, she finally got them into the bathroom where she had to contend with being properly soaked when she was finished with them.

While she had a baby-sitter to assist during the week when she and Mikey had to go to work, they both preferred to take care of the boys on weekends without the help of the sitter. They enjoyed that time to ensure greater bonding with their children. At times, Aisha's mother would spend time with the boys herself, but their energy levels had far surpassed hers and she would lie on the floor laughing when her energy was spent.

Getting them dressed was another event, for Dave was the athletic one who would jump as though the bed was a trampoline. It was while dressing the boys in their room, one evening that Aisha felt a bit ill. She remembered that she had not eaten lunch and chalked it up to that. Mikey had gone to do a showing with a client and was expected back later that evening. She grabbed a bite to eat and after an hour or so she felt fine.

When Mikey came home that evening, they took the boys to the park for them to go outdoors and have some fun. They played to their hearts' delight on the slides and the swings until their parents decided that it was time to go home. On the way home, they stopped for ice-cream. By the time the boys were finished, they needed another bath, for the ice cream was all over their faces and clothes. Aisha could not help but laugh and Mikey took out his phone and snapped a picture of them.

On getting home, both parents helped to bathe the boys and tuck them in their beds. They then sat on the back porch having a beverage and catching up on the day's events. Aisha did not tell Mikey about her sick feeling for she did not wish to alarm him about anything. In fact, since she had grabbed a bite, the feeling was gone. There really was nothing to worry about.

During the next morning, the sick feeling returned with greater intensity. Aisha felt a great deal of fatigue and noted, as well, that her time of the month had passed. In her mind, she had several thoughts which she kept to herself. She decided that she would visit the doctor on her own, to ascertain if there was nothing to be concerned about. She needed to find out first and inform Mikey after.

That morning, she left for work as usual but made a detour to her friend's office. She was greeted warmly by Dr. Patel, who gave her a quick kiss on her cheek. "Hey girl! Have a seat. How are those boys doing? Keeping you both on your toes for sure. Where is Mikey today? Is he coming in?" asked Dr. Patel. "No. I need to find out what is happening to me without causing him any alarm. I am not feeling well these last couple of days and my period is overdue. I just need to know if there will be confirmation of my thoughts, so here I am," Aisha replied forlornly to her friend. "Awww, who knows? It may or may not be what you are thinking about. Nonetheless, let us get some tests done before we arrive at any conclusions," replied her friend reassuringly.

After her usual battery of tests, Aisha and her friend sat to discuss the results which were received from the laboratory. After viewing the document in front of her, Dr. Patel said, "Your thoughts were correct my dear. You are pregnant and perhaps a few months along. You will soon have an addition to the family. Do you wish to know the gender of the baby? I know the last time you all did not wish to find out. How about now?" said Dr. Patel. Aisha then said to her, "This time, you can reveal the gender for me. I will surprise my beloved husband." Dr. Patel responded with a big smile lighting up her face, "Your daughter is now on the way." "What!" exclaimed Aisha. "My goodness! Mikey has been yearning for a daughter for months and I have been brushing away the thought thinking that we would try for another child in one year's time. Can you imagine how excited he would have been if he were here with me? Now I will have to tell him that I was not feeling well at work and came to you because he would want to know why I did not bring him. What I will not tell him is that he is about to have a daughter. I will keep that as a surprise. He will be so delighted!"

"Yes, but you have a bit of iron deficiency, and you will need to eat properly and take your vitamins. Your last pregnancy had complications, and I do not want any for this one," said Dr. Patel sternly.

"Yes, madam," replied Aisha. "I was wondering why I was so fatigued. I will follow your advice." She was then given a prescription to fill out for her medication.

On her way to work, Aisha smiled when she thought of the way her husband would react when he found out that his wish to have a daughter was going to be fulfilled. That night after putting the twins to bed, Aisha and Mikey were themselves preparing to have an early night's sleep since they were both exhausted. Aisha was nervous since she could not contain her excitement much longer. She was particularly anxious to see how her husband would react. As she sat on the bed waiting for Mikey to get into bed, she began smiling. As he took his place next to her, he looked at her and laughed saying, "What is this smiling all about honey? You missed me for the day. Give me a smooch." "If you only knew," she said, continuing to smile. "Know what, hon?" he asked sheepishly. "Mr. Clary, you are about to be a father once again," she said quietly. "Eh! Ha! Ha!" he shouted as he jumped from the bed. "How do you know this?" he asked. She then told him that she was not feeling well and had decided to get a checkup when the pregnancy was revealed. "Oh honey, I am so happy!" he said ecstatically. "Did you find out what gender the baby will be?" "Aisha said to him, "The last time you did not want to know so let us keep it like that for now. I will change my mind at the right time." He then got back in bed and hugged his wife, kissing her passionately. "Babe, this is the girl this time; I just know it," he said as he fell asleep, cuddling his wife in a sweet embrace.

"It's beginning to look a lot like Christmas…" was the sweet melody of the carol being played over the sound system in the house. Christmas was just four days away and Mikey and Aisha had decided that they would have her mother, Aunt Rose, and his sisters over to their home on Christmas Day. Aisha was now six months pregnant, and her doctor had placed her on bed rest for a while. She had hired a babysitter to help her with the boys because they had shown no signs of slowing down their energy levels. While she enjoyed seeing them romp about, she realized that she could not keep up and spent a considerable amount of time in bed, leaving the sitter to tend to their needs.

From time to time, she would check in with the administrative staff for, even though she was on bed rest, she was still doing her legal work while propped up on her pillows. It was during one such check-in that she asked Sandra, her Administrative Assistant, to get her something from the store. Sandra was specifically told not to inform anyone but to collect it and bring it to her house. She had told her, in confidence, why she wanted the item and they both chuckled thinking of the plot that was hatched. That evening, Mikey came home earlier than expected because he wanted to ensure that all was well at home. When Aisha saw him, she was shocked but smiled nervously since she knew that Sandra would arrive at any minute. Nonetheless, she knew that Sandra would think of something so deep down she was not that worried. When the doorbell rang, she heard Mikey speaking to someone. About two minutes later, he came to her saying that Sandra was there with a confidential package, and she did not want to leave it with anyone but her.

She responded by letting out a small laugh and told him to let her go to the back porch where she would meet with her.

When she finally shuffled to the back porch, there she saw Sandra seated, sipping on a glass of ale. Mikey had made sure that she got something to refresh herself while she waited on Aisha. When Aisha entered the porch, he made sure that she was seated comfortably before he left. "Hello Aisha," said Sandra as she smiled and rose to give her a hug, "How are you doing? Sorry to get you out of your bed, but this package came in urgently. It is connected to the matter which you are overseeing currently. She then gave Aisha a brown legal- sized envelope and smiled. Aisha told her that she would check it and get back to her if anything. They spoke about matters at the office and even spoke of looking forward to the Christmas holiday. "Do not forget that we close the office from the day after tomorrow so that staff can get the time to do their shopping and other activities. So, if you need anything further, just holla and your girl will be right here. Your call is my command," said Sandra as they both had a good laugh.

Mikey returned about twenty minutes after to meet two women giggling as though they had been to a comedy show. "What in that package could possibly cause so much laughter between you two?" he asked with a laugh himself. "Well, hon you caught our laughter as well. Be careful, it is infectious," replied Aisha. Sandra then rose from her seat saying that she had to go collect her two girls from school. "You will soon have this to do when those boys must go out to school. Get ready for that. Got to run. Take care of you two!"

After showing Sandra to the door, Mikey returned with the boys in tow. He went out to the lawn and played a ball game with the boys while Aisha sat taking in the view. As she sat looking at them, with a laugh she said, "you need to brush up on those ball skills, hon. Those two will soon beat you in a game." He looked at her and made a funny face before he said to the boys, "Ok. That is enough for now. Let us look to go inside." "Not yet daddy!"

shouted David. "I want to play more. I like this.," he said as he pouted. "David, how about we come back a little later and play another game? Daddy is tired now," pleaded Mikey. He took a seat next to Aisha and opened his arms as the boys ran towards them. David climbed on his father's lap while Dave climbed onto his mother's lap.

With a hug, Dave said to her, "Love you mummy." She then stroked his mop of brown curls and gave him a hug and kiss on his cheek. She then leaned over and gave Dave a kiss as well. "Now, you two, go inside to Ms. Shelly. She will get you something to eat. Love you two," said Aisha to the boys as they rolled off their laps and into the house. She and Mikey had a good laugh and just sat for a while taking in the peace of the backyard surroundings. "Ahhh… this feels good," said Mikey as he closed his eyes. "How are you feeling love?" he asked his wife. "I am good," replied Aisha.

"My sister and Aunt Rose would like to come over to help us with any chores to be done for Christmas. Is there anything that you would want them to assist with?" Mikey inquired. "Oh, that is nice of them to offer," said Aisha. "The curtains must be changed, and I can get Shelly to assist with those in the children's bedroom. Other than that, it is just to plan the lunch for Christmas Day. You should be able to get the items from the grocery store. I will leave it up to you to get the gifts for the boys. You can take out the tree tomorrow and have fun decorating it with them. We will also have to get gifts for the family who will be here as well as for Shelly. That is, it really. I am not too fussy about Christmas. For me, it is really the joy of seeing people, especially children, enjoy themselves with the gift-giving." "Aye! Aye captain! It is your ship," said Mikey, saluting her as he sat there laughing. "I will execute madam."

They spent the rest of the evening catching up on their individual work matters before going inside to get ready for dinner and sleep.

"My goodness! What smells so mouth-watering in this kitchen?" asked Aisha as she walked slowly towards the kitchen. Christmas Day had arrived, and Cindy was baking a ham as well as a turkey. Aunt Rose was helping to cut up vegetables as she sat at the table in the kitchen. Aisha gave them each a hug and said, "Happy Christmas! Well, what is there for me to do?" "Sit around and look as cute as you. Happy Christmas everyone!" said a familiar voice behind her. Mikey then gave a hug from behind as he, too, seated himself at the table. "Listen, I do not want too many of you in my kitchen currently. I want to be able to turn around with ease. I also have a surprise dish, and I do not want any of you to see what it is before lunch is ready. In any case, I run the risk of having the food eaten before it gets to the dining table," she said in gest while the rest of them laughed.

"Well, the two you must worry about have not yet awakened from their sweet slumber. They stayed up all night waiting for Santa and I was able to lift them to their beds when they realized that he was a bit late because of harsh weather from the North Pole. I better help with breakfast and try to stay out of your way, Cindy dear," said Mikey as he gave his sister and Aunt Rose each a hug. The atmosphere was warm and continued even when Aisha's mum arrived in the kitchen. She, too, continued with the laughter and conversation and even helped Mikey to set the table for breakfast.

All this time as Aisha sat there absorbing the atmosphere in the kitchen, she could not help but smile at what she had planned for Mikey. She watched him as he turned around in the kitchen. He was in his element when he had his family around him. She wondered how he would react when she was finished with him.

As she sat sipping on her hot chocolate, she soon felt someone brush against her and realized that Dave was up. "Hey honey, come sit on mommy's lap. Merry Christmas!" she said to him and gave him a kiss on his cheek. "Is David up yet?" He shook his little head indicating that his brother had not yet awakened. "Santa came and you were asleep," she continued. "I wanted to see Santa, but he took so long to get here mummy," replied Dave as he yawned. "Oh my! Santa was busy delivering gifts to so many children! Do not worry, he will have left your gifts, but you must first brush your teeth and have breakfast before we open what he left for you," said Aisha comfortingly to him. Her mother soon came to take him to the bathroom after she and

Mikey had completed the setting of the table for breakfast.

In about twenty minutes, they were all seated around the dining table. David had awakened by then and his grandmother had dealt with getting him and his brother ready for breakfast. Mikey blessed the food, and they all partook in the breakfast of eggs, sausage, toast, and fruits. Hot chocolate, tea and coffee were the choice of beverages. After breakfast, everyone retired to the living room for the opening of the gifts.

The gifts for the boys were opened first and they were in glee when they realized that Santa had left their gifts. Their squeals of delight filled the room as they saw the bright shiny fire truck and the big yellow truck. As the gifts were distributed, she heard Mikey stating, "Where is my gift? No one remembered me this year. Santa forgot me when he brought these two." As everyone was absorbed in the laughter, Aisha asked to be excused stating that she needed to go to the bathroom.

After ten minutes she returned, and a hush fell into the room. There she was dressed in a white smock with a broad, pink satin bow wrapped around her belly. She walked up to her husband and said, "Your gift has arrived. Your daughter is well and doing fine. Just giving her mother, a kick or two." Mikey flew up from the floor and hugged his wife. "Do you mean to tell me that we are going to have a daughter?" he asked with eyes wide open. All Aisha did was nod her head and smile. "I knew for a while now but wanted to wait for the right moment to break the news to you." Mikey then went over to her and kissed her stomach. He unwrapped the pink bow and tied it around his head. Following this, he jumped like a rabbit around the room with the twins in tow thinking he was playing a game with them. Aisha's mum and the rest of the family could not contain their excitement either. The shouts of joy seemed to go on forever. "Hello! Hello! Lunch must be finished! Have you all forgotten about the food?" asked Aisha as she was overwhelmed with hugs and kisses.

"God is good! Thank you, Lord!" he shouted. "Now my family will be complete! Yes! This is a great Christmas gift! Thank you honey!" He continued to do a dance in the living room with his two sons. The rest of the family cleared the table and moved to the kitchen to complete the lunch preparations. Mikey then sat with the boys assisting them with their new toys. In the meantime, Aisha went to the bedroom to remove her gown and bow. She felt great knowing that her little plan had the desired impact on her husband. She had to tell her assistant how that worked out.

While in the bedroom, Mikey entered and hugged her from behind. "Hon, you made me so happy today. I love you!" He gave her a passionate kiss as they stood in their bedroom embracing each other. "You will need to take it easy given some of the issues you had the last time." "I know that Mikey," she replied. "Hence the reason I am on bed rest." "Well, today is no exception. You keep your feet up and let us worry about the food and prepping and even the boys. Whatever you need, just holler," he said as he led her to the bed. "Mikey, I am fine. I am only pregnant, not sick," she said with a laugh. He made sure that she was well propped in the bed before he left her to go help in the kitchen.

Within two hours, he returned to the bedroom to inform her that lunch was ready. He helped her out of the bed and walked with her to the dining table which was laden with all the food. "My goodness! This food is making my mouth water! I cannot wait to dig in!" she said as she took her seat at the table. Once again, Mikey blessed the table and carved the turkey and the ham. The plates were filled, and everyone enjoyed the food. "Wow! This food tastes as great as it looks and smells," said Aisha's mum. "Thank you all so much for having me here. I do not think I would have been able to get through this day on my own. While my heart is saddened with Dave being gone, this has helped me tremendously. I would not want it any other way. To learn that I will soon have a granddaughter is the icing on the cake. I ask God to bless all of you." With that, she smiled and without missing a beat, Aunt Rose said, "I want to raise a toast to life, love and family!" With that, they touched their glasses and drank.

While they were seated at the table, the doorbell rang. Mikey went to answer the door, and a loud shout was heard at the door. Everyone hears him saying, "Well look who is here! Come on in!" There, in the living room, was Hetty and her husband, Garvin. Cindy flew up and hugged her. She and her husband then kissed and hugged Aunt Rose. Hugs were also given to everyone else, and she even gave Aisha a big hug when she realized that she was pregnant. "Did you all think that I was going to let this day go without being around the people that I love? I told Garvin that we will surprise them, and I hope we did." They gave Mikey the gifts they brought with them and were invited to have lunch since there was a lot of food remaining.

The rest of the Christmas Day was spent relaxing, playing Board games, and chatting among themselves. Mikey was like a kid in a Candy store enjoying himself with his family. For a moment, he sat and looked around the room filled with a sense of contentment. This is how he had envisaged his life one day. This is the family life that he yearned for as a child, and he was happy that he could give this to his sons. With that thought, he went and sat next to his wife, placing his arms around her as she settled in his embrace looking on at the activities taking place around them. Cindy soon brought out her surprise Cheesecake dessert with homemade peanut ice-cream and everyone partook of it. "More! More! More! This is simply divine sis!" said Hetty as she moved to the kitchen to get a refill. The rest of the family laughed, and Cindy had no choice but to refill their bowls with her tasty delicacies. Mikey's house was filled with love and laughter. At that moment nothing else mattered, this was the world to him.

In the weeks that followed, Mikey treated Aisha as though she was fragile China- ware. On one such day, she was about to stretch to reach a glass from the top shelf of the cupboard when she stumbled a bit. It did not take Mikey one second before he sprinted from the kitchen sink to hold his wife. She often had to laugh and remind him that he was over-pampering her. His response was always the same: "Precious cargo my love; precious cargo."

He made sure to prepare her meals to ensure that she had the right nutrition and hardly allowed her to do much work around the house. Aisha once told her mother, "My husband thinks that I am a baby at this time. The only thing he is not doing is giving me a bottle." "Enjoy it while it lasts," said her mother in return.

As the days wore on, Aisha spent her time relaxing and taking her medication. She had stopped doing work from home and had passed on her cases to her junior attorneys. She also spent time with the boys making sure not to isolate them from being around her. She recognized that she had to maintain a balance with them.

One evening, when Mikey was not at home, she was sitting on the couch playing a game of Ludo with the boys when a sudden, sharp pain engulfed her. "Ahhh!" she cried out while holding her stomach. "David, call your gramma!" she commanded. The child ran off to get his grandmother while Dave moved towards her. "Mummy are you ok?" asked in all his innocence. "Yeah, baby. Mummy is just feeling some discomfort," she said comfortingly. As she said this, another wave of pain hit her and she bent over, holding her stomach again.

It did not take long for her mother to come to her aid. She noticed that her daughter was looking pale and was now lying down on the couch, rolling pain. She did not hesitate to call Mikey, who stated that he was on his way. She returned to ensure that Aisha was not being overwhelmed and called the baby- sitter to deal with the boys.

"Mum, I am feeling as though the baby is coming," she said, clenching her teeth in pain. "But you are only six months pregnant," replied her mum. "I know. This does not feel good at all," she said to her mother. "Where is Mikey?" asked Aisha. "Right here my love," he said as he rushed into the room, sweat pouring from his face. "What is happening? Try to remain calm, my love. You need to get to the emergency room." He rushed to the bedroom to pack an overnight bag just in case she had to be hospitalized. Aisha began moaning in pain and Mikey did not waste time helping her up from the couch and taking her unconcerned about anyone seeing him. "Why God? Why? Why?" he asked repeatedly. After feeling drained and helpless, he sat back in his chair with his head facing the ceiling with his eyes closed.

He was in that position when Dr. Patel came into the lobby approximately one hour after. "Hey Mikey," she said in a soft tone. She took a seat next to him as both he and his mother-in-law braced themselves for the feedback. "Aisha is resting comfortably now. However, she did have a miscarriage as we suspected and sadly, your beautiful baby did not make it. I know this is a painful experience given the expectations that you had, but I want you to be calm around Aisha. She is going to need your support." Mikey then asked, "We made sure that Aisha took it easy. What could have been the cause of the miscarriage?" "You do recall that during her last pregnancy she was at risk of this happening. Fortunately, it did not, and you were blessed with two healthy boys. Due to cervical insufficiencies, however, this pregnancy did not go to term, and this was the result. I would also recommend that you think about the risks if you really want another child." she replied.

Mikey looked at her as though he was in a daze. "I do not want to put her through something like this again to satisfy my own selfish need to have a daughter. I love my wife too much and I am grateful for the children God has blessed me with. We will have a chat when she gets back on her feet. For now, I will be there for her to make sure she heals mentally and physically. Thanks for your advice doc. Can we see her now?" he asked forlornly. "Sure, follow me," she said. They followed Dr. Patel back to the room where Aisha was resting with a drip bag attached to her arm. "She was sedated so she will not be able to speak at this time. Just allow her to rest. You can come back at any time if you wish. I will be here until this evening so I will be looking in on her periodically," she said. Mikey shook his head and thanked her for her support.

He then sat next to the bed stroking his wife's head as she slept. He quickly wiped away a tear as it rolled down his cheek. Aisha's mum then told him that she would remain with her, and he could go home to make sure that all is well with the boys. He protested for a moment that he wanted to be there when she woke up, but she convinced him that once she did, he would be informed. He hesitatingly left the room and proceeded to the Car Park where he sat in his vehicle for a while before beginning his journey to his home.

On the way home, he had time to think and clear his head. He gave God thanks that at least she was not in any danger and that her life was spared. He promised himself that he would be strong for her and support her through this. "We were so looking forward to the birth of our daughter. We did all that we could to minimize any risks, but God you know best. I cannot question you. All I can say is thanks for having her even for six months in the womb. Take care of my daughter, mama," he mumbled to himself as the tears began to blind him while clutching the steering wheel.

Two months after recovering, Aisha and Mikey visited Dr. Patel who had advised them against having any more babies. They had both agreed that the risks were too great, and they had agreed to tubal ligation. They were happy and focused on their twins who were developing rapidly. Each week they made sure to do some family activity to develop strong bonds with their boys.

On one occasion, Mikey was taking them to a friend's house for a birthday party when he had to pass by the orphanage where he grew up. He had promised himself that he would let his children know about his upbringing when they were at an age to understand. He also made a mental note to one day visit the orphanage. Since he had left the orphanage, he had not returned, and it was not that he held any animosity towards the institution. Yet, he was surprised that he felt a warm tug in his heart as he drove by. He had both positive and negative memories, but he always chose to focus on the positive aspects. It was there that he had a father-figure in Mr. Gosine, whom he had grown to love and respect. It was there that he had met his friend, Chad. It was there that he was given the opportunity to hone his entrepreneurial skills. It was there that he spent time with Ms. Andrea; precious memories which were now treasured in the deep recesses of his mind.

He was so focused on the orphanage that he did not realize that he almost ran up on the curb. All he heard was Aisha's voice shouting, "Mikey!" He had just enough time to react and straighten the vehicle before he collided. He stopped the vehicle and spun around to check on the boys in the backseat. They were, luckily, in their car seats and were not too shaken. "What on earth happened to you?" asked Aisha. "Sorry love. For a moment, my mind wandered, and that was all it took to lose focus. Are you ok?" he said. She replied that she was fine. For the rest of the journey, they chatted about the orphanage, and she even encouraged him to pay a visit. "I recall that is where my dad heard about you," she said with a smile.

The boys had fun at the party and were fast asleep by the time they had returned home that evening. After putting them in their beds, Mikey and Aisha spent the evening relaxing before turning in for the night. His last words to her before falling asleep were, "Honey, you are right. A visit to the orphanage is overdue. I think I will place that on my to-do list for this week."

CHAPTER 13

Dreams Fulfilled

"Life is a cycle; pass the baton."

"I look forward to hearing from you tomorrow and trust that we can close this matter." said Mikey to his clients as they left the property which they had been viewing. This was his last viewing for the morning and after checking his schedule, he realized that he was free for the rest of the day. He grabbed a takeaway lunch and decided to do something that he had promised himself that weekend. He piloted his vehicle onto the freeway and ate his lunch as he drove by to his destination.

In about forty minutes he was at the gate for the orphanage. He identified himself to the security officer and asked to speak with the Head of the Institution. He was informed that the new Director was Ms. Pam Strudel. Mikey smiled when he heard this, for he remembered her as one his counselors when Mr. Gosine was in charge. As he drove slowly into the compound, he took time to stare at the surroundings. Not much had changed for he recognized the field and the dormitories, the school block, the auditorium, and the library. There was one new block which he did not recognize and made a note to inquire about it. HE found a park and walked slowly towards the Director's office.

He remembered the walk quite well and smiled as he recalled some of the events that occurred there. As he strolled by, he observed the children in the home and reflected on how he was once in their position. Soon enough, he was knocking on the Director's door. "Come in!" said a voice from behind the door. He pushed and entered the office. His heart was beating on his chest for he was not sure how Ms. Strudel would react. "Please give me one second," she said without looking up. Mikey stood there looking at her features after so many years. Time was kind to her for she had just a few gray hairs to the front of her head, while she looked the same as when he last saw her.

In about three seconds, she raised her head and greeted Mikey with a smile. "I am sorry, but I needed to deal with what I was working on before I did anything else. Do have a seat and tell me how I can help you," she said without giving a hint that she remembered him. "Hi, my name is Mike Clary, and I am here to see how I can assist the Orphanage in any way." "Mike Clary. Mike Clary. That name sounds quite familiar to me. Were you a resident here before?" she asked with some level of anticipation in her voice. "Yes mam. I was here when Mr. Gosine was the Director and you were a counselor," he said with a smile. "Yes! I remember now. I recalled telling Mr. Gosine that one day you will do something great with your life. Yes Mikey, I remember you quite well. My eyes are blessed to see you today!" she replied. "Come give me a hug! This is indeed a wonderful surprise!" she said as she rose from behind her desk. He obliged by rising and giving her a long warm hug.

After separating, she returned to her chair and continued the conversation. "Well Mr. Gosine retired about four years ago and the baton was passed to me. We have had a few changes over the years, but nothing major. Tell me about yourself though. I am excited to hear about what you did with your life." In response, he told her about his career, his siblings, and the struggle he endured after being placed with the family. Her face registered a look of total shock when she heard some of what he had to deal with. "However, I decided that my life must be positive, and I persevered. I graduated from university, got pulled into Real Estate and I have my own agency now. I am married to a wonderful woman, and we have twin boys," he said with a sense of pride. "Wow! You have accomplished a lot despite the challenges Mikey. What an inspiration you are! I am so proud of you!" she said as she gave him a clap. "Thank you," he said graciously.

"I was passing by with my family recently and felt the urge to do something for the orphanage. Is there anything that needs to be done urgently with which I could assist?" he asked.

"Well, this is timely. You would have noticed a new wing as you entered. That is a new dormitory for the girls. The old dorms as you know have become overcrowded and we were able to get that wing constructed. Yet, it is not completely furnished. There is still some work to be done but we have moved quite a few of the girls across there. "We need beds, closets and other furnishings for the place," she explained.

Mikey shook his head in response and said that he could organize a crew to do a site visit and provide him with a budget. Ms. Strudel then invited him to do a walkthrough to show him, first-hand, the state of things there. He was happy to accompany her, since, for him, it was a walk down Memory Lane.

As he walked beside Ms. Strudel, he felt as though he was back in the classroom listening to his teachers. He recalled how Chad and his other friends were at the time and smiled as he saw the man that Chad had become. As he stepped gingerly into the library, he recalled the library renovation project that he had been instrumental in collaborating with his mates to get done. The library looked the same except for the rearrangement of the books and a few more desks and chairs. He continued smiling as his mind was flooded with memories.

He was then led to the new wing which was on the other side of the field where he used to sit and daydream about moving in with a family and experiencing love. He recalled his days with Ms. Andrea sitting there with him, reminding him to think positively and that everything would work out for him. He felt himself getting teary-eyed and was happy that she was able to see how he had progressed over the years.

As they pushed the door to the new wing, he realized that, as Ms. Strudel had mentioned, it was for the girls. He was given a tour of the new facility, and he believed that the basics were there. However, he looked around to see what else could be done to enhance the place and he made mental notes.

As he and Ms. Strudel were about to exit the building, a little girl about nine years of age walked briskly across to them. "Excuse me, Ms. Strudel," she said with a boldness that reminded Mikey of himself. "I was looking for you to let you know that the tap on the top floor has been leaking for about two days now and no one has done anything to stop it. Sue and I told Ms. Bronte about it but it is still leaking, and the place is always wet. Can you do something about it, Ms. Strudel?"

"No problem, Corina. Thank you for bringing it to my attention. I will make sure that it is attended to today," replied Ms. Strudel with a smile. When she left, Ms. Strudel said, "Corina reminds me of you in many ways. Respectful, bold and a natural leader." "How did she come to be in the Orphanage?" he inquired. "Her parents died in a car accident, and she was left without any other family. As such, she was brought here when she was five and she has been here since. Hopefully, one day, a loving family will embrace her feisty personality. Until then, she remains with us and is a joy to be around at the orphanage." Mikey shook his head and continued his tour.

At the end of an hour or so, he was ready to leave having taken note of what he could assist with. On the drive to his home, he smiled as though he had been given a new toy. His joyful mood overflowed to his household for when Aisha saw him, she inquired as to what had him so perky. "Guess what!" he exclaimed. "I visited the orphanage and boy am I glad that I did.

I was taken on a tour of the orphanage and so many memories flooded my mind; the good as well as the bad. I even remembered the day that I fought and had to be taken to Mr. Gosine's office. Can you imagine a well-behaved gentleman like me fighting in school?" He laughed raucously when he was finished speaking.

Aisha sat looking at him with a smirk on her face. "Well, Mr. Clary, you were certainly no angel, so yes I could picture that taking place," she said. "What do you plan to do for the institution now that you have done well in your life? What are you prepared to give back?"

He informed her of the needs but that his pet project would be to refurbish the girls' dormitory. "Your firm can partner with mine to do the needful. I will have one of my staff go over there tomorrow and get a costing done so that we can have a budget formulated," he said to Aisha. "Sounds like a plan," she replied.

"Oh, I almost forgot to mention that I saw this little girl, about nine, who reminded me of myself. She saw Ms. Strudel and I walking out to my car, and she approached bravely to remind her about a leaking tap that was not fixed. You should have seen the little tyke. Even Ms. Strudel commented that she reminded her of myself." "Oh, ok. I realize that she made an impression on you already." replied Aisha. "I really did not interact with her to form a more informed opinion," he said as he went on to check on the boys who were playing in the backyard with the baby-sitter.

Three months after his visit to the orphanage, new beds and furniture were being moved into the girls' dormitory. Staff from his office as well as Aisha's, had volunteered to do the painting and redesigning of the new wing. Ms. Strudel was excited about the project and she and some of her staff had volunteered to provide the meals for the crew that was working. The day was filled with fun and laughter and even some of the children were there to assist. Among them was Corina, who came to bring refreshments and water from the kitchen.

"Hello," she said to Mikey and some of the crew that was working. "Would any of you like to have water or sandwiches? I have cheese sandwiches and chicken sandwiches." "That sounds great! I will have a chicken sandwich," said one of the young ladies. "What is your name, little lady?" inquired Aisha. "My name is Corina Simon, but my friends call me Cory," she replied without hesitation. "Will it be ok if I call you Cory as well?" asked Aisha. "Sure, that is no problem," she responded. "Ok Cory, I think I will have one of your cheese sandwiches then and a bottle of water," said Aisha to the little girl whose smile lit up her round face. After serving the volunteers, she left to return to the kitchen.

The work continued and at the end of the day the dormitory was transformed into a space that was so inviting for girls. Some of the volunteers even donated stuffed toys and tablets for the children. In their post-project discussion, the volunteers promised that they would return the following month to do the same for the boys' dormitory. "We cannot leave the boys undone," said one of the volunteers from Aisha's firm. Interestingly, all of them agreed and it was a unanimous decision to do the same for the boys. Ms. Strudel was overwhelmed by the generosity of the crew and all she could do was raise her hands in thanks. "Thank you all from the bottom of my heart," she remarked. "This was more than I had expected. Thank you, Mikey. Let me allow one of the girls to give you their thanks, as well."

From the group of children, out stepped Corina, all bright-eyed and bubbly as she came to the front of her colleagues. "I want to say thanks for doing this for us. We are excited to sleep in our new beds and play with our stuffed toys. We also love the pink and purple colors. Thanks," said Corina smiling broadly from ear to ear as the volunteers clapped in appreciation.

Later that day, when Aisha and Mikey were relaxing, Aisha was recapping the day's events when she said, "I now see why you were smitten by little Ms. Corina. She is indeed a brave child. Is it possible for us to have her spend a weekend with us? Is that allowed at all? Perhaps some of our volunteers can even invite some of the children to spend weekends and even organize fun events for them. What are your thoughts hon?"

Mikey rocked back his head and took a while before he responded. He then sat up and said, "This is interesting that you mentioned that love. I was thinking along the same lines. When I saw Corina, I thought of myself when I was her age and had inquired about her background. With the knowledge that she has no family, I was considering having a chat with you about bringing her to spend a weekend. We are thinking alike, and I am happy that you mentioned that. I can speak with Ms. Strudel and hear what she has to say."

Two days after that conversation with his wife, Mikey made a call to Ms. Strudel, and he put forward the idea to her. Without hesitation, she agreed to it, but it was also dependent on whether Corina also wanted to spend time with them. She ended the call by stating that she would have a chat with the child, and she would get back to him. Mikey recalled how he felt when he had spent his first weekend with his siblings and reminded himself that he must never treat any child the way that his adopted mother had treated him. In his heart he felt that he was ready for a girl to be around the house, and this was the direction that he had to take.

Mikey did not receive a call that day, but by midday the next day, he recognized Ms. Strudel's number. He held his breath in anticipation, not knowing whether the child would have agreed to spend the weekend or not. He answered the phone gingerly, "Hello Ms. Strudel. How are you today?" "Hi Mikey, I am doing well thank you. I discussed the proposal with Cory, and she has agreed to spend a weekend with you. She was careful to ask which one of you and I reminded her about who you were. She also remembered your wife and she was comfortable. Please note that she must be collected by 3pm on Friday and returned to the Orphanage by 5pm on Sunday. You can give me a call in the morning to let me know your estimated time of arrival. I look forward to seeing you then. Bye," said Ms. Strudel as she ended the call.

Mikey felt relieved upon getting the feedback. He made a mental note to prepare the boys for their visitor that weekend. He immediately called Aisha and gave her the news. She, too, was elated and mentioned that she would need to shop for some stuff for Corina's visit. He took some time that day to pass and check on Aunt Rose and updated her on his visit to the Orphanage.

She was happy to hear that he was giving back to the home and even said to him, "Why don't you take one of the children to spend some time with you? You were longing to have a little girl. You can adopt a little girl, Mikey."

He looked at her and smiled. He then said, "Aunt Rose you raced ahead of me there. Aisha and I are planning to bring a little girl for the weekend. Her name is Corina. Out of all the children there, she, somehow, piqued my interest. Her attitude reminded me of myself when I was there. So, yes, we are going to take her to spend the weekend and hope that she will enjoy herself. Adoption, however, will be another story for that is a process all by itself and Aisha and I will have to discuss that."

"Hello Corina! Welcome to our home!" said Aisha as she moved forward to hug the little girl. "Is it still ok for me to call you Cory?" The little girl smiled and shook her head. "Come let me introduce you to our little boys. David and Dave please come and meet a special person," said Aisha as she led Corina by the hand to the living room. The two boys ran energetically to meet their visitor. "Boys, please say hello to Corina," said Mikey as he walked behind Aisha. The children shook hands with her, and Dave said, "Do you want to play Snake and Ladders? I have been beating David all morning." "Not true!" shouted David. "He only beat me in one game!" "Ok, ok, there will be no arguments in front of our guest," said Aisha with a laugh. "Allow her to get settled and then she will join you. Come Corina, let me show you to your room."

After settling her in her room, Aisha allowed her to play for a bit with the boys before they agreed to go out to watch a movie. The movie, "Angels and Earthlings," was being shown and it was one that everyone wanted to see. Aisha assisted Corina to get herself dressed and then the family went to the car. On the way to the cinema, the children chatted among themselves. "How old are you?" Corina asked David. "We are both five years of age. We are twins," he replied. "I noticed that" she said. "What is your favorite television show?" asked Dave. "I hardly watch television because I love to read books. But, if I watch, I like cartoons because they make me laugh.

My favorite cartoon is "Popeye the Sailor man," she said with a shrug. The children continued their chatting in the back seat as Aisha and Mikey listened and monitored their conversation. They noted that the children interacted well with each other and hoped it would be that way for the duration of Corina's stay.

The evening passed without any incident, in fact, Corina was in her glee. They all had hot dogs, popcorn, and other refreshments. After the movie, they went to a Play Park in the area. Corina did not seem too keen on some of the games, but she had fun watching the boys trying to hold on to the Merry-go- round. Before they left, however, Mikey challenged her to get a ride on one of the thrill rides. "If you go with me, I will go," she said to him. "Oh boy! What have I done to myself?" he said with a laugh. "Good one Cory! Let us see Mikey on the coaster ride! I bet you he will be scared!" Aisha taunted him.

Soon enough, Corina and Mikey were strapped in the ride, and it was off. Fortunately, the level of challenge for that ride was mild, but not long after it started, they were heard shouting, "Ahhhhh! My gosh! Eeeeeee!" When the ride came to a stop about ten minutes after, they hopped off as though they could not find their feet. Aisha and the boys screeched with laughter. Mikey gave Corina a high-five and told her that she was a brave girl. She was laughing so much that her cheeks seemed to shine. "I had fun Mr. Clary, but you screamed like a big baby," she said, doubling over with laughter. "I agree with you Cory!" said Aisha, who herself was in fits of laughter. "Come my love, let me help you to be steady," she said to Mikey as he placed his arms around her.

On reaching home, it did not take long for the children to shower and get into their beds. Mikey and Aisha made sure that Corina was tucked in and wished her a good night. They then retired to their room where soon enough, Mikey's snores filled the room.

The rest of the weekend was filled with family fun and outdoor activities. Aisha even took Corina to the mall where she bought her a dress and a pair of blue sandals since that wasCorina's favorite color. She seemed to gel well with the little girl. Mikey, too, spent time chatting with her about what she wanted to become and what her hobbies were. In his head, it was as though this was Ms. Andrea chatting with him. "Life is surely a cycle. The baton has been passed to me," he said to himself.

That Sunday when Corina was taken back to the Orphanage, she seemed a bit sad and not her usual bubbly self. She had said little on the way and Mikey had noticed the change. When he pulled into the driveway and parked, he turned to her and said, "I do hope you had a fun time with us. We were so happy to have you. Will you want to spend another time with us?" She smiled shyly and nodded her head. "What is wrong?" Mikey asked as he noticed a small tear in the little girl's eye. "Nothing much," she replied, "I enjoyed the time with you, Ms. Aisha, and the boys. You have a nice family. Thank you, Mr. Clary." "You are welcome, Corina," he said while looking at her with a puzzled expression.

She then got out of the car, and they walked towards the Administration Building where they were met by Ms. Strudel. "Well look who is back! Welcome back Corina! Did you have a fun time?" inquired Ms. Strudel. "Yes, I did," the little girl replied with a smile. "I am going to look for Jada and Terry to tell them about my weekend." With that, she ran off without looking back.

Mikey then spoke further with Ms. Strudel before he left the compound. On his way out, he stopped and looked at the girls' dormitory. He knocked his hand on the steering wheel, looked up in the heavens, smiled and said to himself, "Got to have a conversation with Aisha."

(One year later)

Squeals of laughter filled the air as the children played and tumbled over each other. Mikey sat looking at them and his eyes brimmed with tears. Aisha was embroidering a pillowcase when she looked across and noticed that her husband was emotional. "What is wrong, hon?" she asked tenderly. 'This, this right here is what I wanted for myself when I was growing up. All I ever wanted was a home where I felt loved. Now that I have a home that is filled with love, my life is complete," he responded softly. He then looked across at the framed letter from his biological mother and said, "Yeah mama, your little boy will never forget you nor the journey his life had taken. You will always be in my heart."

As he dried his eyes, the little girl came running up to him and placed her arms around his neck. "Why are you crying daddy?" she asked. "Oh, nothing to worry about Cory. However, I think the time has come for me to have a little chat with you, my three children." They huddled around him as he began, "Many years ago, there was a little boy by the name of Michael Clary, son of Sheila Clary...."

Aisha had snuggled closer to him as well, smiling at the twinkle in her husband's eyes, the radiance on his face as he told his life story to his sons and daughter, he recalled the day that Corina left the Orphanage to take up residence in their home. It was a day that would remain etched in her mind for Mikey had behaved as though he had brought home precious cargo. She smiled as she listened. The final piece to his life's dream was finally accomplished. Life's obstacles did not keep him down; he had kicked those pebbles aside and he made it!

Acknowledgments

My acknowledgement starts with Almighty God for His enduring grace and protection, which He has bestowed upon me as well as His wisdom, knowledge and understanding.

Standford Clark, my English Literature teacher, I say thank you for inspiring me to author this book. I am forever grateful.

My beautiful daughter, Aaliyah Harvey, and niece, Senay Harvey, I say thank you. Your stimulating discussions have motivated me and kept me going.

My parents, Mary, and Ashton Harvey have continuously supported me through thick and thin. Thank you for the moments spent with me in prayer. I have a heartfelt appreciation for your parental presence and words of encouragement.

Finally, my sincerest gratitude goes to my editor, Donna Chapman, for your patience, motivation, and immense knowledge. Your guidance has helped me throughout the writing of this book.

SCANNING...

About the Author

Henry Harvey is the Founder and CEO of 21st Century Security & Electronics Ltd, a company that specializes in biometrics and security services. Henry spent more than fourteen years in law enforcement, a career that he loved. Henry Harvey is happily married and is the father of one daughter and enjoys a very close relationship with his parents. Faith and family are his priorities. He enjoys reading and being on the beach in his spare time, in the beautiful island paradise where he resides.

Notes